Farewell Rio

ALSO BY ROA LYNN

<u>Fiction</u>

O Assassino e a Musa

Persisting

The Barbosa Legacy

<u>Non-Fiction</u>

Brazil in Brief

Brazil and the U.S.A.: What do we have in Common?

Learning Disabilities: An Overview of Theories, Approaches and Politics

Farewell Rio

Roa Lynn

CORCOVADO PRESS

Farewell Rio
Roa Lynn

CORCOVADO PRESS
corcovadopress@verizon.net

ISBN 978-0-9830197-0-1

Printed in the United States of America

A previous version of this book was published in 2001 in Brazil in Portuguese translation as *O Assassino e a Musa* by Livraria Francisco Alves Editora S.A.

This is a work of fiction set against historical events. All the principal characters and their actions are fictional creations.

For my husband, Bernard,
my first reader and constant editor.

CHAPTER ONE

I cannot support this feeling,
This ecstasy,
This transparency
Of give and give,
This crisis of love
Blown over.

E. Catherine Lawrence

I

When my plane landed in Rio de Janeiro in 1967, a week before Christmas, I understood little of Brazil beyond what I had gleaned in New York from Sérgio, my former lover. I had $800 in a money belt under my shirt, and the feeling of power. I was determined to be exuberant, incautious, as if everything I would think and do would carry the permissions, the possibilities, the grandiose delusions set loose in that year. Even before I left Galeão International Airport my lightweight, elegant raincoat was stolen off my arm. As my taxi pulled away from the curb, I realized the culprit was my baggage porter, who blew me a kiss of good luck. His smile invited my forbearance.

My luggage had been stowed under the hood of the dilapidated Volkswagen Beetle taxi with its right front seat removed to clear a passage to the rear. The taxi driver, a scrawny black man, left me no time to think about my loss. He accelerated both his vehicle and his broken English. "Look, lady, I'm a composer, samba composer. Where you from — *França*, you *Americana*? You like samba? You understand me? You make a record of my samba in Hollywood?" The taxi gathered speed in heavy traffic.

"Careful," I said. "Watch out."

"Listen to my samba. *É original,* new." The driver began to sing and beat counterpoint with alternating hands on the steering wheel. The car went still faster.

"I'm not in a hurry."

"You like my music?"

"Please slow down."

"I compose many songs."

"Slow down." I tapped the driver on his shoulder and pointed to his speedometer. *"Calma,"* I said in Portuguese.

"Don't worry. I know the fast way to Ipanema. You like my samba?"

"Muito original," I said.

The driver continued singing energetically, interspersing his catchy song with what I took to be his entire stock of English phrases until we crashed into the rear of a dark blue Ford sedan. The hood of the taxi disappeared on impact. The driver didn't move or speak or sing. My knees were twisted and wedged at a painful angle into the back of the driver's seat.

I tried to get loose but couldn't. I had been thrown forward with my face very near the driver's head. I could smell the pleasant aroma of lime cologne on his cheek. I tried again, one knee at a time, to wiggle free. I wondered if the bulk of my clothes and books had cushioned us in the collision. Were my belongings ruined beyond repair?

The driver of the Ford got out of his car exploding in a tirade, his face contorted. He walked over to the taxi and pried open the driver's door, ready to continue his invective, until he saw that the taxi driver was unconscious. The sound of the crash was still reverberating in my ears. The suddenness and seriousness of what had happened began to sink in. "I'm stuck," I said. "I can't move my legs." The Ford's driver, a middle-aged man in a suit and tie, tried unsuccessfully to extricate me through the opened door. He spoke excitedly in Portuguese and I spoke, with equal excitement, in a mixture of Portuguese and English.

Magnetized by the accident, passers-by surrounded us. The taxi driver was slowly reviving. He spoke a few words, though he didn't attempt any movement. A young man in a bathing suit with a towel thrown over his shoulder opened the passenger door and was able, after some strenuous pulling, to free me. My knees and everything inside me, including my mind, felt shaky. The beach boy helped me to the Ford, opened the passenger door and sat me down. The crowd of spectators was growing. It didn't take long before the police arrived in a black-and-white Volkswagen Beetle cruiser.

Daylight was fading rapidly into twilight, as it does in the tropics. Then abruptly it was dark. I understood only fragments of the Portuguese being hurled at me. I wasn't seriously hurt, and the sedan's driver did not appear injured at all. By the time I left the scene with the police, the taxi-driver/samba-composer was on his feet smiling at his audience of well-wishers.

I arrived at the Hotel Vermont in Ipanema jammed into the back of the Beetle cruiser, two policemen in front, my three mangled suitcases stacked beside me. I nodded my head when the policemen inquired, again, if I was okay and I shook hands with each officer when they left me at the front desk.

The Vermont was a small, inexpensive residential hotel two blocks from the beach and one block from the bar where Tom Jobim and Vinícius de Moraes first observed the girl from Ipanema and put their thoughts on a napkin. My room was on the third floor, facing the street. Its floor was grayish mottled tile; twin beds were separated by a scarred wooden nightstand with a small gooseneck lamp on top.

The low-wattage bulb cast a sallow light, barely adequate for reading. The room cost $8 per night.

My baggage had withstood the impact of the crash remarkably well except that a shard of metal had punctured one of my suitcases, damaging, beyond repair, the left shoe of a pair of sexy black patent-leather, high-heeled sandals. There was nothing to do but throw both of them into the wastebasket.

Waiting for sleep that night, I reviewed my expectations. Sérgio had portrayed Brazil as a country of unmatched physical beauty and high culture (among the upper classes), a self-involved society that "respects its poets." It was poised somewhere between Third World poverty and modern technology, ruled by a military government that had seized power to prevent a communist takeover. One evening over coffee, not long before he left New York for his new posting in Geneva, he held my hand across a red-and-white-checked tablecloth and told me how he longed to go underwater spearfishing at Angra dos Reis on the coast 70 miles from Rio. He boasted of how deep he could dive and how long he could hold his breath. "Your attention can't be divided down there. It clears the mind."

"Take me with you," I said.

"I wish I could." I knew he meant, "Not until I get my divorce."

Sérgio had been the Brazilian Consul General in New York, fluent in five languages, a procrastinator by nature given to extended periods of painful existential introspection. He had been raised in a culture where people were accustomed to taking their emotional temperature minute by minute, acting or not acting depending on the reading. I was both impatient with this attitude and surprisingly attracted to it. I looked forward to experiencing a nation so preoccupied with its mental state.

Sérgio was handsome, politically astute, charming and, like many of his country's diplomats, well schooled in philosophy, history and classical literature. One of his great-grandfathers, a Spanish aristocrat, had owned an enormous coffee plantation in the state of São Paulo. In later generations, the family's fortunes had faded, and they had slid into the upper middle class. His maternal grandfather had been an industrialist who made a modest fortune in copper mining, but the worldwide economic crisis of 1929 and the retrenchment that followed had dissipated his business. Sérgio's father, deceased for 15 years, had been a lawyer, a painter and a part-time politician, having been elected once to the Brazilian Chamber of Deputies.

Three months had passed since our calamitous breakup. It made me wonder whether Brazil might be both a lush paradise and a neurotic hell. I vividly recalled our parting:

* * *

Sérgio is flying to Rio Saturday morning where he is to be briefed for his temporary assignment in Moscow. He has managed to route his trip through New York to see me. He wanted to tell me in person that he has his Brazilian separation and within six weeks he will have a Swiss divorce. We have been apart for nearly 14 months.

I am shy. I am in his arms again. The presents he brought me are spread out with our clothes on the hotel arm chair. I am complete. Even when he kisses me, I surround his kiss with exuberant chatter. We plan our marriage. My friends who advised me to forget him were wrong. He moves inside my body. I cannot stop talking. "Be quiet, Kate." Finally I am.

I pull the sheet up to my waist, rearrange the pillows, plump them and lean nearly upright against them, smiling softly into space. I am too weak to stand. He walks to the bathroom. As he shaves, we talk, lovers' talk, private talk. I can see half his face reflected in the mirror above the dresser. It's a beautiful, chiseled face. His black wavy hair is perfectly clipped. We shower together, dress, go out to greet New York. The sun has not quite set in the late-September sky. The horizon is magenta.

We visit our old haunts and discover new ones. I briefly telephone my girlfriends Joyce and Marta to tell them the happy news — that Sérgio and I are discussing wedding plans. Sérgio's colleagues think he is flying directly to Rio from Geneva. They don't know he has arranged to pass through New York. I told my secretary I was taking the next two days off. "I will be unreachable," I said.

We eat, make love, eat, go to a movie, make love. We visit no one, sleep little. We have no schedule of day or night, breakfast or dinner. I haven't had a moment to phone my parents or his colleague, Paulo, who had, over the last three months, become my friend. I will phone them later. I show Sérgio all my new poems and the prize I won for a poem about my two years in the Peace Corps. He speaks to me in Portuguese: "Practice for your new life. I hope you won't be disappointed with Brazil."

"I can't wait to see it. I confess I've built a pyramid of fantasies."

We go to The Museum of Modern Art. I wear all his gifts at once — a pin in 18-carat gold in the shape of a stylized leaf, Chanel No. 5 behind my ears, Je Reviens on my wrists, French sunglasses, a blue Hermès scarf.

Friday, sometime in the early afternoon, as he is in the bathroom showering off our love, I use the moment to take stock. Lying in bed, damp with coition, I dial Paulo's office number. "Kate, you deserve to be happy. Tell Sérgio hello for me."

6

"I'm sort of in a state of delirium. We've been waiting for the final decree."

Sérgio walks into the room, naked, catching the last part of my conversation. His face is tranquil. After rapturous lovemaking his feelings and his face are one. I hang up the phone and lean into his soft, languorous mood. "Who was that?" he asks.

"Paulo Costa Souto. I wanted to tell him our news."

After a moment he says, "I didn't hear the phone ring."

"I called him."

"You did? ... But why call him now? What's your hurry?"

"No hurry, really. I'm just so happy I want to share it."

"It's not enough to share it with me? There's something wrong here, Catherine. I don't see the logic ... What's going on? ... You're hiding something."

"I have nothing to hide."

"But you must be ... I see it." Sérgio grabs a towel off the back of the desk chair and snaps it around his waist. His voice cracks with rage. "You're having an affair with Paulo behind my back. My God, how could you? How dare you talk to me about our wedding plans one minute and call your lover the next? Three months ... that's what we just agreed on. Does that give you time enough to break off with Paulo?"

I hurry to get up, throw on a robe and sit on the edge of the bed. This isn't the kind of conversation one can continue naked. "Sérgio, for God's sake. I'm not having an affair with Paulo. You know me better than that."

"You think you can change lovers like horses? Is that what you think? What kind of a person are you, Kate? How can I trust you now?" His fury is rising but his voice is low — steely cold and threatening. He

7

dresses hastily, out of my sight, the bathroom door closed. He returns to the room.

"I don't believe you, Kate. You and Paulo are lovers. There's no other explanation why you would be calling Paulo Costa Souto at this moment. What did you want to tell him? Change the time when you could meet him? What, Catherine? What did you want to tell your lover? Tell me. Did you have to choose my vice-consul? The boy who was my protégé? There are no other men in New York?"

"I can't believe you're saying this. Sérgio, listen to me, for God's sake. Be quiet a moment and listen . . . "

"Tell me, Kate. How long have you been lovers?"

I jump up, take my clothes into the bathroom, pull them over my perspiring, trembling body. I smell of love. I throw cold water on my face, squirt toothpaste onto my index finger and rub it over my front teeth, rinse my mouth with water, run a comb through my matted hair and enter the room. Sérgio is sitting rigidly in the straight-backed chair next to the small desk piled with a jumble of items from his suitcase. "I'm waiting for your answer, Kate. Be careful what you say. I know you. A lie won't work."

"I telephoned Paulo just now because I wanted to tell him our good news. We've had dinner together a few times while you were away. We talked mostly about you, about Brazil, what the military government is up to, restaurants . . . If what you're saying wasn't so patently ridiculous and hysterical, it would be funny."

"There's a saying among the experts, Kate, believe me. 'A woman who talks to a man about another man is as good as in bed.' What did you want to tell Paulo? Just tell me. I think I'll call Varig Airlines right now and change my reservation from tomorrow and leave for Rio tonight."

"Please don't, Sérgio. Call Paulo. Ask him, if you don't believe me."

I collapse onto the bed, hold my hands over my ears. Sérgio pulls his chair next to me. "Paulo was always ambivalent toward me, Kate. Always competing with my intelligence. I'm convinced he cares for you, in his own way, as a sort of tender and exciting doll." He picks up the bedside phone, hesitates, then puts the receiver down without dialing. "Why don't you just say it was an impulsive act taking up with Paulo? A reaction to being alone so much while I've been in Geneva and not seeing how things were going to work out. You could start there. What you tell me now will affect us for the rest of our lives."

He does not call Paulo as he threatens, or change his airline reservation. He will leave New York on Saturday as planned. In the evening, quite late, we go to the Russian Tea Room for caviar and blini and vodka. Back at the hotel he wavers — should he make love to me once more before he leaves? He decides he will. He cries when he enters me. We cry together. I try to express with my body what I have been unable to convince him of with words. That Paulo is not my lover. Never has been. Could never be.

I accompany Sérgio to Kennedy Airport in a taxi. I sit with him at the Varig gate, holding his hand until his flight is called. We kiss. He joins the queue to board his plane. I wait beside him as the line moves forward. I feel giddy. "The future has to be rebuilt, since the past is past," he murmurs. "It's like going back to the main road."

I nod, noncommittally. We approach the door to the ramp. The agent takes his ticket and motions him through. I stand aside. He turns around to look for me. He touches his earlobe, giving it a small tug — the same gesture of delight and affection he used when he returned from one of his trips to Brazil and spotted me waiting in the throng outside customs.

"Goodbye. Goodbye," I say, not sure if he hears me. I slowly blow him a kiss off the palm of my hand, keeping my eyes fixed on his face.

9

But we don't rebuild the future and a series of stinging letters from Sérgio makes it clear we never will.

* * *

After the first time my father met Sérgio he had warned me: "I've seen this play before, Catherine, and so have you." In the weeks after Sérgio's angry departure, I asked myself again and again what hunger had made me persist with him despite my own good sense and the misgivings of those around me. I felt I owed myself an explanation.

Still in shock, I heard myself say to an editor of an airline magazine, "Why not do a story on Rio in their early summer? You know, off-season in the Southern Hemisphere. The real Rio. Everybody writes about Carnival."

I had read in a guidebook that Rio had 16 distinct beaches. "The Sixteen Beaches of Rio de Janeiro" became the working title for my assignment. My contract stipulated a plane ticket, $250 for expenses, a modest payment when I delivered the story and even a kill fee if the editor didn't like what I wrote.

I called Berlitz and set up private Portuguese conversation lessons three evenings a week and dropped my less-intensive Portuguese grammar classes at The New School. I told my employer, Macmillan Publishing Co., that I needed a leave of absence.

Over four years I had progressed from low-level administrative work to reading unsolicited manuscripts from the slush pile to proposing book projects and editing manuscripts. For most of a year I had put aside the question that nagged me at Macmillan. Was my editing job compatible with my ambitions as a poet? It used up my literary energies and kept me pinned down in New York. I needed time to think, to travel the world, to have experiences that would inspire poems, to take risks, to keep my eye to the keyhole. When I expected to be a diplomat's wife, I didn't need an answer. Now, once again, I did.

Thomas Duncan Mayhew, the executive editor, looked at me over his half-glasses and lighted a cigarette. "I'll agree to your leave of absence if, while you're down there unwinding, you look around for promising authors. Find me a Brazilian Borges. I'll work out a stipend." I hadn't expected him to agree to my request for a five-week leave. I accepted his reluctant consent with, I feared, excessive girlish gratefulness. Attempting to cover my effusiveness with a lame quip, I asked if the Brazilian author had to be blind.

II

Eight days after I arrived in Brazil, bruised and still stiff, I found myself holding conversations in Portuguese with a confidence that surprised me. It wasn't easy to locate all the beaches of Rio. They were scattered from the North Zone of the city near the international airport to the other side of the mountains in the south. I planned to visit one or two a day, starting with the obvious ones in the South Zone — Copacabana, followed by Ipanema and its neighbor, Leblon.

Before my first morning's outing, *senhor* Gonçalves, the very correct hotel front-desk clerk, stopped me. "Permit me to say, miss, that you must watch your valuables on the beach. The beach is crowded with all sorts of people. If you leave your camera unguarded while you swim, you may not find it again." I assured *senhor* Gonçalves that, as an international traveler, I knew how to take precautions. "Ah, you have been to Europe then?"

"And also to North Africa," I said. "Six years ago, just after I graduated from college, I was in the Peace Corps in Tunisia."

11

Senhor Gonçalves seemed quite impressed with those credentials, but he continued to watch over me and offer advice. He was an elderly man of dignity and reserve — a pensioner, he said, a bachelor, with no close family still alive. He wore his thin gray hair neatly parted in the middle, his antique, round, wire-rimmed glasses and old-world manners seeming to serve as amulets against casual indecorum.

Each morning a porter brought breakfast to my room on a tray — coffee with warm milk, a finger banana, an orange partly peeled in a decorative spiral, two hard rolls, butter and guava jelly. I ate, showered, gathered up my maps, my camera, tanning oil, notebook and sunglasses and went off to a beach. I struck up conversations with strangers everywhere I went. My color was turning a burnished golden brown, a shade the sun of Cape Cod couldn't produce on the sunniest days. At night my skin prickled as I lay, gingerly, on coarse sheets.

When I ate lunch alone in a restaurant, men invited me to dinner or to parties at their friends' apartments. I accepted a few of these invitations knowing that the men hoped for sex. I invented elaborate dodges at the end of the evening, escaped their unsubtle maneuvers, but used the occasions to gather information on intoxicating Rio.

Brazilian girls on dates, I learned, found protection from unwanted advances by linking up with acquaintances during their evenings out. One night I went to the movies with an attractive date who, I judged early on, was earnestly plotting his move to take me to bed. I foiled him just as a Brazilian girl would do by chatting in the lobby with a group of people I'd met at a party the night before. We all found seats in the same row. After the film it was only natural for the group to have a drink together. We drove in three cars to a restaurant in Copacabana, drank beer, ate little cheese sandwiches and argued about whether the film's director had a coherent vision. On the way home, with another couple in the car, I was insistent that my date drop me at my hotel first.

"It's right on your way," I said, breezing over his dismay. "It's late and I'm expecting my father to call me very early tomorrow morning."

I glanced at Carlos' face as I got out of the car. It had lost all its attractiveness. I thought I heard him whisper "American bitch" under his breath.

At the beach I interviewed women who were accompanied by their young children. The mothers guarded my belongings while I splashed in the sea. I quickly discovered that, most of the time, the waves came in hard and fast and real swimming was next to impossible.

My notebook filled up with observations and anecdotes. I located beaches in the North Zone of the city that natives of the South Zone didn't know existed and vice versa. The North was petit bourgeois, industrial and commercial; the South was chic, residential and rich. Rio's numerous *favelas,* or shantytowns, didn't observe geographical boundaries. Devoid of municipal services, they marched straight up the city's forested mountains or squatted on scattered flat marginal lands.

I was filling my notebook with the practical things the reader of my article would want to know: that all the beaches in Rio are free, that there are no restrooms, that oceanside hotels do not provide private cabanas, that volleyball players eager to set up their nets may unceremoniously disrupt your peaceful sunbathing, that skinny black vendors incessantly march up and down the beach blowing whistles to hawk their ripe coconuts, pineapple slices, salted peanuts, skewered bits of steak, sunglasses, Coca-Cola.

I kept musing, however, about the beach at night. After dark the shouts of young men playing volleyball vanished. I imagined I could hear the sound of the fleas jumping in the filthy sand. On Friday nights, *macumba* priests would arrive to honor Iemanjá, goddess of the sea. Worshipers dressed all in white lighted candles whose flames

13

fluttered in the warm breeze. They offered gifts that a proud woman would esteem: lipsticks, fragments of mirror, combs, hair ribbons, fresh flowers, perfume. Pretty girls walked by on the wave-patterned mosaic sidewalk that bordered the sand. In places, here and there, the sidewalk's small square charcoal and ivory stones were missing. These incursions were minimal, but they could provoke a twisted ankle. Placed at intervals along the sidewalk were rough-hewn concrete benches. Lovers sat on them, entwined in each other's legs and arms.

In Copacabana, from a high floor of an apartment building overlooking the broad beach and the ocean, the details of life became irrelevant. Looking out the windows at night, residents did not see their maids making love on the beach, the fences receiving their stolen wares, a drunk staggering out of a nightclub to lurch toward the sand, vomit, and then stumble back inside. Nor did they see the midnight fishermen casting their lines, participating in an unspoken fellowship with the prostitutes plying their beckoning romance. From the tenth floor, the residents and their guests looked past the evening pantomime on the beach to follow the lights of an ocean vessel gliding through the luscious night.

By half past three in the morning, the movement stopped. Almost everyone in Rio was asleep. A few who were very poor indeed slept fitfully on the beach. They couldn't afford even a *favela* shack with its roof of tin cans pounded flat. Finally exhaustion would overtake them too, as they lay on the bare sand covered with newspapers or pieces of cardboard. As they dozed they prayed that some unfeeling citizen, secure in his employment, wouldn't toss a lighted match at them. It had happened.

The rhythms of life waited for sunrise.

CHAPTER TWO

A nine-year-old Captain Marvel
Went sailing
Out his bedroom window
To his death
In Copacabana.
It serves him right:
Dreams are dreams.

E. Catherine Lawrence

After three and a half weeks I had nearly completed my magazine assignment. Sitting at a sidewalk café and feeling lonely, I decided to return to my hotel, change into my white maillot and plunge into the Atlantic. A brisk swim would restore my spirits. I put my notebook down on my towel and picked my way through sunbathers to the water's edge at Ipanema's beach.

A man laden with cameras and lenses stood ankle-deep in the sea. A Nikon was at his eye; he seemed intent on his left thumb, which he held upright at the end of his outstretched arm. He was thirtyish with close-cropped sandy hair and wore cutoff jeans. I was wondering what he saw in the empty ocean when a girl in a white maillot, very similar to mine, leapt from the swell of a wave into the air. The photographer clicked his shutter and signaled for her to do it again.

I stood with a group of onlookers to watch the professionals at work. When they finished I started back to my towel to make a few notes. The photographer rushed to my side. "I must photograph you. I'd like to take a shot of you and Helena together. Do you mind? You could almost be twins."

"You must see something I don't," I said.

"You have a good accent in Portuguese. Are you British?"

"American. What do you do with the pictures?"

"Oh, I'm famous for my pictures of gorgeous women in white bathing suits soaked to the skin. I'm Nelson Claudio Carvalho. How do you do?"

"Kate Lawrence. I've had some interesting invitations since I arrived in Rio —"

"Say yes. You are from New York? Every American I meet in Rio is from New York. Or else California. You know the saying, 'I never read the book but I didn't like it.' I've never been to New York but I love it." He took a pack of Gauloises cigarettes out of his pocket and hungrily lighted one. I shook my head no when he held out the pack to me.

"I do live in New York but I'm from Boston. I love Rio. It's hard not to."

"I'm serious about the picture. I don't have enough budget to pay you, but you'll be able to see your picture in a magazine. Maybe you've seen my photographs in *Manchete* or *O Cruzeiro*? I had one in *Manchete* last month of Bibi Dantas — page eight. She was wearing a white bikini. I took her picture under a small waterfall. She was holding her long blonde hair over her head and laughing because the water was very cold. My models tell me I make them suffer, but they are always pleased with the pictures."

"Is this what you do for a living?"

"I don't just photograph models. I have regular corporate clients. Last week I took photos for General Motors. The wet bathing suit pictures are my signature. I not only photograph beautiful women. I shoot beautiful men, too."

"I really need to take a swim. I'm hot and sticky." I walked into the water up to my knees.

The model came up to me. "Hi. I'm Helena."

"Hello." I extended my hand. I still wasn't accustomed to kissing everyone I greeted on each cheek, right to left. "Kate Lawrence. Is he serious? Are his pictures really good?"

"Nelson Claudio is one of our best photographers. He wants to take one of us together. He has a terrific eye. Trust him. Everybody does."

Helena and I ducked into the water, jumped straight up, walked arm in arm in the surf, batted a volleyball back and forth. Finally Nelson Claudio said he had what he wanted. "You were great, Kate. I can't thank you enough. Where can I send your pictures? I'm not sure when or where they will be published. There are three magazines that want photos of Helena. She appears on one of our soap operas. Did she tell you?"

"I'm leaving Rio in a week. I'll give you my address in New York." I wrote it out for him in his notebook. "I'll look forward to seeing them. My friends will be surprised."

"You'll have a picture for your boyfriend."

"If I had one." I turned and began walking out into deeper water.

Nelson Claudio called after me: "Careful of the undertow." I pushed off the sandy bottom into a lazy sidestroke. He watched me for a few minutes, then cupped his hands and shouted. I couldn't hear what he said, so I swam back to him and stood up in the shallow surf. "Would you like to go to a party with me tonight? It's at David Bernardes'. Have you heard of him? Kim Novak will probably be there."

"She's in Rio? I'd love to meet her."

"So come. If you don't go to too many, David's parties are amusing."

"I'm writing a travel piece on Rio, how can I resist?"

17

In the late afternoon, *senhor* Gonçalves was on duty. He rose from his chair behind the front desk as soon as he saw me enter the lobby. He had become one of my chief informants on Brazilian deportment. I quizzed him about David Bernardes. "It's said he's just this side of a roué, but he has great charm and, need I mention, great wealth. And he has a famous collection of American jazz records — historical records from the artists who invented jazz. I stop with the greats, *dona* Kate. Mozart, Bach and a few Brazilian composers."

"When I was on the beach this morning I met a photographer who took my picture and invited me to a party at David's apartment."

"David is always having a *festa*. Several times a week, it seems. His parties are very sophisticated, with movie stars, musicians, intellectuals, businessmen. His son, David Jr., sometimes brings his student friends."

"Have you been to his parties, *senhor* Gonçalves?"

"My goodness, no. But I have a distant cousin who sometimes goes. He's a writer and he also translates poetry from English and French to Portuguese."

"How interesting. What's his name?"

"Exactly the same as mine, Oswaldo Gonçalves."

"Have you ever heard of Nelson Claudio? ...Now I can't remember his last name."

"Carvalho?"

"That's it. He's the photographer who invited me to David's party."

"His work is a little modern for me — I prefer landscapes — but he's quite known. If my cousin is there, by all means tell him you are staying at the hotel."

Senhor Gonçalves seemed to know about everybody in Rio and have opinions on many matters of high culture. When I inquired discreetly about his background he directed my attention to a pile of newspapers and leather-bound books sitting on a shelf under the desk. "Reading, miss. Reading can make a nobody a somebody."

"You aren't a nobody, *senhor* Gonçalves."

"Thank you for saying so."

Nelson Claudio and I had agreed to meet on the street at 10 o'clock in front of David Bernardes' Copacabana apartment building. He was waiting for me, enjoying his cigarette, when my taxi pulled up. "You even look wonderful in clothes," he said as he helped me out.

I inclined my head to accept one kiss on each cheek. In my high heels I was four inches taller than he. His face was round and his features were undistinguished. I would have considered him unattractive, except that his lopsided smile was completely engaging.

David Bernardes greeted us at the door. He was a small bald man with vivid green eyes behind horn-rimmed glasses. He held his cigarette between his third and fourth fingers, the way I'd seen artists on the Left Bank hold theirs. "I do hope you're enjoying yourself in Rio. It's stunning, isn't it? Our city's final victory of caprice over fact. Wouldn't you agree?"

"With hedonism, poverty, fantasy and I don't know what else thrown in," I said.

"So you do agree." David pressed my forearm. "Good, I like you already. The music room is upstairs. Nelson Claudio will show you. Play anything you wish. My collection of jazz records is without parallel, even in your own country, if I may say so. You like jazz?"

"I do, but I'm not the expert I'm told you are."

"You probably prefer English groups. The Beatles? The Hollies? What about soul music? So plastic, it's a sellout. Such a shame, really."

Nelson Claudio knew everyone and everyone knew him. We made the round of the public rooms. David's apartment was immense. Rich nut-wood burled paneling, the color of caramel candy, came halfway up the ivory walls. Etched-glass art deco cocktail tables were interspersed between vanilla-colored sofas and ottomans. The living room, dining room and library were satiny smooth and sumptuous. A long, narrow balcony overlooked Avenida Atlântica, the wide crescent-shaped Copacabana Beach and the open sea beyond. We stopped at the dining table and sampled the roasted baby pig served with *farofa*, the essential Brazilian side dish of coarsely-ground manioc flour sautéed with onions in butter and palm oil that tastes like delicious birdseed.

"When David's wife was diagnosed with cancer," Nelson Claudio said, "David changed completely. He used to complain about his wife's shortcomings in the beds of other women. But when Patricia's cancer was discovered and she was forced to live without pretense, she gave up her quest for the latest fashion. She even stopped wearing makeup. And David became a faithful husband. He jilted all his mistresses."

"Is she all right now?"

"She died. Three years ago. It was very sad. David rented a fishing boat in Salvador, where Patricia was born, so he could scatter her ashes in Todos os Santos Bay. But once at sea he remembered he had left her urn on the seat next to his on the airplane. The ashes disappeared. The cleaning crew probably thought they were dirt and dumped them down the toilet. David's a playboy again."

I lingered on the periphery of several conversations. Well-groomed guests, fully enjoying David's luxurious quarters and lavish hospitality, criticized current conditions in the world with an undercurrent of glib resentment of the United States. I didn't join in because I didn't want to have to explain the incomprehensible — why the United States was in Vietnam.

20

Kim Novak arrived after midnight. Out of the corner of my eye I caught glimpses of her. Wherever she moved in the room there were ripples of commotion. One of the guests asked me if she was Czech. "Bohemian," David answered from behind my shoulder. "Come, let me introduce you. Marilyn Pauline Novak, may I present Kate Lawrence and Nelson Claudio Carvalho."

Our conversation was brief. We had interrupted an intense argument between Kim and a Brazilian movie critic about the way Alfred Hitchcock had framed a scene in *Vertigo*. After a few pleasantries they resumed their discussion. We listened for several minutes. "I didn't expect her to be so thoughtful," I said to Nelson Claudio after we had walked into another room. "I wonder what she thinks of Rio."

"You can be sure she's seeing a rather rarefied view. She just got divorced. She's dating David."

"Who's that?" I asked. I had noticed a young man surrounded by courtiers delivering an oration in a corner of the room.

"Oh, that's Walter Decker holding forth. Let me introduce you to him. He's brilliant."

"He looks like a student."

"At heart he is, even though I don't think he ever went to the university. He writes diatribes. Everybody admires them. He's totally unique. Presses his pants by putting them under his mattress when he sleeps."

"How do you know that?"

"Everybody knows. Besides, you have only to look."

We walked over to Walter's court. He was at ease in his role as the center of attention; he beamed with pleasure. "It's not just the São Paulo businessmen who put our government in place. And now the military's grip on power is complete. Nobody's fooled. Who's

21

fighting the cold war 90 miles off their shores and needs allies in Latin America?"

When Walter paused to take a breath, Nelson Claudio introduced me as a writer from New York. "I've just been telling Kate that you write incredible polemics and stories."

"I guess incredible is the word," Walter said. "Is it not incredible the situation we find ourselves in? Your world — the developed world, that is — maintains its luxuries. Even though you face lack of capital just as we do, the industrialized world maintains the possibility of choice. They leave us no such luxury. I'm talking about economic imperialism."

"I know the United States acted as an imperial power in the Philippines and in Panama," I said, "but I'm not aware we have taken any such posture toward Brazil. Don't you think you're making excuses for problems that arise out of your own culture? We didn't force you to spend millions building Brasília when you already had a marvelous capital here in Rio."

"I'm not saying the Yanks are sending troops here, or are ever going to. It's more subtle and insidious than that." He adjusted his glasses and smiled broadly. "You can't know Brazil or even Rio by going to David's *festas*. You need to see and taste the interior. This," he waved his arm around the room, "is the pseudo-intelligentsia and high society. Eva, my girlfriend, brought me. She likes to come to David's parties to see who's here. I oblige her now and then. I only don't object because of David's records."

Nelson Claudio turned to me and said: "I should have told you Walter's also a very good musician and songwriter."

"*Bossa nova*?" I asked.

"*Bossa nova* is where we've been," Walter immediately responded, "not where we're going. We're a country of extremes. Our music has

22

to be open to all valid aesthetic influences — samba mixed with Jimi Hendrix. The atomic age and indigenous rhythms — our own delirious blending."

"I love *bossa nova*. I thought everyone did."

"You see . . . an assumption."

"I have only one more week in Rio. I'm afraid I'm going home having missed a lot."

"I challenge you to stay. Get to know us. My friends and I are changing everything."

"I wish I could stay, but I have a job I have to get back to. I'm worried I've already stretched my boss's goodwill."

"What do you write?" He seemed genuinely interested. Despite his leftish ranting, he radiated a feeling of receptivity and benevolence.

"Actually I'm an editor at Macmillan Publishing. I have to go home or starve."

"I don't believe in editors. They're cowards."

"If I could figure out a way to support myself writing poetry, I'd spend my time doing that. For the moment, though, I'm taking a bit of a career detour to come down here to write a magazine piece about Rio's 16 beaches."

"We have that many? I only go to three. No, four." Walter drew in his breath, leaned back and put his hands on his hips. "If you're a poet, you should write, not edit other people's work. Poets belong on the streets, poking their noses into life, getting to the bottom of life's mysteries. Editors sit behind desks. Am I not right?" I nodded. "Then do it. By every means, stay in Brazil. Experience our special hypocrisy."

We both smiled. A petite, vivacious blonde in her twenties joined us and slipped her arm through Walter's. "Eva, meet an American editor from New York — Kate Lawrence." He winked at me.

"Much pleasure, Kate. Are you editing a book here?" Like Walter, Eva seemed open and sincere.

"I wish I were. I'm writing a travel piece and trying to figure out Brazilian men. One especially."

"Good luck. Is he here?" Eva looked around the room.

"He's living in Geneva now, but I met him in New York."

"Have you had something to eat? David's food is always marvelous."

"Thanks. I've already overeaten. It was delicious."

"You'll excuse me. I'm really hungry." She withdrew her arm from Walter's. "I admire your courage to research Brazilian men."

"Imagine what it's like to live in a folkloric ambiance, looking backward," Walter said, looking at me quizzically and resuming his lecture.

"Is that what Brazil does? Looks backward?"

"No. And yes."

Walter winked again. "I don't have the chance to talk to Americans very often. My Brazilian friends already know my positions."

"I don't accept, *prima facie,* your statements about American imperialism," I said.

"Believe me, it's real in Brazil."

Nelson Claudio came back to my side. "Enough," he said. "I'm taking Kate away. You both look too serious."

"Think about my counsel," Walter said.

"To forget my job and stay in Brazil?"

"Precisely." He squeezed my hand. Walter rejoined his group of fans and continued his disquisition.

Of course Nelson Claudio wanted to take me home to his bed. At 3 in the morning we had a prolonged discussion of my plans on the street in front of David's building. "I'll be quite busy in my remaining time in Rio. I really enjoyed David's party," I said and meant it. "Thanks for inviting me."

"Partial payment for being patient this afternoon."

"It's hard work being a model."

"That's not really why I invited you. I think you're beautiful, but not only that. I was intrigued because you didn't want your picture taken and most beautiful women do. I wanted to get to know you."

"I've never liked having my picture taken. It just seems boring."

"You held your ground with Walter. That's impressive, too. He loves excess. Some so-called adults — in other words, members of our military — think he's either puerile or dangerous. They aren't sure which."

"He may be puerile but he doesn't seem dangerous — quite the opposite. Please be sure to send me the pictures."

"You can count on it, though I don't vouch for our post office. It's not the world's most reliable." He held my hand. "I'd really like to take you to dinner. Or for a *cafezinho* in the afternoon. Whatever's convenient. My schedule next week is flexible. I may even have your pictures ready. You have my agent's phone number. Leave me a message."

"If I can, I will, Nelson Claudio. It's late. I'll take a taxi back to my hotel. I do it all the time."

"As you wish." He hailed a taxi. We kissed on each cheek, farewell, and I got in. "Watch out for the undertow, it really is dangerous," he said as he closed the door.

CHAPTER THREE

Trapped, disheveled, kicking around Rio wondering
Where to sleep, or with whom, if necessary.
Education means so much, I can always speak English
And use a hotel telephone ...

E. Catherine Lawrence

I

The next morning I was in the Vermont's small lobby, taking refuge from the threat of a downpour, considering my day's program, when I saw, for only the second time, a Brazilian man cry. The sobbing man, in his early twenties, sat slumped in a corner. His clothes, like his bearing, suggested the provinces. He wore a brown shirt over flared, russet pants and white, patent leather, slip-on shoes. *Senhor* Gonçalves, dressed in his usual frayed blue blazer and gray trousers, officiated over him with a stiff earnestness, offering balm without the least success. The young man seemed beyond consolation. A second comforter, a middle-aged businessman wearing a narrow-waisted navy suit of Italian design, nervously ran his hand through his hair. I sat on a couch close by, pretending to read the South American edition of *Time*.

The provincial struggled to gain control of himself: "How could I have known? All my life, my family and Maria Carolina's have been friends. Our marriage was inevitable from the time we were both 12. I ask you sincerely, how could I have known?"

The businessman assured him, "There was no way for you to know. Heloísa Marques has this effect on many women. She is a force of nature."

"This force has come into my life and destroyed it. A fraud, a fraud, a fraud ... " He repeated the word over and over as if its repetition, though not its meaning, would stop the pain.

"*Meu filho*, I am more than sorry," *senhor* Gonçalves said. "At this moment things look black but I assure you, you will recover though you may not think so now. You will even find another wife. One that deserves you."

The provincial blew his nose and attempted a lame half-smile. The businessman said, "As Heloísa's manager I apologize to you for this disgrace, but I don't know what can be done now. What has happened has happened. Go home to Barra do Garças. Forget about this unhappy and shocking event."

Senhor Gonçalves added: "Time is the better solution. I promise you."

I understood most of the words I overheard but I couldn't yet put them in context. Heloísa Marques was a famous singer who was staying at the Hotel Vermont during her two-week engagement at a nearby theater, where sold-out audiences attended her highly original show of songs and artful stories. I had seen the show. Midway through her performance Heloísa fell forward toward the audience on her outstretched, slender arms and hands, catching her fall before her face hit the stage, then instantly pivoting onto her back while she raised one arm in a salute. A single spotlight found her hand and narrowed until the stage went black with shock. Curtain. Intermission.

Heloísa had a throaty voice and a boyish body hardened — it was reported in the press — by cigarettes, red wine and steak tartare. She wore bell-bottom trousers and a man's shirt tied around her bare midriff, exposing the leanest of waists. Her adornments were many, literally dozens of necklaces made out of ivory, silver, gold, dark-polished jacaranda wood. Her arms were filled with bracelets, and no finger, not even her thumbs, lacked multiple slim silver bands. Her skin was the color of milky coffee. Her gaze was unforgiving.

Later in the day *senhor* Gonçalves filled in the gaps for me. "Heloísa is a notorious lesbian. It is our shame. Our men are too brutal and the women turn to each other for comfort."

The sobbing man, he explained, had much to lament. He was on his honeymoon, visiting Rio de Janeiro for the first time from a cattle-raising prairie town on the Mato Grosso plateau. The marriage festivities had been planned and saved for by both families for many years. The honeymoon was in its second week when the new wife, Maria Carolina, encountered Heloísa in the lobby. The bride, still giddy from her nuptials, had never heard of Heloísa who was, at that moment, by herself, without her manager, without her enthusiasts who went with her everywhere, including to her hotel room. *Senhor* Gonçalves saw her, holding a glass half drained of its red wine, entering the elevator with Maria Carolina. While the groom fished for marlin in the Atlantic bay, Maria Carolina and Heloísa went to bed.

When the groom returned to the hotel at dusk, stinking of fish, Maria Carolina announced her mistake and begged her husband's forgiveness. She was, she said very plainly, remaining with Heloísa forever. She would ask for an annulment because she had discovered, thank God, before it was too late, that her marriage was "a fraud."

The drama was still unfolding when Walter, the polemicist from David's party, walked in from the street. I observed him from behind my magazine. He took in the scene at the front desk with care and listened, a look of sympathy but not surprise crossing his face. Although he had paused near the entrance, just a few feet away from me, he didn't glance in my direction. After a moment, he turned to withdraw to the street, sacrificing, perhaps, whatever errand he had come on. *Senhor* Gonçalves was so engrossed in his ministrations, he momentarily forgot his duties. At the last second he caught a glimpse of Walter and hurried to the entrance. "At your orders," *senhor* Gonçalves said with a slight bow.

"You needn't have interrupted your important conversation for me," Walter said. "I have an appointment with *senhor* Rui Lima for lunch. I'll just wait outside."

"*Senhor* Lima has already left the hotel, about half an hour ago. Do you wish to leave a message?" *Senhor* Gonçalves was at attention; he leaned forward on the balls of his feet.

Walter looked only faintly disappointed at his missed connection. He was on the verge of departing when I put down my magazine and waved to him. He came over to greet me. "Well, do you accept my advice?" he asked.

I looked up at him. "You mean to stay on in Brazil?"

He nodded. "You made a big impression at David's party. You Americans, how do you do it? You come here and immediately know everyone in Brazil. Two years ago I spent three months in New York and all I met were Brazilians."

"You didn't tell me you've been in New York."

"I've been to Miami, too. For three days. Does one narrate his entire life at a *festa?*" We both smiled. "Eva moves easily among the elegant and powerful, even though she is not from their society. It amuses me to see how David's guests respond to the vitality of someone from the humbler classes. I know I am a curiosity for them."

"You play your part," I said.

He winked. "I have my biases, but I'm a responsible guest."

While the bridegroom's predicament continued to dominate the lobby, Walter and I left the hotel for one of the ubiquitous neighborhood stands selling *cafezinhos* (demitasses) for a couple of cents. Each stand had several bar stools arranged on the sidewalk, their cushions usually covered with dark red cracked vinyl. At 2 in the morning, for the brief time the stands were closed, metal gates were padlocked across their open mouths. Although modest, these stands attempted a display of sanitation. The attendant scrupulously avoided touching the bowl of a spoon when presenting it.

Customers, at the slightest provocation, perched on the stools several times a day, downing their little cups of over-sweet coffee. A *cafezinho*, with its caffeine wallop, brought ceremony to everyday life. In addition to selling coffee at the price set by law and shots of *cachaça* (the potent rum of the poor, made from fermented sugar-cane juice), these stands offered ham-and-cheese sandwiches, my usual lunch, and *vitaminas* (fruit drinks prepared in a blender, combining any type of fruit with milk and sugar). They also dispensed sticky-looking pastry from a glass display case. The inviting glaze was camouflage; the pastries were absolutely tasteless.

Walter ordered a bottle of still water and a sandwich. I had a *cafezinho* without sugar. "Poor guy," Walter said between gulps. "It's obvious. He married a lesbian and they both just found out."

"I really have been thinking about what you said at David's *festa*. Your challenge to stay in Brazil —"

"To confront the backlands, not only Rio?"

"Rio is absorbing enough for me. I wish I could find a way to stay longer. I asked the hotel desk clerk if he could find me cheaper lodgings, perhaps with a Brazilian family."

"Has he had success?"

"Unfortunately not."

"What about your editing job?"

"I'm thinking of asking for a few months of leave beyond the weeks I've already taken. Unpaid, of course. Throwing caution to the winds, as we say in English."

"You can stay with me and Eva. I don't pay rent. It's not a problem."

"That's extremely generous, but I couldn't impose ..."

"Hotels are for mindless tourists. As far as I'm concerned, it's settled."

II

I woke in a shoebox-shaped room on a platform bed, really a wooden plank, nailed well above seated height into a stucco wall. A decaying green-and-white-striped mattress belonging to some outdoor furniture had been thrown on top. A crude wooden two-rung stepladder was built into the side of the bed. Underneath the platform were several large storage drawers. The room had no other furniture except a long wooden shelf attached to the wall above the bed.

By my pacing, my new windowless bedroom was six-and-a-half feet wide and nine feet long. Opposite the bed, just below the ceiling, a triple row of glass bricks, a meaningless clerestory of sorts, was set into the wall separating my room from the living room of the two-bedroom apartment. Below the clerestory was the door to the living room and, to its left, a large abstract painting in bold colors. I liked the painting. It pumped energy into the windowless space. The room was mine, rent free. The only strings attached were the ropes of my nerves. I was living with a free-floating gang of students, writers, middle-class girls who held normal jobs, hangers-on and millionaires.

I occupied my narrow room with a jittery unease. The southern two feet of my room served as a foyer connecting the living room with the apartment's only bathroom. Anyone wanting to use the bathroom in the middle of the night had first to open the door between the living room and the foyer, then step into my room to close the living room door so it wouldn't block the bathroom door. Likewise, I had to walk through the living room, exposing myself to the couple bedded there on the fold-out couch, to get into or out of my pinched quarters.

Our four-room commune was on the eighth floor of a white 10-story concrete building, three blocks from Copacabana Beach. It was filthy. My efforts at cleaning were seen as aggressive attacks on the statement of disorder. The dirt was political. Hiring a maid was exploitation.

The owner of the apartment was David Bernardes' only child, David Jr. He was 18 and finishing high school. It turned out he had painted the canvas on the wall of my cell, as well as several life studies scattered about the apartment. When David Jr. had reached 17, his father had decided it was time to rent his son a bachelor apartment. In David Sr.'s social circle, a few sons had such arrangements. The small apartment remained the after-hours retreat of the young man, who still lived at home with his parents. Until the young man's marriage, the apartment was used for conquests and, when needed, as a retreat to study for Brazil's highly competitive placement exams for higher education and civil service. Then it was officially given up in favor of a large apartment to be shared with a wife and children. David Jr. did not follow this custom. In essence, he had given his bachelor apartment over to Walter in support of Walter's writings and music. Occasionally, David Jr. would visit with his friend Paulo.

The commune had four permanent residents: Walter, Eva, Jaime and Ana Maria. Walter was unemployed, but Eva was the secretary to the president of a large textile company. Jaime was a vagabond writer who occasionally picked up odd clerical jobs; his girlfriend, Ana Maria, was a travel agent.

The activities of the group revolved around the likes and dislikes, the things thought virtuous and those thought a waste of time, of Walter alone. He, with his puzzled, solicitous face, was the sweet acknowledged leader of the gang, its prophet, guiding his admirers to be true to their own inner lights. Walter ate irregularly but never haphazardly. He washed down his meals with Coca-Cola, carefully and vigorously stirred with a spoon until he had removed the carbonation. He never drank alcohol, never drank coffee or smoked. Once in a while he accepted marijuana passed around at a party because he thought it less injurious to his health than alcohol or tobacco.

A real meal didn't come until late at night. Often the gang would troop off together to a simple restaurant for plain staples of meat or fish. To vary our diet, we would have Chinese food, sometimes eaten in a cheap restaurant and sometimes purchased by Jaime and brought to the apartment in paper cones. Occasionally, we indulged in sumptuous feasts; occasionally, just Coca-Cola accompanied by black Portuguese olives, bread, butter and radishes.

Like many residences in Rio, David Jr.'s had no phone. During my first week in the apartment I used a street pay phone to leave a message for Nelson Claudio at his agent's office. The next day he joined the group for dinner at a Chinese restaurant. Ana Maria had invited a new acquaintance, Jane, to join us.

"I'm leaving Sunday for a two-week trip to Argentina," Nelson Claudio said after we ordered. "My agent's been trying for months to get me an assignment from this glossy German travel magazine. I'm going everywhere — Bariloche, Córdoba, Mar del Plata. Of course, Buenos Aires."

"Sounds like fun," I said.

"I've only been to Argentina once, and just to Buenos Aires," he continued. It's going to be hard work. My Spanish isn't very good. It's outstanding you decided to stay in Rio, Kate. Will you be here when I get back?"

"I expect to be."

Over dinner Nelson Claudio and Walter had an elaborate discussion about plantations — the economic significance of, and cultural

33

differences between, Brazil's *fazendas* and Argentina's *estancias*. I recalled Sérgio telling me he had learned to shoot a hunting rifle on an enormous coffee *fazenda* that belonged to his favorite cousin. He had described his cousin as a charming, eccentric character to whom he would like to introduce me one day.

While the men talked to each other, I fell into conversation with Jane, a lively English redhead with porcelain skin. She was a free spirit, traveling around the world and stopping opportunistically where she could find work to finance the next leg of her adventure. She had worked as a journalist in Hong Kong and as a secretary in India. In Rio she was learning Portuguese and supporting herself by doing errands for a film production company. We made a date to have a tête-à-tête later in the week.

The seven of us polished off 10 delicious Cantonese dishes; Nelson Claudio paid the bill.

I asked Macmillan for additional leave, unpaid, and received a telegram back from Mr. Mayhew: "Wish you well. See me your return. No guarantee what position, if any, open 2 months hence. All best." Whatever apprehensions I had about postponing my return I brushed aside unexamined.

At first I was an honored guest in the commune, welcome to observe its potpourri of sloth and ambition. Within two weeks, though, because of my prodding for order and cleanliness and my disciplined writing schedule, I was an outcast to everyone except Walter, Eva and David Jr. I began to feel I was serving a strange, self-imposed sentence. For Jaime, especially, my bourgeois expectations took on the character of unwelcome demands. While I recognized that a sort of fellowship bound up our lives together, I didn't like its anarchic undertones.

My privileged status briefly returned when I got a letter from New York announcing that my piece about Rio's beaches had been accepted. The money order for $250 impressed everyone, including me. Getting paid real money plus expenses and a plane ticket set me apart from the writers in Walter's circle. Later in my stay, when everybody was once again thoroughly fed up with my attempts to impose everyday habits of cleanliness, news that I had received $5 from a U.S. academic quarterly for two poems did little to increase their esteem.

At first I was enthusiastic about integrating myself into this outpost of the intellectual/hippie side of Brazil. The feeling faded as I began to discover, painfully, that my assumptions and understandings were so different from those of my new Brazilian berthmates, it was fruitless to discuss them. At bottom, the apartment's inhabitants resented Americans as much as the conventional values of their own prosperous parents.

I was learning, drowning, wallowing, suspending my career in New York. When it came to insight into Brazilian culture Walter was, by his own admission, the fount of sagacity. He challenged my intuitive understandings, reinterpreted my observations, took exception to 50 percent of my conclusions. I wished he could help me with my inexact understanding of myself.

Walter showed me his prose:

> Terrible things will happen. Soon in Asia, Africa, America Latina. It's not for nothing that these three names begin with 'A'. 'A' is the beginning. The beginning of the tempest. Because of that everyone should follow his own way. And it is within each one that this way exists.

I found his writing naive and pretentious but also oddly fresh, unlike the predictable prose of young American polemicists. One morning at the beach Walter abandoned his usual lecture to instruct instead by parable and illustration. He repeated a story told to him by a left-wing student: "Marcelo was on a rich man's yacht when they came close to a ship. Nothing about the ship attracted their attention. Suddenly they heard screams carried over the water. They went closer to listen. They heard a woman's scream. Within seconds guards ran onto the deck holding machine guns. They pointed their weapons at the yacht and fired a warning shot. Later they found out that, for secrecy, the military government had ordered several merchant ships to be refitted as prisons and anchored off the coast."

"I'm skeptical," Jaime said.

"So you should be," Walter replied, "but only of the details. The story contains poetic truth."

CHAPTER FOUR

A woman
Trying to get a bargain
Stuck her umbrella in Eduardo's nose
Because, a woman
Isn't true unless she's a virgin.

E. Catherine Lawrence

I

Confined in my windowless box, hemmed in, no adequate light to read, I would find myself still fretful at 4 in the morning. David Jr.'s apartment slept as I kept vigil over bodies younger than mine. Late at night the apartment breathed sadly in unison. When, at last, David Jr.'s bachelor pad (sans David Jr.) settled down for the night, I would lie awake, breathing the rank smell from the bathroom and question my long-range plans. Sometimes I would indulge my sadness over the breakup with Sérgio. I did not believe Walter and Eva, tangled together in the bedroom, were happy, nor Jaime and Ana Maria sleeping on the living-room couch, nor whatever odd souls might have set up camp on mattresses in the unused kitchen.

In fact, I thought everyone I knew in Rio de Janeiro was sad in a way that had no cure and, perhaps, no cause. I excepted the bridegroom from the Mato Grosso prairie. He had a reason. Sadness, a vague loneliness that crept inside the heart, came unbeckoned in the dusk. It was nursed in a feminine breath, heavy, sweet and warm — the breath of Rio itself. For brief moments it could be quenched by a glance, a promise, a few seconds of engaging conversation.

A beautiful cashier could confer not only correct change but a wordless consent to a subtle approach; she could make your heart stop. A secretary could do more than type a letter. She could be a mistress, fidgety and wet with desire, anticipating the arrival of her married lover. Wives spent their days in one of Rio's 2,581 beauty parlors and their early evenings waiting by the windows of bourgeois apartments, looking for half-truths in the street, waiting for the sounds of their husbands' keys in the door.

The whole city was in love and out of love at the same time and it made everyone miserable. Even scientists and engineers succumbed. Effortlessly, the city itself stimulated the general sadness by lying invitingly curled around the blue-green bay like a languid woman pressed against the buttocks of her lover. By day her hair was adorned with butterflies, flowers, fleecy clouds. At night she wore a string of glowing lights — strands of diamonds entwining the tall buildings, the mountains and the outstretched arms of Christ the Redeemer. Her movements were slow, easy. Rio, the woman, was not in a hurry.

Love was a lottery over which there was no control. Politics, however, was steady, ongoing, eternal. No need to draw a winning number. A melancholy lover, exhausted from fornication, could always stumble out of bed and fall straight into the comforting arms of politics. Anyone, anytime, could score by talking to a cabdriver about former President Castelo Branco's last official act decreeing a new security law, or by exchanging *cruzeiros* for black-market dollars, by talking to a parent about money for education or a shopkeeper about devaluation. Life seemed to be a series of events strung together to offer variety and relief from love and from sadness. Events could add money or take it away, and this complicated love and kept everything fresh and painful. Reversals in fortune could come from any quarter at any time, and always landed a man or a woman in bed.

I explained my theory to Walter. "I disagree," he said. "In fact, it's the reverse. Politics is connected to displaced libido. People turn to politics because of unacknowledged lack of sexual intercourse."

"You think there's not enough sex in Rio?" I said.

"It's all bound up in perceptions. People have sexual energy and they don't know what to do with it. We're a Catholic country, baby."

"It seems to me everybody feels guilty and miserable when they're having sex and just as guilty and miserable when they're not. We're saying the same thing, Walter, from opposite sides. What about love?"

"A complication, just as you say."

Weekday mornings Eva and Ana Maria got up and dressed for work in the dirty surroundings, but miraculously they turned out fresh, clean-smelling, impeccably groomed. How did they perform so successfully a feat beyond my abilities? I tried to spy on them to discover their secrets but the bathroom door was closed, and besides, not all the miracles took place there. They had only to walk through the few rooms of the apartment for glamour to leap out to them and stick to their perfect, supple bodies. They wore beautiful, fashionable sports clothes perfectly washed and ironed as if by maids whom no one saw. Their hair shone with good health and each vibrant strand contributed to an enviable composition. Their skin was suntanned evenly and each had, by another miracle, a real mole next to her full lips.

I looked around the apartment for the French makeup artist who must have passed through the outside wall into the apartment. This prestidigitator, I imagined, was the one who applied the shiny black eyeliner to Eva's and Ana Maria's lovely brown eyes in small vertical strokes to exaggerate their lower lashes. Clown makeup was the mode of the moment. The fashion agreed with both young women — Eva, small, well-proportioned, natural blonde, and Ana Maria, tall and rounded, with long brown hair.

Furtively, I recorded the apartment's daily life. While the parents of Walter, Jaime, Eva, Ana Maria and the other hangers-on worked in their antique shops, saw patients in their clinics or ran their manufacturing businesses, their offspring divided into two camps: male and female. The women went to downtown offices; the men stayed home.

The young men spent much of their time simply hanging around. They often left David Jr.'s apartment around 10 in the morning, gathering up volumes of Nietzsche, Kierkegaard, Hemingway, Ferlinghetti, e e cummings and Pound to read on Copacabana Beach. The glorification of Nietzsche's superman theory was intoxicating to Walter and to the powerless students who attended him. They cheered a literature that spoke of chaos, because dislocation and demise were exactly what they all hoped would befall bourgeois society in Brazil. They were sad for the revolution they had never had.

One day a Chilean boy, Guillermo, a new arrival in the apartment, his hair bleached chrome yellow by the sun, accompanied us to the beach.

"Let it rain down on our heads," Walter said, recalling for his listeners the 12 years that Ezra Pound spent confined in a mental hospital in Washington, D.C. "Kultur with a 'K'. Kaos with a 'K'. It's all the same, baby. Who was really the madman, Pound or his judge?"

Walter's question was not addressed to anyone in particular. Everyone nodded, including me, as we continued to squint directly into the sun. The beach began to fill up with vendors. It wasn't the first time I had heard Walter use mystic alliteration to tie up his philosophy of clarity through confusion. I rather enjoyed the cadence of his rants and their literary allusions. I wandered off to buy fresh pineapple slices from a skinny black hawker. The Chilean boy tagged along after me. "Isn't he wonderful?" Guillermo said. Without waiting for me to agree, he continued, "I love him."

The night before, on my way through the living room to my cubicle, I couldn't avoid observing Walter's fingers interlaced in Guillermo's luxuriant blond hair as they sat together on the sofa. "Who gave you your hair?" Walter had asked softly. "Was it the moon or the sun?"

When I returned with my pineapple, Walter had not run out of steam: "The Fascists were wrong, but so are the Americans who want only profit. Business has filled the pockets of the politicians in Brazil who cling to the coattails of the United States. There are backdoor interests attached to every dollar America invests in America Latina."

"You're full of shit, Walter," I said. "Even so, I love you anyway."

"Wait 'til the whole story comes out. We'll see who's right."

"What story?"

"The story of the U.S.'s backroom deal to put our military in power. And not only that — their continuing maneuvers to keep them there. You have a hell of a big embassy in Brazil. Christ, you'd think we were Germany or something."

"Brazil's a big country. We probably need a large staff."

"Think about it. Who are all those people working in your embassy? Doing what? Holding classes on fiscal responsibility? Besides, Brazil has a way of correcting its problems. It always has."

After a morning on the beach the young men often had a leisurely snack at one of several restaurants on Avenida Atlântica that had large open terraces facing the beach. In the afternoons they would take classes in English, French, sometimes German or guitar. They also spent countless hours in the peculiarly Brazilian activity known as "looking for someone." Since telephones had minds of their own, connecting by phone was next to impossible. It could take hours of frantically clicking the disconnect button just to get a dial tone. After that the

41

chances of completing a call were only 50-50. In addition, people had to wait years to get telephones installed in their offices or apartments. Many potential subscribers went without.

Brazilians are resourceful if nothing else. They still used their hundred-year-old pre-telephone system to get around their inability to make instant connections. They hired legmen — adolescent boys and older men who carried messages in leather briefcases back and forth. The notes covered the entire range of human interactions from invitations for a business lunch to messages of regret for canceled love affairs. The legmen didn't dawdle.

Lack of money wasn't the only reason Walter and his followers didn't employ legmen. They preferred to do the work themselves. Their version of the enterprise was to station themselves at popular bars and restaurants in Copacabana and Ipanema where their quarry was known to spend time. Drinking Coca-Cola and eating raw vegetables, they would wait for the object of their search to appear. It could take a week or more of intermittent waiting and then, by agreement, their business was never completed. The conclusion of one meeting immediately initiated the beginning of the next period of looking for the same person. It started as soon as the principals shook hands good-bye.

The first time I accompanied Walter and Jaime on such a mission we ran into another friend who claimed to have seen the object of their quest the night before at the very same bar. "At what time?" Walter inquired.

"About half past 9," the friend said.

Of course they had left at quarter past 9 to go to a movie, having given up hope for that day. We decided to stick around the bar and got into a discussion about ambition. Walter surprised us: "I'm half a fake, you know, because I still want to make movies, write books, compose songs that become popular."

42

"Still?" I asked.

Walter furrowed his brow in mock seriousness. "Naked ambition is wrong in a prophet."

Looking for someone could and did eat up lives but if you weren't otherwise occupied, and were of a patient nature, it was an agreeable career. Walter tolerated the activity without questioning too closely why it was necessary. In fairness, I don't believe he ever thought of it as an end in itself.

"Brazilians like to make simple things hard to avoid confronting life's real questions," I said.

Walter smiled. "We toil away at pleasure."

The women in the group carried on a very different and, in my opinion, harsh life compared with the men's life of ease. They worked in downtown offices, or in shops or schools. Each took her pay in cash and carried her neat bundle of bills back to David Jr.'s apartment on Fridays to take care of her needs, the needs of the young man she seriously loved and his friends. They had the abortions, suffered the infidelities, and despite extreme heat, maintained a standard of fashion that would have been the envy of New York or London. Their arms never tired from the weight of dozens of bangles. Each finger had the correct balance of modish, twisted silver and gold bands. The polish on their tapered nails was never chipped. Whatever subject or style they chose to explore, they attacked with maximum enthusiasm.

The young women who lived in David Jr.'s apartment adorned not only themselves but Rio itself. They walked with the assurance that all eyes were upon them. Walter, the intellectual, was duty-bound not to acknowledge Eva's beauty or her sensuality. If anyone had questioned him on the subject of Eva's grace he would have had to take the moral position that such things were, correctly, beyond his notice.

Eva had her own moral responsibilities. Hers, however, included such practical considerations as getting to her job each morning roughly on time. Eva and Ana Maria read the newspapers every day so that they could inform the men which movies were showing or which plays or art galleries had openings. The young women often arrived at the apartment at twilight with theater tickets for everyone in their purses.

In general, the women in Rio were both gorgeous and inquisitive. They turned heads with the sway of their hips. Their carriage was erect and proud. They liked to practice their English with strangers, and they paid full attention to new ideas, promptly incorporating them into their cosmopolitan, assured approach to the world.

Jane and I became comrades in voluntary hand-to-mouth existence. When Jane wasn't busy scouting locations and finding exotic props for her film company (a parrot that spoke French, an antique pearl-handled pistol, black satin bedsheets) we would meet and, out of earshot of our Brazilian friends, exchange observations. Walter would have disparaged our discussions. I looked forward to the more normal conversations I could have with Jane. She was my natural ally.

One night over dinner she asked, "If you could have any man in this restaurant, who would it be?"

I surveyed the animated diners. "No one. They're all too homely. I don't understand it. There are two races in Brazil, the beautiful women and the unattractive men. In New York I met incredibly handsome Brazilian men, but in Rio they're mostly plain. They must give passports only to the handsome ones. The beautiful men are for spreading false impressions about Brazil abroad."

Jane laughed. "The other day I read a profile of a Chilean poet, Nicanor Parra. He said the Chilean women are pretty and intelligent but the ordinary Chilean man is short-legged and not so very clever." She leaned back in her seat and studied me with a deliberate glance. "So who were these beautiful Brazilian men in New York?"

"I had an affair with a Brazilian diplomat. He wasn't just beautiful — he used to edit my poems. He was good at it. He was the Brazilian Consul General in New York."

Jane kept probing. "I understand better why you came here. Did you think he was going to marry you?"

"I did," I said. "I worried about being a diplomat's wife." Sérgio's colleagues, I told her, expected a kind of domestic servitude from their wives that was repellent to me. None of these women worked, although they were very well-educated and each spoke several languages. Whenever they appeared in public they were beautifully turned out. They had, on average, three and one-half children, they attended official receptions, gave elaborate cocktail parties in their tasteful apartments, suffered the idiosyncrasies of their imported maids, visited the museums and the Madison Avenue art galleries on Saturday afternoons, believed Brazil was the best country in the world, read books and slept late. "They got the pick of the handsome Brazilian men," I said, "the ones allowed to go abroad, but —"

Jane interrupted, "Sentenced to life in a gilded cage with no career in sight. It does sound wasteful and boring."

We commiserated over the sad state of affairs that forced beautiful, generous, responsible women at home in Brazil to involve themselves with homely, irresponsible, unfaithful men. They came together because nature knew no other way, but it was exploitation.

"The men here are cynical, completely charming bastards," Jane said. "The country wouldn't be a go without its women."

We vowed to visit Uruguay to compare. Suddenly I couldn't hold back vivid images of my breakup with Sérgio. Jane stared at me with growing concern. "Are you okay?" she asked as I reached inside my purse for a tissue.

"I was remembering my last three days with Sérgio. I'm fine, really."

"From the look on your face, I'm not so sure."

"I'm fine, but our split-up still hurts. And rankles. I know where Sérgio stands — he doused the flame."

Jane's expression was skeptical. "He's the reason you came here."

"He took me away to another reality. I wanted to experience it myself — the positive side and all the flaws."

"Then will your life be back on track?"

"Absolutely. I've promised myself."

"I think you're doing penance living with Walter and his merry gang."

"If I am, it's for a crime I didn't commit except in Sérgio's imagination."

"Don't tell me — he said you were unfaithful."

She smiled knowingly when I nodded. "With one of his subordinates," I said.

"I could have guessed that part, too. Your Sérgio decided he'd gotten in too deep and was looking for an excuse to break off. Accusation, indignation, tears — and he's free. Old story."

"You're a cynic."

"After two years here, you bet I am."

"I don't believe he was planning to break up with me when he did. He was just a few weeks away from getting his Swiss divorce and we were planning our wedding."

46

"He'd probably been lying to himself as much as to you about his intentions. He seized an opportunity."

Walter moved between women and men, loving each in turn, but at the time I resided with the gang Eva was the one he returned to. I never asked Walter, and it certainly was none of my business, but I knew the answer: Walter accepted each relationship for the sweetness it offered. He promised nothing. He lied about nothing in return for the hospitality.

When Eva met Walter she was 22 and had already had two abortions. She had another while I was an occupant of the apartment. She was then 24. Ana Maria and I observed as she prepared for her third abortion. Around midnight Eva counted out a huge stack of bills and sorted them neatly by denomination on the battered coffee table until the tally was correct. She rolled the stacks of *cruzeiros* into businesslike bundles, secured them with green rubber bands and put the bills inside her stylish purse. Then she went to sleep. The next morning I heard her leave the apartment much earlier than usual. When she came back at dinnertime, not pregnant, having worked all day, she never mentioned her ordeal nor showed any sign of needing to rest. I didn't wonder about her choice not to have a baby, but I wondered about her willingness to be incautious repeatedly.

I continued to delve into Rio's mysteries, gathering my strong emotions, putting them into poems and journals. Walter accused me of strip-mining, and he was right. I had become besotted with a city that was slightly Victorian, slightly mad, confident, tantalizing, concerned with its prestige and unfailingly tolerant of dawdling. No misstep was fatal, no conversation more interesting than one concerning the complications of love.

One morning I trudged up one of the city's granite mountains to visit a *favela*. People told me it was dangerous. I ignored their warnings. From a distance the colorful cantilevered shacks looked like tarnished ornaments. Close up, the raw poverty made me angry. I put my feelings in a poem:

> Will she believe it, the young wife,
> That her husband was caught in a fight?
> Her belly is round in agreement,
> She is missing several teeth …

Later in my journal I wrote: "I pray for anger. We write against the distress of our lives. Writing is a revolt. To remember is to renew."

II

Eventually the bathroom at the apartment and I parted company. Its stench and unsavory hygiene overwhelmed my ingenuity. With the availability of low-wage household help, the other Brazilian apartments I had visited — from lavish to very modest — were notably clean and tidy. David Jr.'s was a bohemian aberration. I had learned, after a fashion, how to shower and brush my teeth and use the toilet without touching any slimy surface. I had also learned how to hold my breath for long periods. I would gulp a bite of stale air as I entered the bathroom, hold my breath as long as I could, open the door a crack when my breath gave out, exhale and inhale deeply and continue my toilette. It usually took 18 breaths to complete my ablutions.

Toward the middle of my trying encampment, an unconscious plan evolved. I had joined the gang gathered in the living room to celebrate the publication of Jaime's poem by an important São Paulo newspaper. Before going to bed, quite out of character, I drank a liter bottle of beer. I woke up having to use the toilet and walked into the bathroom to discover the floor flooded with some disgustingly malodorous deluge. Since it was impossible to enter I couldn't identify the source of the flooding. It probably was the toilet but it could have been anything. Unpalatable sources were not in short supply. I didn't want to speculate further at that hour. As the beer pressed against my bladder, I reached for my clothes in the dark and threw them on. I ran my fingers quickly through my hair, tucking it behind my ears, opened the door to my room and walked quietly through the living room, trying not to stare at the two sleeping bodies silhouetted on the couch.

Once outside on the street, shaking with urgency, I ran the three blocks to the Copacabana Palace Hotel straight past the dozing uniformed doorman and into the clean, pleasant ladies' room. I then sleepily retraced my steps to David Jr.'s apartment and slipped peacefully onto my shelf.

The next day the flood still was not cleaned up. David Jr., the boy with the money, had to be located to set the repairs in motion. Jaime went "looking for" him and learned that David Jr. was visiting his grandmother in Salvador. I had no idea how my fellow freeloaders managed to live with this disaster but everyone looked clean and scrubbed as usual.

My plan to deal with the bathroom catastrophe centered on the wonderful Copacabana Palace, one of Rio's few hotels in the luxury class. The large and immaculate ladies' room had peach sinks and marble counters. Peach terrycloth hand towels were stacked in thick piles between the sinks and scattered about were pastel boxes of soft facial tissue. Compared with my bivouac, the luxury was overwhelming.

For days, long after the bathroom had been returned to its usual grubby condition, I gathered up my toothbrush and paste, my Noxzema cleansing cream and my makeup and sauntered off to the hotel to get properly cleaned up. I took wonderful bird baths in the graceful sinks, clasping the absorbent towels to my washed, wet limbs, and relaxed in the tastefully wallpapered ladies' sitting room adjacent to the bathroom. There, for no money at all, I could sit on a pink velvet couch and read and write and think in splendor.

I entered the lobby early each morning in clothes that lacked a wealthy tourist's attention to fashion and pressing. Still, the doorman greeted me as if I belonged. I knew he was responding to the education he saw shining through my rumpled attire, and I received his greeting as my due. The cheerful attendant in the ladies' room came and went throughout the day in a professional round of scouring, refilling supplies, collecting tips, never questioning my hanging about. I was an American and therefore rich and entitled.

In the middle of the night I made the trip to my secret island of fastidiousness and luxe with increasing abandon. After a while I stopped taking care to avoid noise as I let myself out into the corridor. The topsy-turvy household be damned. I never explained my nocturnal wanderings to the inhabitants of the apartment. Walter and Jaime could think I met a married lover or bought drugs.

Several days into my routine I confessed my invasions of the Copacabana Palace to David Jr. Since his mother had been half American, I thought he would appreciate my Yankee ingenuity. He smiled wanly, not really registering what I said: "My father owns the hotel, actually 51 percent of it." That evening when I went to a party at David Sr.'s I enjoyed the irony of washing up in his hotel and then returning to sleep in his son's squalor.

CHAPTER FIVE

Will she believe it, the young wife,
That her husband was caught in a fight?
Her belly is round in agreement,
She is missing several teeth.
She is lavender-smelling, spontaneous, clean
In the *favela* midst of urine, orange pulp,
And stained flowers cowering on cheap cotton.
There was an overall plan to her loveliness.
She knows only the responses of day-to-day,
Rain, carnival, treacherous rain tumbling newsprint shacks,
Cachaça, samba, rain. The beach is for light skin,
But the pavements are for the black prostitutes
Who wriggle their revenge outside the Copacabana Palace.
No need to cure diseases, life expectancy
Is just not to expect.

E. Catherine Lawrence

I

Twice a week at least, to bring variety into my diet of hippie cuisine and rhetoric, I would accept an invitation to a party or a dinner date. After Nelson Claudio returned from Argentina, he would show up at the apartment with some regularity. Sometimes we went out with the gang; other times he took me out alone.

One hot afternoon Walter was in the living room playing his guitar. I was lying on my mattress, writing in my journal. Walter called me to join him. Everyone was out. Gone with the apartment's inhabitants was his need to be the leader, to posture. "You're in a whimsical mood," I said.

"How can you tell?"

"By your playing."

"Ah, well, you can only be whimsical occasionally when your ancestry is German. Even when it's far back, like mine."

We talked against the mellow sound of his strumming. After half an hour he allowed his playing to become more purposeful. We stopped talking. Before he or I fully realized it, he had composed a song that recounted his first evening in New York City.

Walter had told me the story before. He had arrived in New York in August 1966 full of wonderment. After checking into a hotel on Lexington Avenue, he dropped his luggage in his room and rushed outside to take his first walk on the streets of New York. He hadn't walked more than a few blocks, gathering impressions, when he was attacked by two young black men who demanded his wallet and his watch. One of them, the taller of the two, made sure Walter saw a hunting knife he held half-in and half-out of his jacket pocket. Walter's wallet was stuffed with *cruzeiros* and dollars. The shorter man punched him hard in the temple, cracking his eyeglasses. Then he knocked Walter to the pavement.

"I just arrived in America, man. It's all the money I have in the world." It was the truth.

"Shit, man," the taller man snapped, threatening Walter's face with the toe of his shoe as the shorter man took his wallet, unbuckled his watch and tossed them to his partner.

"Please, mister."

"Shit, man," the tall man cursed again.

Before fleeing, he opened Walter's wallet, took out a $5 bill and threw it on the sidewalk near Walter's head. "Have a good time," he barked over his shoulder as he and his buddy took off. They had taken a few bounds down the sidewalk when the shorter man ran back to

Walter, bent down on the pavement, grabbed him by both his shoulders and kissed him fully and sensuously on the lips. "Yeah, have fun, man."

Walter had cleverly woven all this information into his new composition. When Eva and Ana Maria arrived a few hours later, Walter had polished his song into a fine jewel. He feigned casualness to the young women about his afternoon's endeavors, but I knew he was anxious for their approval. When Walter sang the final surprising line about being kissed on the lips by his mugger, tears welled in Eva's eyes. "It's amazing, Walter," she said. "So moving. It's the best song you've done, ever."

Later the song was recorded in São Paulo. It became a minor hit in that city and in Rio. It also placed first in the annual Rio song festival, beating a song by one of Brazil's most popular composer-performers. Walter titled his song *Dedos Amarelos* (Yellow Fingers) because his mugging took place a block away from that well-known New York restaurant.

II

The summer rainy season was half over. Feeling at the end of my financial and emotional resources, knowing I had to leave Brazil soon, I sat cross-legged after dinner on my fetid mattress listening to Walter play his guitar in the next room. A flying insect buzzed at my face. I could feel the advance of Carnival beginning to invade my life. Ash Wednesday was 11 days away.

Some *cariocas* — natives of Rio — would not wait for the three days of happiness to begin. For them, the first steps of the season would be danced at the Artists' Ball, beginning in a few hours at the Hotel Gloria. And next Saturday, before the official launch of Carnival, the Rio Yacht Club would hold its exclusive Hawaiian Night. Invitations were brokered and fussed over months in advance.

Preparations for the annual rite had begun in late December. I became aware of them when I first heard the gentle throb of drums coming from the *favela* perched precariously on the hill behind David Jr.'s apartment. The compelling beat mingled with the ordinary sounds of the city at work. At night the drums grew louder and voices were added. A fast-paced chanting in a hypnotic, nasal singsong broke into my meditations.

During January and early February Walter and the others paid no attention to what was coming. The dissonant sounds of whistles, drums, triangles and a weird, wheezing instrument — the *cuíca* — increased as Rio readied itself for its revel. The sounds not only came from the surrounding hillsides but also erupted on the streets as impromptu parades streamed down from the *favelas*, clogging the Copacabana evening traffic. While the countdown ticked away, seamstresses all over town doubled their prices as they worked throughout the nights, sleepily attaching the final excesses to elaborate tinsel and satin costumes.

I would have been curious to be thrown into a Carnival ball's perspiring, crowded whiskey breath, but I couldn't afford a ticket. At midnight, I had just put down my book, ready to go to sleep, when Nelson Claudio, out of breath and dressed in a white tuxedo, showed up at the apartment. "I got two press passes to the Artists' Ball at the last minute, Kate. Come with me."

"Fantastic, but I don't have a costume."

"It's not strict. You can wear anything — a ball gown, a costume, jeans — it doesn't matter. Get ready. It started two hours ago."

"It's café society, Kate," Walter called over from the sofa. "I feel obligated to look out for your interests. All the balls are nothing but drunks, bare flesh, embracing and waving arms. But do what you want."

"Walter's right," Nelson Claudio said. "But you should experience a Carnival ball at least once."

"Of course I'm going. I wouldn't miss it."

In the end neither of us went to the ball. As we left the apartment Nelson Claudio got a riveting chest pain that practically glued his feet to the sidewalk. He could barely speak. I didn't wait for him to recover his breath. I hailed a taxi and told the driver to rush us to the nearest hospital.

When we arrived at the emergency entrance, no one was on duty. I helped Nelson Claudio to a chair, ran down a deserted, dimly lighted hospital corridor and at last found a nurse sitting in a small office peacefully reading a *foto-novela* — a romance in comic-book format. I shouted to her to come with me at once. When we got back to the emergency entrance Nelson Claudio was slumped over, looking more dead than alive. His tuxedo jacket was soaked through with sweat and his round face was ashen. The nurse grabbed his wrist for a pulse and said, "It's good you got him here." She ran to a nearby intercom and shouted for assistance. It arrived quite promptly despite the late hour and the general slowdown in all forms of service that accompanied the approach of Carnival. Nelson Claudio was helped onto a gurney and wheeled down the corridor out of sight. The tickets to the Artists' Ball in his pocket would probably be discovered by a hospital employee, who would use them at the end of the shift.

Everything had happened so fast. It took me some minutes to fully appreciate where I was and how I was dressed — in a slinky red evening gown borrowed from Ana Maria. The hospital seemed so foreign, more like a snoozing tropical barracks than a place to get well. I wandered outside into the hot night to look for a taxi.

When I arrived back at the apartment at 3 in the morning, everyone was out. I needed to get in touch with Nelson Claudio's family but I had no idea where they lived. I fretted and paced the living room in Ana Maria's expensive gown for another hour until Jaime arrived. He knew Nelson Claudio's cousin. I left the details up to him.

III

The next day I learned from Jaime that Nelson Claudio had had a heart attack of medium severity. He was resting comfortably in an oxygen tent. I had suspected heart trouble but promptly dismissed my diagnosis because he was too young. It seemed everyone was shocked, including the attending resident.

Jaime conveyed the thanks of Nelson Claudio's mother for my "very American" reaction to the crisis. She believed Nelson Claudio's Brazilian girlfriends might have suggested they sit on one of the stone benches along the beach sidewalk and wait for him to catch his breath.

During the following 16 days I wanted to visit Nelson Claudio in the hospital but was told by Jaime that, except for family, visitors were not allowed. Finally, Tuesday night, as Jaime and Ana Maria were leaving for the Monte Líbano Ball, Carnival's grand finale, Jaime said Nelson Claudio could receive visitors.

Ash Wednesday dawned bright and hot. I left the apartment at 9 to take a bus to the hospital. Rio was a shambles. Sleeping bodies lay everywhere. Drunks sitting on curbs held their heads between their knees. Tattered princesses, stumbling viceroys, dazed Arab chieftains wandered in the middle of semi-deserted back streets. Couples in all stages of dress and undress slumped together in doorways or lay in each other's arms at the bases of staircases. Bushes, too, provided refuge for the exhausted. Collapsed courtiers breathed foul-smelling *cachaça* into my path as I walked by. In the distance I heard a never-say-die samba band winding down. Street sweepers were beginning to tackle the tons of debris left behind by the revelers. It was a huge job for a city that did not exalt maintenance.

I took a bus to the public hospital, Miguel Couto, in Gávea, where I had taken Nelson Claudio. I got off too soon and had to walk three blocks to the hospital. As I approached the building I saw an ambulance driving slowly into a secluded rear entryway, followed closely by two police cars. I thought it odd that the ambulance didn't pull up to the emergency entrance.

Nelson Claudio was in good spirits when I entered the ward he shared with four other patients. He was not inside the oxygen tent. His mother, a small, intense, dark-haired woman, sat at his bedside. They were both full of thanks and vows to be of service to me while I visited Brazil. "I appreciate your offer," I said. "Unfortunately I'm leaving Rio in a few weeks. I've got to go back to work."

Nelson Claudio tired before my eyes as we chatted about my experiences in Brazil. The effort to *fazer charme* (make charm) was obviously exhausting. I wished him a speedy recovery and left.

I was on my way out of the hospital when I noticed a commotion in a corridor just off the main entrance. Two uniformed policemen were conferring with a group of white-coated hospital staff. It was still early and I had no definite plans for the day. I stopped to listen. The cops were describing the condition of a body they had found in the Botanical Garden. I overheard one of the cops say a pedestrian, an older woman, had informed him that a man dressed in ordinary street clothes was sleeping on top of some exotic plants near the entrance. The woman said she walked there every day and knew that all the plants and trees in the Botanical Garden were protected by law and that he should sleep it off somewhere else. Then a maintenance worker rushed out of the garden with very much the same story. "I went in to have a look," one of the policeman said. "The guy wasn't asleep. He was dead."

I was vaguely curious about the story, but not enough to continue listening. As I was turning to leave, I thought I heard the second policeman say "shot." I moved closer to the group and took a seat, putting on the face of a stoic patient waiting to be seen by a doctor. I thought perhaps this was one of those anomalous stories I had been encountering in Rio — stories I challenged myself to turn into poems.

Within minutes a man in plainclothes joined the group. "The victim wasn't killed where we found him," he said. "He was dumped there. From his appearance and clothes, he could be a wealthy European tourist. No wallet." The plainclothes guy flipped open a small notebook and read aloud. "Male, mid-to-late fifties, large, heavyset. Pale blue eyes. Blond hair, thin and graying." He turned to a man in a white coat. "We need the autopsy report. Hurry it up. Some foreign government could be contacting us about a missing person who came to Rio for Carnival."

I left my seat and went back up to Nelson Claudio's room. His mother wasn't there. Nelson Claudio looked very drowsy. I moved close to his bed, leaned over and told him what I had overheard. "Please ask your nurse if she can find out anything," I said. "The joy of Carnival and murder mixed together. Just the kind of juxtaposition I like to write about." Nelson Claudio nodded his head and drifted into sleep.

Two days later, Friday, Jaime told me Nelson Claudio wanted to see me. When I got to the hospital, Nelson Claudio was alert and excited. "Kate, you've got good ears. Or should I say good instincts? And you're in luck. Turns out one of my nurses has a boyfriend who works in hospital administration. She found out they did an autopsy on that guy but the hospital isn't releasing any information."

"Isn't that normal, not talking about a police case?"

"Sure. Sure. And it could just be a simple case of assault and robbery. But I suspect something else. Fátima said her boyfriend was very guarded about what he told her."

"Have they got the name of the victim?"

"If they do, I don't think I can find it out. You said you overheard a cop say he thought the guy was European. What's a European doing in the Botanical Garden during Carnival? Normally very few tourists go there, though it's worth seeing. But during Carnival nobody would go. The action's on the downtown streets and in Copacabana. It doesn't make sense."

"Something tells me it isn't a simple robbery," I said. "I'll try to interview someone at the morgue. The real story might make an interesting poem. Thanks for asking around."

"I wish I could fill in more blanks for you."

A nurse came in to tell me I had used up my visiting time. Before I slipped out, I asked Nelson Claudio to tell me what he knew about the layout of the Botanical Garden.

CHAPTER SIX

I think of unmixed wants, a bed with sheets, not
Some stinking mattress speaking of departed love,
An antiseptic bath dusted off with a tender kiss
And a signed contract for a good day tomorrow.

E. Catherine Lawrence

I

Saturday morning I got up early to buy *Jornal do Brasil,* the Brazilian equivalent of *The New York Times,* still intrigued by the juxtaposition of Carnival with homicide. I wanted to see if the murder had been picked up by the press. A story headlined "Carnival 1968 About as Deadly as Last Year" caught my attention. The title reminded me of those stories in American newspapers listing all the traffic fatalities over Labor Day weekend. The statistics included Flávio Gruber, age 52, who had been found murdered in the Botanical Garden.

The story stated that a maintenance worker had found the body lying on some rare tropical plants near the entrance. The police doubted robbery was the motive because he was still wearing an expensive Rolex watch. Flávio Gruber had resided in Ipanema with his wife and three sons. Gruber's wife had reported her husband missing on Ash Wednesday. She had last seen him Tuesday night when he went out to walk their dog. Based on her description, the police had taken her Thursday to Miguel Couto Hospital to see if she could identify a body being held in the morgue. The article went on to say that Flávio Gruber owned the Arpoador Bowling Alley in Copacabana.

Walter disdained bowling as the current chichi pastime of café society. Both of Rio's bowling alleys were in Copacabana. Jaime, who occasionally bowled, had told me they were expensive and poorly equipped for the game. They served food, had elaborate bars, played *yé yé yé* music and were hangouts for David Jr. and his crowd of wealthy schoolmates.

The Arpoador Bowling Alley was lifeless when I entered its cavernous space at 11 a.m. It was dressed for evening and looked shabby in its nocturnal lighting with sunlight filtering in through the front window. A man of about 30, dusky complexion, wearing the latest Italian mode, was arranging glasses behind the bar. He looked distracted. We were alone in the gloomy space. I ordered a *Guaraná*, the ubiquitous Brazilian soft drink made out of a fruit from the Amazon rich in caffeine. The man behind the bar was eager to talk about the murder of his boss. He told me Flávio Gruber had been born in Munich. I had learned from a morgue attendant at the hospital that the victim's Rolex watch had a German inscription on the back: "*Meinem geliebten Friedrich* (For my beloved Friedrich)." "Maybe Flávio was a World War II refugee," I said.

"I never heard him talk about the war. You might be right. I never asked him. He prided himself on efficiency. He knew how to run a business. He once told me he managed 3,000 workers."

I continued to probe discreetly. It turned out that the man behind the bar was the manager. When I thought I had extracted everything he was willing to tell me, I paid for my drink and left.

An incredible idea was working its way through my brain. Flávio was a Nazi. Somebody had fingered him. Flávio Gruber, possibly Friedrich Gruber, was 52 when he died. That would make him 24 when the war started. According to the manager's story, Flávio must have been around 30 when he arrived in Brazil. He had started out as a waiter and been involved in the restaurant business ever since. The only way he could have managed a workforce of 3,000 would have been as an officer in a munitions factory or mine that used slave labor.

61

When I returned to the apartment Walter and Eva, relaxed and tanned, were just settling in after three days at the historic beach town of Cabo Frio. They had left Rio to avoid Carnival. I disappeared into my cubicle to write.

I tried writing a narrative poem about Gruber's death, modeled on one I had written in New York after Paulo told me the story of a Brazilian businessman who electrocuted his wife by throwing her radio into her bath. As my crumpled failures mounted up, it occurred to me that what I had was a news story, not a poem. Maybe this was a chance to stretch myself in a new direction. I decided to try writing an impressionistic newspaper piece.

I needed more than just guesswork. Thinking the Botanical Garden was a good place to start, I took a bus there. After wandering around for a while, I found the maintenance worker who had discovered Gruber's body. He showed me the plants on which it had been lying near the entrance, a place where it was sure to be discovered. I asked if he had seen a lot of blood. "No," he said, "The cops got a surprise, though. There was an envelope with some writing on it pinned to the guy's shirt. One cop read it aloud: 'Those who will never forget.' The other cop said, 'That's a new one,' and the first cop put the envelope in his pocket."

When I got back to the apartment, I told Walter about the message on the envelope. He said it sounded familiar. He recalled that a Nazi living in Brazil had been taken to Montevideo and killed. "It was a big story a few years ago," he said. "The killers left a message."

"You're sure about that?"

He nodded.

"Christ, Walter, I need to check that out."

He suggested I try the archive at *Jornal do Brasil.* I took a bus downtown to the newspaper's office. I found my way to a helpful clerk who handed me clips about the killing of Herberts Cukurs, a famous prewar aviator who had become an SS officer. He had fled Germany with the retreating Nazi troops and turned up in Brazil in 1946. He was so sure Brazil wouldn't extradite him that he lived in São Paulo under his real name, married, had children and set up a thriving tourist-excursion business. In 1964 he was lured to Montevideo, where he was shot to death in an isolated beach house. The killers had sent messages to the press signed, "Those who will never forget," saying that Cukurs had been found guilty of murdering thousands of Jews in Latvia and had been executed for his crimes. The messages told the Uruguayan police where to find his body. Pinned to Cukurs's shirt were the charges leveled against him and the verdict of death.

II

"Very interesting, Kate," Walter said when I showed him the third draft of my story about the drumbeat of Carnival drowning out the sound of a gunshot. "At least you haven't written about the usual nauseating Carnival insanity that everyone else rehashes year after year. Pierrots and Pierrettes dancing samba. All that crap. I'm sure you can get your piece published. I haven't a doubt."

A few hours later he walked into my muggy cubicle with a copy of William Shirer's book, *The Rise and Fall of the Third Reich.* He said, "I borrowed this for you from a friend."

In the index were several references to slave labor camps. One paragraph mentioned a Nazi officer, Friedrich Grabenz, who had brutally mistreated 3,000 women slave laborers at Essen. High-ranking Nazi commanders had found Grabenz remarkably able. He followed to the letter the dictates of barbarous exploitation laid down by Fritz Sauckel, Plenipotentiary General for the Allocation of Labor. I believed Flávio Gruber and Friedrich Grabenz could be one and the same.

I located the police station nearest to the bowling alley, walked in and asked to talk to the officer in charge. "We're aware of the rumors," the chief said in answer to my question about Nazis living in Rio. "Anything's possible." He dismissed me: "Talk to the Minister of Justice." We shook hands and I left.

All weekend I worked furiously in my miserable quarters, typing on Walter's portable Olivetti perched on my lap, subsisting on *Guaraná* and finger bananas. During intermittent forays into the streets of Copacabana for therapeutic walks I consumed cups of *cafezinho* and ate stale, sticky pastries.

Late Monday night I showed my completed story to Walter. "Are you crazy?" he said. "You actually walked into a police station. Christ, you should know better than that by now. Nobody in his right mind talks to the police. Come on, baby, let's walk over to the Velloso and see if Bernardo Braga's there. He can show your story to his editor at *Jornal do Brasil*. The paper might buy it."

Bernardo wasn't at the Velloso Bar. Walter suggested we try Jangadeiros, a restaurant popular with journalists. Bernardo wasn't there, either. We gave up.

Tuesday morning I decided to go downtown to the press section at the American Embassy, a nondescript, boxy, modern glass building. I found my way to James W. Donaldson III, the dour information officer newly arrived from Oslo. We talked in a government-issue reception area that probably registered near 90 degrees Fahrenheit. He didn't hesitate to tell me he wished he could be reposted to a phlegmatic, cool country. He longed for Oslo. Nothing about Rio suited him.

"I've written a story about a murder during Carnival. I was hoping I might get it published. Could you give me some advice?" My enthusiasm and naiveté must have seemed pathetic. It didn't help that the embassy's air-conditioning system had been out of order for 10 scorching days.

"I don't have time to read your story right now, Miss Lawrence. I suggest you try taking it around to the wire services. Try UPI and the AP. You could also try Copley. If those suggestions don't work, let me know. Maybe I can think of something else."

III

The United Press International bureau was on the sixth floor of the same building that housed *Jornal do Brasil*. When I entered, a reporter looked up briefly from his typewriter and pointed out the office of John Ford Wadson, the news director. His door was open. He signaled me to enter. He was lean, wearing caramel-colored horn-rimmed glasses and letting a crew cut grow out. His face and carriage were boyish, though I guessed he was in his mid-to-late thirties. "Let's take a look at your story," he said. He spoke with a Canadian accent and looked like a Royal Canadian Mounted Policeman in civilian attire.

I handed him my folder. A smile skittered across his mouth and eyes as he read. I liked his face. It was assured in a society where nothing was sure. While I waited, I looked around his office and was surprised to see Walter's collected essays on a bookshelf alongside an almanac, dictionaries, other political writings in Portuguese and English and some government publications. I looked at his left hand. No ring.

"E. Catherine Lawrence. Is that the name you use? Why not e c lawrence with lowercase 'e', 'c' and 'l'?"

"I sign my name E. Catherine Lawrence because I use Catherine, not my first name, Edwina. My mother was Edwina. Most people call me Kate. I like the e c lawrence, though. It never occurred to me."

"You've got an interesting story, Kate. A bit speculative, don't you think, suggesting that Gruber might have been killed in retaliation for activities he undertook during the war? What got you started on it?"

"A friend had a heart attack and I took him to the hospital. By accident I overheard a cop talking about a shooting victim found in the Botanical Garden. They'd just brought in the body. I was curious so I poked around."

"Who'd you talk to?"

"An attendant at the morgue. The manager at Gruber's bowling alley. The Botanical Garden maintenance worker who discovered the body. The police. I tracked down some rumors."

"I like your take on the story, blending the distraction of Carnival with murder, and the subtle way you used the Cukurs case to imply Gruber might have been a Nazi without actually saying so. Unfortunately, though, UPI doesn't buy pieces from freelancers. I've tried in the past, but our vice president in Buenos Aires always vetoes it."

"That's very disappointing."

"There are real Nazis in South America. They don't hesitate to do what's needed to protect themselves. Weren't you a little nervous asking around?"

"I didn't think about it."

"You could go see my competitor, Charlie Wall, at the Associated Press. I think the AP buys freelancers' stuff. Let me know how it turns out."

The AP office was a few blocks from UPI on the same street. In my high-heeled pumps, my gait invited street comment. A man with an umbrella pressed firmly against the side of his pot belly called out to me: "*Olá, bomba atômica.*" He invited me to run away with him, the sooner the better. I acknowledged his attention with a barely perceptible sashay.

I felt the muscles in my face soften, thinking about John Wadson. He intrigued me. Did he read poetry? e e cummings? I saw him

66

stretched out at night with a book, happily absorbed. I would have guessed by his appearance that his taste ran to Hemingway. Or, in the opposite direction, to Durrell.

Charlie Wall, a balding redhead with a gray beard, read my story, bought it and paid me $40 in cash on the spot. Normally, he said, a check would have had to come from New York.

I returned to UPI to thank John Wadson for his suggestion. He was out of the office on a story. I was surprised by the depth of my disappointment. I wrote a graceful thank-you note and left it for him. I thought about giving him my address but decided against it. I was leaving Brazil. My tourism was over.

The AP money bought me a number of pleasures. I thought I would spend part of my earnings luxuriating for a night back at the Hotel Vermont, sleeping on clean sheets, primping in a slime-free bathroom. I wanted to get away from the gang for at least 24 hours. I hadn't been alone for weeks. I needed privacy.

I returned to the apartment hoping to slip into my cubicle, gather up a change of clothes and slip out. It was nearly noon when I turned my key in the door. Two young men I had never seen before walked out of the kitchen, bleary-eyed. They looked innocent and childlike.

Walter was waking up, as he often did, by going through the tai chi form. I didn't want to disturb his meditative state. I pulled a few crumpled, dirty garments out of the drawer beneath my sleeping shelf, put them into a plastic sack, picked up my toiletries bag and wrote a note, which I left on my mattress:

To Whom It May Concern: I will return tomorrow afternoon.

I retraced my steps past Walter's floating arms to the front door. "How'd you do? Success?" Walter called out without breaking his form.

"I sold it to the AP. I'm exhausted. Finding the Shirer book was essential, Walter. Thanks. And thanks for all your suggestions. See you tomorrow."

Senhor Gonçalves welcomed me back to the hotel as a favored guest. My old room was available, and he gave it to me at the discounted price of $7.

Jane and I had dinner together that night at the Zeppelin, an Ipanema restaurant where we liked the food and the crowd of intellectuals and artists. When the bill came, I grandly paid the entire amount, equivalent in *cruzeiros* to $3.90. "Be careful with your money, Kate," Jane warned.

"Since I'm leaving soon, I can afford to splurge," I said.

Her caution was particularly impressive since I knew she thought nothing of treating herself, whenever the fancy took her, to a bouquet of cut flowers, or to a stylish leather belt or purse, or to sugary Brazilian champagne. "Don't you get tired of living out of a suitcase?" I asked. "It's wearing on me."

"I'm used to it. It's definitely better than living at home with dear old Mum. She's slightly deranged and definitely possessive. I like to keep at least one country between us."

After dinner I returned to my hotel room, picked up my sack of toiletries and entered the bathroom. Luxury, at last! I arranged my toothbrush and paste, shampoo, the Noxzema cream I used instead of soap to cleanse my face, deodorant, pressed face powder, mascara, the dark gray luminous liquid I used to paint false lashes under my hazel eyes, perfume, rosy liquid blush, Visine, blue-gray eye shadow,

68

hairbrush and large hair rollers on a glass shelf above the sink. No one else would set foot in that bathroom to disrupt or use my armaments. I had been aching for this private space for nearly six weeks.

The sink, the toilet, the bidet, the bathtub, the clean tile floor were mine alone. Also mine was an accoutrement unknown in America and, as far as I knew, unknown in Europe — a gas heater just like the one at David Jr.'s apartment, rectangular, about 20 inches high by 15 inches wide by 7 inches deep, attached to the wall at standing height near the bathtub. The jet protruding from the bottom needed to be opened carefully to release gas. When the gas hissed out, one had to light the invisible fumes immediately with a match. There was no other way to get warm water for a bath or a shower. Some gas heaters were self-lighting but, unfortunately, not the ones I encountered. These snarling jets scared me because of the way the gas erupted in a smelly fire-clap. Jaime had told me of his 14-year-old cousin who had been killed in a freak explosion lighting a gas heater for his bath. At David Jr.'s I often took a cold shower.

With tears in my eyes I surveyed my toilette utensils. Now that I had escaped, I intended never to return to the hospitality of David Jr.'s bivouac, even it meant the immediate end of my Brazilian odyssey. I recalled Mr. Mayhew's half-joking instruction to find "a Brazilian Borges" and sign him up as a Macmillan author. In my remaining time, perhaps I should do exactly that. I had met two candidates but I hadn't taken the initiative. Maybe now I should.

The next morning I bought *Jornal do Brasil* to see if it had picked up my story from the AP wire. No mention of it. In the afternoon I checked *O Globo*. Nothing.

When I told *senhor* Gonçalves I would stay on for three more days, he broke off his duties at the antiquated switchboard behind the reception desk and bowed. "I remain at your orders, *dona* Kate."

Late in the afternoon I walked back to the apartment, hoping every-one would be out. When I stepped off the elevator, Walter was on his way out the door. "Congratulations, Kate," he said, "the police would have covered up the fact that Gruber was a Nazi if it hadn't been for you."

"My story hasn't appeared."

"It will." He gave me a genial kiss on the cheek and sailed off down the corridor.

I called after him. "I'm going to treat myself to a few days at the Hotel Vermont with the money I got from the AP. See you soon."

I entered my rotting cubicle, gathered up a few more clothes and left a note on top of men's clothes piled on my mattress:

Moving out. I'll pick up my things by Friday. Kate

After dropping off my clothes at the Hotel Vermont, I took a bus to the hospital to tell Nelson Claudio I had sold my story to the AP. By now he and I had a bond. While I certainly would never remind him I owed my story to his heart attack, it was true.

When I arrived at the hospital, at first I couldn't find him. He had been moved to a nicer room, which he shared with only two other patients. He looked pale and fed up. He brightened when he saw me. "Thank Christ I'm leaving tomorrow. Do you realize I've been here for 25 bloody days? The damn doctor convinced my mother I should stay a few extra days for observation or I would have been gone last week. I have to get back to work. I'm desperate and bored. I need a cigarette. Have you got one?"

"Are you mad? Besides, I don't smoke except occasionally a Tiparillo when I'm writing. I brought some from New York."

"Fine. I'll smoke that."

"I don't have one with me."

"*Merda*."

"I've got some good news. The AP bought the piece I wrote about the murder."

"*Puxa vida*. That's sensational. Have you got a copy?"

"Of course." I handed him the copy I had made for him. "Don't bother reading it now."

"What's next? Will you write more stories?"

"I don't think so. I'm only going to stay in Rio till my money runs out, which will be soon, then go home. Anyway it would be hard to find another story as offbeat as Gruber's murder."

"So that's his name, Gruber? Sounds German."

"It is."

I told Nelson Claudio who I thought Gruber really was and how I had put the pieces together. He was stunned.

"Brazil has stories everywhere you look. I can lie right here and give you a few ideas without even trying very hard."

"Really. What?"

"Have you heard about the town in the interior that consists solely of a prison?"

"No."

"The prisoners, all murderers, run the prison on their own and even lock themselves in at night. No one ever escapes. They keep a schedule of everyone's sentence. When someone has served his sentence, the prisoner just walks away. Four times a year an official shows up to bring mail and to check on things."

71

"How efficient. It sounds like a fascinating arrangement. What do the prisoners do all day?"

"They play billiards. Sit in church. The town has three churches but no priest to say mass, except on Easter. No one lives in the town, just the prisoners. I can think of other stories for you."

"I want to hear them, Nelson Claudio, but I can't right now. I have to find another place to live until I leave Brazil. Yesterday I moved to the Hotel Vermont in Ipanema but I can't afford to stay there for many more days unless I decide to go home sooner than I intended. I adore Walter and David Jr. but I can't bear the filth and odd comings and goings at the apartment one more day. Can we meet after you get out of the hospital? I really just wanted to stop by to say hello and tell you about Gruber. I wasn't even sure you'd still be here."

Nelson Claudio moved upright in bed. "I hope you don't think staying with Walter Decker and his friends in that apartment is representative of Rio," he said. "By no means." He laughed. "It's a hippie flophouse, like you have in San Francisco, no? You're welcome to stay with us. My parents' house in Santa Teresa is quite large. My father isn't there very often. He has a girlfriend. My mother has had boarders for years. Usually it's a relative who wants to stay in Rio. But there aren't any relatives at this moment. A cousin left after Carnival."

"I wouldn't want to inconvenience your family. To be frank, what I really would like is to be on my own."

"You can't afford it. You can have all the privacy you need at my parents' house. No one resists Santa Teresa's charm. Have you been there? And it's very convenient to downtown — to everywhere, really. A lot of foreigners live there, especially Americans and Canadians, because it's picturesque and historic. Say yes, Kate." Nelson Claudio saw me waver. "The maid prepares breakfast. She can wash your clothes, too."

Should I accept his proposition sight unseen? I hesitated. Finally I said, "You're very generous, Nelson Claudio, and I'll keep your offer in mind, but I really think I have to get back to New York."

The next day I again bought Rio's leading newspapers to look for my story. Nothing. The front pages were full of a story about a bomb that was thrown at the residence of the U.S. air attaché in Rio. No one had been hurt. I stayed in my room at the hotel and wrote in my journal:

> The hypocrisy of charm. The neurotic machismo that is
> Brazil. Brazilians respect nothing and no one. Rio is a
> city of stunning beauty full of tropical Walter Mittys.

Feeling fidgety, I decided to walk back to the apartment to pick up a few more of my things. Jaime was lounging on the sofa, reading, looking sheepish. I chatted with him briefly about the bombing. He said it was an inaugural salvo. Inaugurating what, I wondered, but I didn't ask.

In my cubicle I found my books buried among clothes that were not mine. One of my high-heeled pumps was lying forlornly on the floor at the foot of the bed. I looked for its mate. I couldn't find it. Then I noticed that a sandal and another high-heeled shoe were also missing their mates. I looked everywhere, praying that each corner, each mess I poked into, would yield the missing shoes. I had three right shoes and no lefts.

I had intended to leave my clothes at the apartment another two days while I decided where I was going next. Seeing my possessions in disarray, I knew I needed to pack on the spot and take my two suitcases back to the hotel. I was beginning to suspect that the disappearance of my left shoes was somebody's idea of a joke, or even a sick retribution against an American who seemed to have too much, to be too lucky. Did Jaime have them? Without mentioning my missing shoes to him, I picked up my bulky valises and clumsily let myself out of the apartment.

The next day at noon I walked over to the Copacabana Palace Hotel, bought *Jornal do Brasil* at the newsstand, took a table at the elegant poolside café and splurged on a sandwich and a *Guaraná*. Page three carried the news:

Nazi Killed in Botanical Garden
During Carnival

It was a UPI story with no byline. In essence the article said that Friedrich Grabenz, commandant of a forced-labor camp at the Krupp armaments works in Essen, had been found murdered in Rio de Janeiro's Botanical Garden. It was suspected that the execution was carried out by an individual or group dedicated to meting out justice to Nazis.

The Israeli government denied any knowledge of the murder. *Senhora* Margarida Gruber stated that Flávio Gruber was a model husband and father. She and her three teenage sons did not believe the wartime malefactions attributed to him. They insisted it was a case of mistaken identity, although West German authorities confirmed Grabenz's crimes and said Gruber had distinguishing characteristics that matched their description of Grabenz. An envelope found on the body contained a note stating that Grabenz had been condemned to death for killing slave laborers. It resembled messages sent to the press by the people who killed Herberts Cukurs in Montevideo. I read the story again to make sure I wasn't misreading.

The waiter brought my sandwich. The instant he put the plate down, I asked for the bill. I took two bites, hurriedly left the hotel and hailed a taxi to take me downtown to UPI.

How had John Wadson found out what was in the envelope? Did the cops know that Gruber was Grabenz all along? Maybe Grabenz had been paying off a governor or a general for years to keep his secret.

Without waiting for the elevator in the *Jornal do Brasil* building I dashed to the stairs, took them two at a time and rushed, out of breath, into the UPI offices on the sixth floor. John Wadson was pecking away rapidly on a typewriter with two fingers, surrounded by reporters who were using all their fingers to beat out a steady rhythm. "How'd you tie Gruber to Grabenz?" I said.

He smiled, hit several keys, stopped and looked up with an even broader smile. The reporters around him looked up, too, but they didn't stop typing. "I'm glad you're here," he said. "I didn't know how to get in touch with you." He stood up. "Come to my office."

"How'd you do it?"

"I've got good contacts. But you found the story and did the leg-work. I might not have known about the envelope if you hadn't reported it."

I wanted to ask if he knew Walter, but I didn't think I was being invited to dig. We entered his office and Wadson sat down behind his desk. Too excited to take the seat opposite him, I remained standing.

"You should've put your telephone number and address in your note. What if I wanted to get in touch with you?"

"I don't have a phone. My address is pretty temporary. Did the AP also make the connection to Grabenz? *Jornal do Brasil* carried your story, not the AP's."

His grin was openly amused and confident. "The AP transmitted your story just about the way you wrote it. I checked. They didn't add a thing. Charlie thanked me for sending you over to him, by the way."

I feigned an air of casualness. I suspected that pleased him. "I was treating myself to an expensive sandwich at the Copa and starting to look at the paper when I saw your story. You must have some fascinating contacts."

"I guess I do." He smiled. "Did you finish your sandwich?"

"No."

"Perhaps you would be interested in doing some reporting for UPI?" The way he asked the question suggested he damn well knew my answer. With a pleasant shock, it struck me he was right. "That's why I wanted to get in touch with you. I can offer you three months on a trial basis. No guarantee beyond that. I don't even really have a position open right now. You'll be a local employee. Sorry, but the pay scale's local, too. What's your visa status, Catherine Lawrence?"

"My tourist visa expires in two and a half months. I didn't expect to stay in Brazil."

"Technically you should get a work permit. It's not that hard." He rapidly typed out a two-paragraph employment contract. "You better walk this over to the Labor Ministry today. That'll get the ball rolling. The Ministry will send its authorization to any Brazilian Embassy or Consulate you request. The embassy issues you a new visa that allows you to work. Use Montevideo. That's the most convenient. You can go down there before the end of the month and pick it up."

"I can't afford the trip right now."

"Normally we wouldn't pay an advance to somebody on a three-month tryout. We'll work something out."

We shook hands. "Was that a yes?" he asked.

"Yes," I said without asking how much the job would pay.

I assumed it would pay enough to let me stay on in Rio. It would also provide a credential that would open doors. I was curious about John Wadson, a bit mystified, and more than a bit attracted. As soon as I wondered why I was allowing myself to be drawn to an expatriate in Brazil, it occurred to me that it was this unexplored side of my character, the heedless side, I had come to Brazil to probe, so far without success.

When I wrote my news to Richard Brooks, my friend and mentor at Macmillan, would I sound like a fabulist? I imagined him replying: "Kate, you have arrived in a country of indulgence and contradiction. Take it; it's yours. I await your byline."

I reached Nelson Claudio at his agent's office and asked if his offer was really open to me. It was. We settled on a modest price that included rolls and coffee in the morning. I hoped breakfast would include fruit, but I didn't ask.

I started work at UPI Monday morning, March 11, 1968.

CHAPTER SEVEN

But Brazil, it is a dye, a red dye.
Not more.
Don't become political.
Didn't you say this is a matter of love?

(Brazilwood, the tropical source of a red dye
valued by the Portuguese,
has given its name
to a country in South America.)

E. Catherine Lawrence

I

Four reporters were typing furiously when I entered the newsroom directly from the elevator corridor. Sitting at small desks in two cramped rows, they seemed at once very focused and nonchalant. All four young men were dressed in the reporter's uniform — a dashed-together ensemble of blue jeans and striped, button-down shirt with the sleeves casually rolled up to mid-forearm. No ties. Each wore a sportsman's watch on a well-worn, wide, safari-style watchband.

The newsroom — large, square, noisy and suffused with energy — seemed glamorous to me because of the nature of the enterprise. It reminded me of frantic newsrooms from screwball comedies of the 1930s and '40s. The blustery, cynical, fast-talking movie protagonist was always ruthless in pursuit of "the big story" but had the interests of "the little guy" at heart.

Separated from the young reporters were 10 more desks in a cluster of rows. One woman in her late thirties, who wore no makeup, and six men of varying ages were typing there. Later I was told they were translators, providing UPI's unique service of translating the news from the mainstream languages — Spanish and English — into Portuguese.

One reporter, whose mien lacked his colleagues' untamed air, saw me, stopped typing, and addressed me from his post: "Something's just come up in São Paulo. John'll be tied up on the phone for a while. He told me you'd be starting work today. As soon as I finish this story, which should be just a few more minutes, I'll introduce you around. I'm Ed Tanner, by the way, from Salt Lake City."

He had to extricate his legs from his tight quarters to stand up. I maneuvered between several empty desks to shake hands with him. "Kate Lawrence, originally from Boston." While the other reporters had long brown hair, Ed's was dirty blond and cut short. His handshake was surprisingly soft.

"From Boston. Good, John's hired another state-capital reporter. We can always use someone with that experience. It's a quick turnaround down here. I cleaned off a desk for you." He pointed to a small, partly cleared, pockmarked wooden desk in the row behind his, sat down and immediately resumed typing. Our conversation hadn't broken his train of thought.

Five teletype machines along the rear wall never let up. Three operators beat out a steady rhythm on Model 19s; two machines noisily received news reports. Bells chimed signaling the arrival of breaking news. As I moved about the room I encountered pockets where the bitter smell of stale ashtrays filled the air.

The newsroom's perimeter consisted of numerous doorways leading to small passageways. Wadson's private office was midway along the left side of the room as one faced the teletype machines. That morning his door was half-shut. I couldn't see him or hear his clipped speech over the chatter of the machines. I was anxious. Wasn't there something I should be doing? How did I look?

79

I watched photographers, loaded down with equipment, come and go through the square room. I had no idea where they sat between assignments. They dressed differently from the reporters — in cheap brown pants, white patent-leather slip-on shoes and faded pastel short-sleeved shirts.

Before Ed had finished his story, Wadson hurried out of his office. He was excited, on edge, slamming his knuckles into the palm of his hand. Humming an unrecognizable song under his breath, lost in thought, he walked right by my desk, then noticed me and turned around. "Did Ed get you squared away, Kate? Today's going to be a mess." We shook hands. "A bomb went off at the U.S. Consulate in São Paulo this morning ... People injured. Don't know how many yet. I may have to jump on a plane and go down there. I wanted to be able to spend some time with you ... " He looked around the room, counting heads in a loud voice. "Where's Mike?"

"He'll be right back," someone called out.

"Bases covered," Wadson announced to no one in particular. He turned to me. "Are you ready to do a story? I've got something I'd like you to do ... unrelated to this mess in São Paulo."

He sent me off to Galeão Airport to talk to customs officials. I took a taxi to the airport, conducted three interviews and rushed back to the office at 2 without eating lunch. I examined my notes, wrote down a formal outline and nervously began typing a news story, my second.

> Rio de Janeiro, March 11 (UPI)—Customs officials today opened a 60-pound teddy bear they found lying on a bench at Galeão International Airport in Rio de Janeiro. The bear contained 311 women's nylon panties and 82 dresses. Customs officials said that within the past three months they have seized about U.S. $450,000 worth of contraband, including nine machine guns, 7,600 electric razors and 770 pounds of human hair.

A spokesman said that they are dealing with two classes of smugglers: Those who go to New York and bring home merchandise for resale in violation of Brazil's customs regulations and those who smuggle small arms from Europe. Over the past three months, six Brazilians, including one woman, have been arrested at the airport for arms smuggling. The woman, Maria Carla Duarte, was expelled from the country last week. She went to Zurich, Switzerland.

Carlos Batista, a senior customs official at the airport, stated: "Many of the Brazilian tourists who visited the United States last year (17,000, according to sources) tried to finance their trips by bringing home merchandise to sell. We overlook much of it, and people know it. I assure you, we do not overlook arms smugglers."

I looked around for Wadson. He was busy. I turned to Ed Tanner, "Would you mind taking a look at this? I want to make sure it fits UPI's style."

"Who told you the name of the woman and where she went?" he asked. "You need to put that in."

I added the attribution, grateful for his critique. My story was transmitted to UPI headquarters in New York by radio broadcast at 4 o'clock in the afternoon, along with other minor news. From New York my piece would move over the "Chester" wire — the name given, no one knew why, to UPI's Latin American wire. It might have been named after a town in New Jersey or for a teletype operator.

The big story of the day, the one that had Wadson and my eager male colleagues on the run, continued to unfold throughout the afternoon. The United States Consulate in São Paulo had been smashed by two powerful homemade bombs. Walls, windows, books and furniture had been wrecked. Three Brazilians who worked at the consulate had been injured seriously. One was not expected to live. The police believed at least one of the perpetrators had also been hurt in the explosions. The bombers got away, leaving a bloodstained trail.

The American Ambassador in Rio had to be interviewed, as did Brazilian officials at the Ministry of External Relations. The Rio police were interviewed regarding security. The Minister of the Army was interviewed. Wadson was on the verge of flying down to São Paulo to assist the São Paulo bureau, but in the end he sent Mike Evans, a seasoned reporter.

Around 6 Wadson interrupted his hike around the newsroom to stop at my desk. He looked triumphant and tired: "We outdid the AP and Reuters. We got the national perspective, not just the story from São Paulo. I could use a beer. How about meeting me at the Olimpia bar at 7?"

Just before I left to meet him, UPI's São Paulo-based senior business correspondent, Jim Webster, telexed his third story of the day to Rio for transmission to New York. I read it hurriedly on my way out the door. The police in São Paulo were investigating "strange groups" who they believed were advocating chaos in Brazil. I wondered if any members of these "strange groups" were known to Walter or Jaime.

Politics — at least the kind I was used to, with contested issues, campaigns and regularly scheduled elections — didn't exist in Brazil under the military government. Instead, what passed for political activity was limited to intense rhetoric. The president, with the help of the military and conservative businessmen, had shut down everything but this cocktail palaver. The change from endless talk to open confrontation came just as I joined UPI. Suddenly troops were moving through the jungle northeast of Rio checking on reports of leftist guerrilla activity. In one day, I felt I had gone from a poet's leisurely, impressionistic stroll through Rio to playing the part of a cub reporter in one of those frenzied classic newsroom movies.

I arrived at the Olimpia, a short walk from the bureau, promptly at 7. Wadson was 10 minutes late. I ordered vodka and tonic. The waiter didn't ask Wadson what he wanted; he brought him a Brahma Chopp and a small bowl of peanuts to go with his ice-cold draft beer. Wadson took a long quaff and settled back in his chair: "You got off to a good start with your smuggling story. Want to know why I hired you?"

"I know. I have the inside track on Nazis. But then, you do too."

"Your Carnival story was the work of a real writer. I respect real writers. It's a hard way to earn a living. You've got a problem, Catherine. A few real writers, like Hemingway and John O'Hara, earned their living as journalists. It's a strenuous life. Most reporters burn out early, especially the dedicated ones. But it makes sense for you to try. You could earn a living as someone's wife. Have you tried that?"

"I could be a customs inspector like Edwin Arlington Robinson or a bank clerk like T. S. Eliot."

"They're poets. Different sensibility."

"I write poems, too."

"I bet that didn't pay well."

I smiled. "You never asked me for a résumé. I was an editor at Macmillan. That's part of what brought me to Brazil. I've been asking myself whether my editing job left room for experience, whether it didn't use up my literary energies on other people's work. Rio's full of material. I've written a lot while I've been here."

Wadson sipped his drink slowly. "A résumé wouldn't have told me what I needed to know. I saw what you wrote. Ed Tanner's going back to Salt Lake City in four months to get married. After he gets his fill of skiing and having kids with his Mormon wife, he'll be begging UPI

83

for a transfer to some exotic hot spot. I wasn't actively looking for his replacement when you came along." He held my gaze. "Quite seriously, I wanted to give you a chance to try this business, Kate. A wire service is a good place to start." My elbows rested lightly on the table. I leaned into his words. "I expect good work — solid work — from you, but you don't have to dissemble. If you don't know something, ask me."

"You like to size people up," I said. "You're good at it."

"Did I do okay with you?"

"I intend to make it my business to dumbfound you."

He laughed. "We'll see." After one beer Wadson said he had to go back to the office to check the telexes coming in from São Paulo. He was worried that the bombing victim might have died. It was obvious neither of us wanted our conversation to end. "It's late, but you should come back to the bureau with me and see how this story wraps up."

He dropped some money on the black-mirrored cocktail table and we walked back to the bureau. I hung around, pulled copy off the teletype, read dispatches. Fortunately, the bombing victim was still holding his own in the hospital. Wadson accompanied me to the *bonde*, the diminutive, open-sided yellow trolley that would take me straight up the mountainside to Santa Teresa, home to many of Rio's artists and now my aerie.

"No filtering what you write through your emotions, Kate. Rule Number One."

I started to shake hands but he caught my hand and kissed it gallantly. The *bonde* rattled to a stop. "And never misspell a person's name — Rule Number Two." I got on the trolley. "People feel very strongly about the sanctity of their names," he called after me.

84

I had every intention of being punctual on Tuesday, but *dona* Rita, Nelson Claudio's mother, prevented it. Her migraine headache that morning was so fierce, her screams of pain so loud, that the entire household was turned upside down.

Dona Rita's bedroom was adjacent to the parlor. I was grateful that the guest room I occupied was in the back of the house, behind the dining room. I slept on a vinyl-upholstered sofa that converted to a single bed. Nelson Claudio's bedroom and mine shared a wall.

Nelson Claudio and I arrived at the same moment looking for breakfast, but nothing was set out. Never mind, I thought, I could easily do without coffee and rolls to avoid being late. I had had the shock of a cold morning shower because the hot water wasn't functioning. On Saturday a plumber had come to fix a leak but neglected to bring some essential parts. He took the household's only bathroom apart and left without reassembling all the pipes.

Dona Rita, age 51, looked every second of her age and then some. Nelson Claudio had explained that his mother "understood" while her husband lived mostly "away from home." He had said that she was a conscientious housewife, arranging flowers in the parlor just so, seeing to it that the maid adhered to an immutable schedule of housecleaning. She herself visited the neighborhood open-air food market twice weekly, returning with two blue string bags full of kale, beef, oranges, carrots, pork, squash and eggplant. Every Saturday, when Nelson Claudio's father left his mistress and came home for a hearty lunch, she cooked a big pot of *feijoada* — a complicated dish of air-dried beef, smoked sausage, tongue and pig's ears and tails served with rice, black beans, *farofa* (manioc flour sautéed in butter), orange slices and collard greens.

She did all this despite suffering excruciating migraines nearly every day. Usually they hit after lunch. "When Nelson Claudio was born," she told me, "they gave me a spinal injection. Afterward, when I got out of bed to go to the bathroom, I fell to the floor because of the pain in my head. It has never left. *Foi o diabo*! Thirty-five years of this suffering. I couldn't even think of having another child after such an experience."

"What can we do for your mother?" I asked Nelson Claudio. "I feel so sorry for her."

"Sometimes strong black coffee helps if her medicine isn't working."

Nelson Claudio sat at the empty dining table, looking glum. I went into the kitchen to find the maid. "Where's Maria?" I asked, stepping back into the dining room.

"Probably hiding. When my mother starts screaming, she disappears. Superstition. She's a back-country, stupid girl."

I made strong coffee and took it into *dona* Rita's bedroom. Her small body was lying on the double bed diagonally, as if it were the only position she could bear. Her eyes were rolled back in her head, not focusing. She was dressed in a worn but starched white cotton nightgown. "I brought you coffee, *dona* Rita."

"Where's that girl, Maria of the Devil?"

"Try a little," I said. "Nelson Claudio thought it might help." I sat on the edge of the bed to assist. I held her head as she raised the cup to sip the unsweetened coffee.

"That helps. I don't know why. Thank you." She took several more sips and sank back onto the bed in a calmer state.

Nelson Claudio walked into the room and put a cold compress on his mother's forehead. The muscles in her face relaxed. "Coffee puts her to sleep," he said. We tiptoed out of *dona* Rita's room.

As I descended the six long flights of concrete stairs to reach the street, I saw Maria sitting sideways on the bottom step staring straight ahead. She didn't adjust her gaze or move her position as I approached. I had to step over her thighs on my way to catch the *bonde*.

I was going to be late. On the trolley ride downtown I imagined what Wadson would say: "This is a deadline business. I expect my reporters to be on time." He caught my eye when I walked into the newsroom. He smiled, took an exaggerated look at his watch, but didn't say anything.

That night Wadson invited me to meet him at the Olimpia again. After our first drink I asked, "What if, for the rest of your life, you had just two weeks to travel — would you go to Versailles or to Hadrian's Villa?"

"Neither," he said. "I'd go to the Blue Mosque in Istanbul and then I'd take a boat up the Bosporus."

We got a little bit drunk and quite silly and argued about which was Hemingway's best novel and whether dogs were better pets than cats. Wadson said he would prove that cats were inferior by buying me a Persian. "Or how about a ... Oh, shit, I can't think of the ideal thing right now."

"Goldfish," I said. "You don't have to run home to walk them.'

"Two days on the job and you already think I'm working you too hard? My dear Catherine, what could be more fun, more gratifying, more absurd, than getting paid to snoop? Everybody wants to know what goes on behind the closed door. It teaches us how to live. And that's what we're all looking for — lessons on how to live. Because, at bottom, nobody really knows how."

Every evening that first week, after our day of reporting foolishness and mayhem, John and I would rendezvous at the Olimpia. By the end of the week, the waiter knew me. Unasked, he brought me a vodka and tonic with a slice of lime. The Olimpia was on a side street, a few steps downstairs, blissfully remote from the rush-hour traffic and the restive feel of Brazilian politics around us. We had our table, small and square, with a shiny black surface. I could look down, and often did, to watch our reactions, our smiles, our pleasures, our displeasures, reflected back at me.

John had the self-assurance of a handsome, well-built man accustomed to good fortune. His personality radiated authority kept in check by an easy, slightly bemused smile. He was 6 feet 2, 7 inches taller than I, and agile. His brown hair was fine and straight. He had a slight suntan, not the kind of tan cultivated at the beach. Behind his glasses, his gray-blue eyes bespoke warmth mixed with wariness. He was too attractive not to have a girlfriend, I thought. And if he didn't, why not?

Friday evening he marched into the Olimpia in an agitated mood. "The lid's off, I can feel it." He sat down across from me, reached for my hand and held it for a moment. "Christ, your ambassador is holding secret meetings with opposition politicians — guys who are leading the coalition that's planning to blow Brazil apart. Your ambassador said they discussed the dispute over Brazil's exports of instant coffee. I don't buy it." John's manner made it clear he believed fully in his own instincts.

"When I lived with Walter Decker and his student friends in a dump of an apartment in Copacabana, I got hints all the time about their close ties with groups on the left."

"Decker, the polemicist? I read his book."

"I saw it in your office. Do you know him?"

"Just through his book. Didn't it try your patience to be a captive audience for his casual anti-Americanism and his leftist cant?"

"There's another side to Walter."

"He's an engaging writer — not all his ideas are half-baked. Stay in touch with him, Kate. He could be a good contact."

"I consider him a good friend."

John ordered another round of drinks. I examined his upside-down face in reflection. The vodka put me in a silky mood. "Walter was a big help with my Gruber story," I said. "First, when I told him about the message on the envelope, it reminded him of the killing of another Nazi living in Brazil and he suggested I check the newspaper files. Then Walter got me a copy of *The Rise and Fall of the Third Reich*. Another big help."

"Find anything interesting in the book?"

"I did. I pieced together a plausible story about who Gruber might be. I came up with Friedrich Grabenz."

"Why in hell didn't you tell me?"

"I didn't mention it because I was afraid you'd think I was an amateur and dismiss my whole story, even the parts I was sure of. I've been waiting to tell you the rest. I wanted to astonish you."

"You have."

I recounted my meeting with the bowling alley manager, how he had unintentionally given me clues about what Gruber might have done for the Reich and how I had found out about the inscription on the back of Gruber's watch from a morgue attendant. "Friedrich had to be Gruber's first name."

"Your story said the cops were looking into rumors that Gruber was a Nazi, so I went to talk to them," John said. "My source told me he was sorry to see the money run out. Grabenz had been paying Brazilian authorities for years not to tip off the West Germans. When the cops found out from the message in the envelope who he was and what he had done, they thought they should have been paid more. They went ahead and let the West Germans identify him, posthumously. Grabenz had three lipomas on his left cheek. All they needed was a photograph."

"Why didn't Charlie Wall go to the police?"

"He did, but he didn't have the right contact. He put your story on the AP wire the day before I wrote mine. For Nazi hunters, Grabenz wasn't a major target. I had UPI check in Europe and Israel. I'm guessing he was taken out in such a dramatic way to make a point to the Brazilian government. It was a very professional hit."

"I've been trying to imagine the thoughts of a person who takes on that kind of retribution, even when it's manifestly justified. Wouldn't he feel morally compromised?"

"He sees himself as a soldier fighting for his country. The only difference is he's fighting alone. Consider how many lives would have been spared if someone had killed Hitler early in his career. He killed off all his political rivals in '34 in his Blood Purge. One of his challengers should have taken care of him while he had the chance."

"My father was a soldier. And my great-great grandfather was a sharpshooter in the Civil War. I see your point."

"Thank goodness! I was afraid I'd have to give you a whole lecture."

"But don't you think Grabenz should have been brought to trial?" I said.

"I bet any surviving Nazis are more afraid of being picked off on a dark night than being tried. Jurisprudence can falter even when the evidence is irrefutable."

"You sound like a lawyer."

"I almost was, once."

"Now I'm really curious."

"Some other day. I've got to get back to the bureau tonight."

"Do you work all the time?"

"I've had my share of distractions. None at the moment, though."

We finished our drinks and John walked with me to Lapa, the seedy area that was the downtown terminus of the *bonde*.

"You were late Tuesday morning. If you want, you can make up for it by working tomorrow."

"On Saturday?" I had made a noon date to meet Walter and Eva at the beach in Copacabana. It was too late to change it.

"I'll be in at 10." He appeared ready to say something else, but didn't. He brushed my cheek with his lips, turned and walked away.

I did go to the bureau at 10, but not because I felt duty bound to compensate for having been late Tuesday. When I arrived, John was furiously filing a breaking story about a capsule containing deadly radioactive strontium-90 that had been forgotten in a taxi by a hospital employee. The material was used for treating cancer. One thousand soldiers and police were searching for it. "That's a good use for the military," John said as he moved around the newsroom surveying people's desks, scanning the teletype machines, pacing.

I spent an hour reading wire copy and newspapers, jotting down ideas for stories. We drank coffee while I sat at my desk and he settled, facing me, on top of an empty desk in the next row. He put his feet on the seat of the battered chair, leaned on his elbows and paid complete attention to me for several penetrating seconds until I became uncomfortable.

91

"Okay, I confess," I blurted out. He continued to study my face. "Would you like to know why I took this job?" He nodded. "Partly because it gives me a chance to live out my mother's unfulfilled dream. She died 12 years ago of breast cancer. I always thought that when my brother Jeff and I grew up, she'd travel the world and write stories."

"What about your father?"

"He was very sad my mom missed the chance to have adventures. That's why he didn't try to persuade me to go to graduate school instead of joining the Peace Corps. He's a school superintendent in Boston and my stepmother's a doctor. Tell me about your family."

"Straightforward story. My father worked for the provincial government of Ontario. My mother was a teacher until she married. I have two sisters. One older, one younger. They're both in Toronto. I was a Boy Scout, earned a lot of badges. Just your average striving middle child."

"Did you get good grades in school?"

"Yep, I did, skipped third grade."

I glanced at my watch. It was nearly 11; I was worried about the time. John could see I was nervous. "Are you going to stick around?" he asked.

"I wish I could, but I've already made plans to meet friends at the beach."

IV

Like a true *carioca* I had worn my bikini underneath my clothes. When I got to the beach I stripped off my jeans and shirt and sat on them, sunning myself, while I waited for Walter and Eva to turn up. When I saw them coming toward me, slogging through the sand, I was surprised by my feelings. They had become family. After my frenetic, exhilarating week I was relieved to see their faces. They looked dear.

92

"Well, baby, how do you like covering our national misery?" Walter said as kissed me hello. "You must lose yourself in the greatest of the darkness to find the greatest light, right?" That day Walter's assessment of Brazil's political situation was, in a strange way, reassuring: "If we're going to begin to talk about political revolution, let's have a revolution in behavior while we're at it." His words sounded so remote, so unlike a call to arms, that it was almost as if I were being invited to dismiss the recent bombings as isolated incidents, the pranks of overzealous kids.

The three of us went back to David Jr.'s apartment to wash off the salt from our swim. Nothing in the environment had changed — it was as squalid as ever. I wondered how I had survived those weeks living in such disorder and filth. It was like old times — both the good and the bad.

Someone, not present, had moved into my cage. David Jr.'s painting had been replaced with another, even larger. As I walked past my former mattress, I doffed an imaginary hat to wish the current occupant good luck. In what I knew was a futile gesture, I glanced around to look for my three left shoes.

I showered, using my old trick of holding my breath against the bathroom's effluvium. There wasn't any hand soap in the bathroom. I found a bottle of lemon shampoo wedged behind the toilet and used it. Walter sniffed me when I sat beside him on the living room sofa. "Nice smell!"

In spite of the hazardous hygiene, I left for dinner and the movies that evening feeling refreshed. Six of us, including Jaime, Ana Maria, and David Jr., split up into two taxis for the familiar trip to China Town, the Chinese restaurant in Ipanema that served a gelatinous, but tasty, version of *moo goo gai pan*.

Sunday night, the Rio television stations were still issuing warnings about the strontium-90 capsule. *Dona* Rita was transfixed before

93

the set. The warnings interrupted her favorite musical variety show. I watched the program with her. Nelson Claudio walked in and out of the parlor, staying only long enough to take in the alerts. "They haven't found the capsule yet? I love it. Extreme carelessness. Radioactive Rio! Chaos. Here we go!"

"You've spent too much time with Walter," I said.

Monday, when I got to the bureau, the crisis was over. The capsule had been recovered.

Tuesday night, March 19, 1968, an incident occurred that was later seen as the trigger for the watershed year in Brazil's continuing "revolution." The police found it necessary to fire into a group of demonstrators protesting delays in completing a state-run university restaurant. A 17-year-old high school student who liked to play the piano was killed.

On Wednesday 20,000 marchers shouting *"Viva* Che Guevara!" escorted the body of Manoel Corrêa from the State Assembly House to the cemetery. It had been a year since Ernesto "Che" Guevara, M.D., had been captured and executed by Bolivian army special forces with the assistance of the CIA. For the marching students, an executed Che was a more potent symbol of countercultural resistance than if he had lived. John and Ed Tanner covered the funeral procession from beginning to end. Everyone in the bureau was involved with the story in one way or another. I interviewed a police supervisor who was charged with keeping order.

When I got home to Santa Teresa it was late in the evening. *Dona* Rita was sleeping. Nelson Claudio was playing solitaire in the parlor, listening to one of his favorite records — Miles Davis' *Sketches of Spain*. The fiercely brooding *Concierto* filled the room. He looked up when I entered. "I've been waiting for you, Kate. The demonstration today is going to be followed by more protest strikes. Violent strikes.

In Rio and all over Brazil. The students are armed. Demonstrations could break out tomorrow, but definitely within the week. I've been talking to someone who knows the organizers. Some of the people involved are living right here in Santa Teresa. I didn't know that myself until today." He slapped down a red king and moved a pile of cards. "By the way, Manoel Corrêa died a virgin."

"How'd you know that?"

"I know his sister very well. Manoel's girlfriend, Claudia, agreed to make love with him, but only if it was anal sex. Claudia wanted to preserve her virginity until their marriage."

"His sister knew that? Told you that?"

"Why not?"

"I don't believe you. I don't believe his sister told you that and I don't believe —"

"Virginity's a serious business. Some girls have operations to get it restored. I'm sure in Uncle Sam's country you do the same."

"We don't."

He reached for his ever-present blue pack of Gauloises, lighted one, and exhaled slowly. "Why not?"

"No need. American girls wear chastity belts."

He surveyed his cards. "*Merda*, I lost again even though I cheated twice." He scooped up the deck and shuffled it clumsily.

I went to my room, dug around in a drawer and found my last box of filter-tip Tiparillos. As I walked back through the darkened dining room to the parlor, I wondered if I would ever be at ease in this world whose madness was governed by an enigmatic logic. I entered the parlor and offered a cigar to Nelson Claudio. "Thanks, I'll stick with my Gauloises. They're stronger."

"You shouldn't be smoking at all."

95

"I know. My cardiologist told me to stop."

"Thanks for your warning, Nelson Claudio, about tomorrow."

"You're interested?"

"You know I am."

He dealt himself another hand of solitaire, which he quickly lost. We smoked together. Nelson Claudio concentrated on his drags. In the background, Miles' trumpet cried for the dead bullfighter. I couldn't get that Andalusian melody of loneliness out of my mind for weeks.

CHAPTER EIGHT

My *Brasileiro*, my darling,
Vice-Consul, João, Excellency.
His hair blacker than the hours
Which separate our meetings,
Blackest now, like permanent night.
No more, no more.
There was this man,
You see, there was.

E. Catherine Lawrence

I

Thursday morning, based on the intelligence I passed on from Nelson Claudio, John called an editorial meeting for noon. He invited all the reporters, interpreters and photographers to attend. One of the interpreters observed that, in his 13 years of working for UPI, there had never been a bureau-wide editorial meeting. Another old-timer agreed. Twenty of us draped ourselves around a corner of the newsroom, as far from the clanging teletype machines as we could get. José, our all-purpose porter and legman, made coffee. We sat around drinking it while John outlined how we were going to organize ourselves to cover disorder in the streets.

José swelled with pride when John gave him a formal assignment at the meeting. "From now on, José," John said, "getting a telephone line for the reporters is your top priority and everything else takes a back seat, including serving *cafezinho*. Whoever's got a minute makes the coffee. Clear?"

97

Informally, when José wasn't otherwise engaged, one of his duties had been to sit at a vacant desk in the newsroom with a telephone receiver glued to his ear and repeatedly tap the disconnect button until he got a telephone line to the outside world. When he heard the right noise — which could take from 5 to 15 minutes or more — he would yell out to a reporter who was trying to make a call: "I have a line." The reporter would instantly grab the phone and, fingers crossed, dial his number. Sometimes we got through to our party, sometimes not. By acting as intermediary between the bureau's telephones and the unknowable Bell cosmos, José saved the reporters valuable time.

By late afternoon I began to feel distinctly uncomfortable. After my bombshell about armed students planning more demonstrations, John sent us out to canvass the city center. The streets in Rio and everywhere throughout Brazil were clogged with nothing but the usual commerce and traffic. I was afraid my confreres would think the bureau's only female reporter cultivated unreliable sources.

That evening I brought one of my poems, *The Red Dye,* with me to show John at the Olimpia. It was a meditation on my feelings of loss after Sérgio left New York for his new posting in Geneva. I was putting us to a test, showing John the poem. If it wasn't going to go well, I would rather know earlier than later.

He was waiting for me on the banquette when I got to the bar. We always left the bureau separately for our assignations. No need to supply the office gossip mill. The UPI staff didn't patronize the Olimpia; they could drink in plenty of other places that were cheaper and nearer the bureau.

Our table was tucked into a cool, hushed, dark corner. We could sit either facing each other or side by side on the banquette. Many calculations would go into the unconscious choice of how we arranged ourselves — the heat of the day, the danger we had faced on the streets, what stories we might be telling from our pasts. In this way our table gradually evolved into a confessional.

"Here," I said as I slipped onto the banquette beside him and handed him my poem. Our thighs touched lightly. "Talk to me after you've finished reading it."

He was already drinking his usual Brahma Chopp. The waiter brought me my vodka and tonic with lime. John began reading. I sipped my drink nervously. John fiddled with his eyeglasses. When he finished, John looked up slowly. I was barely breathing. "That's another reason why you're here. João."

I nodded, yes.

"It's a strong poem."

"I feel exposed right now."

"You should. You weren't obliged to confess." He took a sip of his beer. "I'm searching for the felicitous thing to say. I feel a little bit at a loss." I could feel the tension in my leg next to his. "I like the series of disappearances. Confused frontiers, nothing where it should be. The narrator mad with love, desperate to find her lover. Citizens of the countries bordering Brazil trying to be helpful, reciting logical-illogical truths. Musically, you've organized your poem like a cantata — passionate songs alternating with recitative."

"Are you a musician?" I asked.

"I played clarinet in my high school band." He paused and took my hand, which was cold. "Is it published?" I shook my head. "It should be."

"Poetry is my incessant inner voice. Since I've become a reporter I haven't written a polished line, just fragments."

"I'm honored you showed it to me." I squeezed his hand. "Why'd you leave Boston, Kate? You should have married a banker or a doctor so you could write poetry without having to worry about money, gardened — that sort of life."

"I did have a boyfriend in Boston. Stuart Anthony Bryant. He became a banker."

"What happened with you and Stuart?"

"I went away to college and discovered other men I liked better. If I had still loved Stuart, I would have married him. And maybe gardened. Do you still play the clarinet?"

"Sometimes. Is it over? With João? I don't suppose that's his name."

"Not because I wanted it to be. His name is Sérgio."

"What if you could get him back?"

"That's one of the reasons I came to Brazil. To probe that question. Now I have." I took a sip of my drink. It was mostly melted ice. John handed me my poem. I put it back in my purse. "The answer is no, I wouldn't want him back."

II

Friday morning Nelson Claudio had an early photo session, so he accompanied me downtown on the *bonde*. Segments of the track were supported by the lofty arcs of a colonial Portuguese aqueduct. The ride was always glorious, offering a glimpse of Guanabara Bay and views of numerous public staircases that wound in stages to neighborhoods hundreds of feet below.

Nelson Claudio was truly the quintessential internal Brazilian man. According to the theory I had developed for Jane, he shouldn't have been issued a passport to travel abroad. He was short, ugly — except when he smiled — smart, generous, charming, had a refined sense of aesthetics and was definitely interested in me. How could it be otherwise — a 28-year-old woman, American and therefore exotic, sleeping on the other side of the wall from his bed?

In the two weeks since I had moved into his household, Nelson Claudio had invited me to dinner, to the movies, to the beach, to photography sessions, to parties, to bowling, to bed. He dated models and some of them stayed the night with him, but I must have been especially on his mind when he slept in his bed alone, which was about 70 percent of the time.

"At noon I'm going to be at the beach doing a fashion shoot. Want to come? I'd like to take more shots of you ... maybe riding a motor scooter along the packed sand."

"Actually, Nelson Claudio, as much as I was reluctant to let you take those pictures of me with Helena, I have to admit they were very good photos."

"*Manchete* thought so too."

"My family was shocked." I smiled.

"They weren't indiscreet."

"It wasn't that. They were surprised I was willing to pose."

"How about another, alone, in your white maillot?"

"Maybe this weekend."

Nelson Claudio's "wet/white" signature photos were increasingly bringing him money and notoriety. I still have the ones he took of me.

We got off the *bonde* at Lapa. I'd been carrying his tripod for him. I handed it back. "I'm not an invalid, Kate. I had a minor heart attack from which I've recovered phenomenally well. But I may give up smoking." He kissed me on each cheek and marched off, loaded down with his gear.

I headed northwest toward the bureau, negotiating Rio's ubiquitous mosaic sidewalks in a new pair of low-heeled shoes. Every few yards, due to poor maintenance, there were stones missing from the intricate patterns. It was easy to turn an ankle. A headline at a newsstand caught my eye: The Federal Congress in Brasília and the Assembly of the State of Guanabara (which included Rio) were calling for three days of mourning in honor of Manoel Corrêa.

"Which way'd you walk to the office?" Ed Tanner wanted to know as soon as I set foot in the newsroom.

"From Lapa."

"I guess you missed it."

"Missed what?"

"There're marines on Avenida Rio Branco stopping cars, hunting for student demonstrators. Last night there was a confrontation between the cops and students outside one of the movie theaters in Cinelândia. Wadson's somewhere on Rio Branco. He wants us to help him cover."

I took a few large-denomination *cruzeiro* notes out of my purse and stuffed them into my shirt pocket. I pinned on my press badge, grabbed a ballpoint pen and a small notebook and rushed out of the office with Ed. One lesson John had already taught me was to travel light when there might be pushing and shoving. "No purses, please. Nothing anybody can grab onto and nothing that can slow you down if you have to run. No high heels, either."

Ed and I walked up Avenida Rio Branco a short distance toward Guanabara Bay, the opposite direction from Lapa, until we ran into a police barrier blocking the sidewalk. A swarthy marine asked where we worked. Two more marines quickly joined him. "Press," we said simultaneously. The three marines eyed our photo badges.

"There's a roadblock ahead. You'll have to detour."

"What's the problem?" I asked.

"No problem."

"You said there's a roadblock."

Ed took my elbow and steered me away from the marines. "You're not going to get anything from them."

Ed walked down *Rua* Uruguaiana. I doubled back to Rio Branco. I saw more marines and police milling about. Behind me cars were lined up at the roadblock with their windows rolled down. I could feel the drivers' impatience. A crowd of office workers stood around watching the scene. I approached a man in a dark business suit.

"What's happening?"

"The marines are stopping cars, searching inside for guns."

I walked north toward Avenida Presidente Vargas, interviewing pedestrians and marines as I went. It occurred to me that the road-block was effective in one direction only — stopping cars traveling south. "They're idiots," I thought. I retraced my steps back to the bureau. When I arrived, John was typing at a desk in the newsroom.

He looked up. "I bumped into Ed. I told him to stay on Rio Branco just in case something breaks. What d'you have?"

"Not much beyond what Ed told me when I got in."

"I see you're dressed properly. No encumbrances."

"There's a lot of pent-up feeling on the street," I said. "I'm going back."

When I got outside I could feel energy building in the government's show of force. It was matched, fidget for fidget, shove for shove, by a growing crowd of demonstrators. Suddenly people were screaming and running. I tried to push my way through to the nucleus of the mob, where I thought something was happening. I couldn't make headway. I rushed back to the bureau to get John. "Something's up. Hurry."

Seconds later Mike Evans raced into the bureau. "A guy just got killed on Rio Branco. The marines clubbed him. I tried to telephone from the street but a kid in yellow John Lennon sunglasses was monop-olizing the phone. Ed's down there somewhere."

"Oh boy, here we go!" John yelled. "Marcio, stay here and be ready to write. You, you, and you ... " he pointed to every reporter in the room except Marcio. "... where the hell's Luiz? Christ. Someone get him." Luiz, a photographer, was working in the darkroom. Mike hurried to get him. John barked and pointed at Luiz when he rushed out, "Get your camera." John moved toward the door at a gallop, half-singing, "We're off to see the wizard." He paused at the door to call out, "Careful, everyone. No heroics."

We all took the elevator down to the street together. For a while we went our separate ways, but once John found me again, he kept me close. The demonstrators were armed. Now his lessons on streetcraft continued under fire. "One of the tricks is just to outwalk everybody," he shouted. He moved so quickly, I was half-running to keep up. "Another is to know where the public phones are. I know every goddamn public phone in downtown Rio. Half of them don't work, but sometimes you get lucky and save time by phoning something in. I always beat Charlie Wall to a phone. But don't waste too much time trying to find a phone that functions."

John's instincts were uncanny. He always seemed to know where to be and where not to be. Slipping between shoving demonstrators and police brandishing rifles, I watched myself sidestep a dangerous knot in the crowd. Faces were sweaty. Someone handed me a mimeographed one-page manifesto. I caught the name Trotsky across the top. The mob was excited, pious, happy. Tear gas canisters fired. They sounded like dull pops. People stumbled away, wiping their eyes, coughing.

John and I avoided the worst of the gas. Once we were clear of the crowd and the fumes, he grabbed me by the shoulders and kissed me quickly on the lips. "I can trust you not to get really hurt," he said as he let me go. We coughed for several minutes. "Clears out the lungs, doesn't it? We'll go to Paraty the weekend after next and do a nice little fishing village story. You deserve R and R."

104

"I could use the R and R right now, immediately."

John put his arm around my waist; I rested my head on his shoulder. He stroked my hair. "You're okay, aren't you? I'd say this weekend except the boss wants me to meet him in São Paulo. He's flying up from Buenos Aires. I'm not senior enough to say no."

By Friday at midnight the streets had gone quiet. Two people were dead. The police held 150 students and agitators in jail pending an investigation. Forty demonstrators were in hospitals, injured. Twenty others had been taken to hospitals, treated for injuries and released. Seventeen policemen were wounded. No UPI reporters were injured or detained by the police, but one UPI photographer had been roughed up. Giant masses had been held all over Brazil for Manoel Corrêa, the virgin piano player. The bureau worked through the night filing thousands of words and transmitting black-and-white photos on facsimile equipment with a noisy revolving drum.

The Governor of Guanabara, elected by voters opposed to the military, had to subdue the students or risk being dismissed from office by the military government. He authorized the police to use arms. This order injected a new seriousness into future resistance. In the minds of the rightists it also legitimized the police's previous use of firearms. The Governor closed all institutions of higher learning without saying when they would reopen. The war was on.

III

I looked forward to the dinner I had scheduled Saturday night with Jane. I had told her plenty about Wadson, the astute, attractive, competent, energetic UPI news director who had hired me. Now I wanted to tell her about John, the UPI news director who had invited me to spend the weekend with him.

"A new, exciting career, interesting man, not Brazilian. Good for you, Kate. I guess you won't be leaving Rio anytime soon. For myself, I've had enough of Brazil. For one thing, I've got a vaginal fungus infection I can't get rid of. So much for lazy topaz afternoons in the tropics and tropical sex."

"You can't leave, Jane. You're my reality down here."

"You've got John Wadson. He sounds solid."

"You know that's premature. We're still on our best behavior. I need to understand why I am even open to looking for a man down here."

"Are you? I never got that impression. I thought you were doing the opposite — you came here to exorcise a man. Sérgio sounded like a bad habit to me. Glamorous though he may have been."

"With Sérgio I leapt, I didn't look if there was water in the pool. There's lots I don't know about John. He's something of a mystery. What's he doing in Brazil? Why isn't he married? I need to pry."

"I hope you're not still obsessed with Sérgio?"

"When I dream he crops up, but it's involuntary. When are you planning to leave?"

"In 15 days. As soon as I get my last paycheck from the film company. While your voyage of self-discovery isn't over, mine is. And the verdict is in. I'm a nomad, a minimalist, I don't collect stuff. If I ever found a man I really liked, I would start an argument immediately so I could break off before any little possessive tentacles could ensnare me."

"I wish I were as sure of my feelings, Jane, as you are of yours."

"I've actually decided to placate my Mum on her turf for a while. Time for a visit. She's getting old. Then, knowing me, I'll push on. Maybe back to Hong Kong."

"You're amazing."

We talked about whether Brazil could become a Communist country like Cuba, about the sophistry around us, the unrest. "Brazil is no place for the English," Jane said. "It's non-stop pleasure seeking and self-absorption down here. Everything comes down to emotion. Not our sensibility at all. They excuse the crime of passion. We don't. Maybe it just comes down to that. Did you know that in Brazil a man can kill his unfaithful wife and get acquitted by claiming he did it to restore his honor? I had to look into some cases for a film we're doing. It doesn't work the other way around, of course."

"I'm not surprised. The other day our Brasília stringer filed a wonderful story. Congress was debating the regulation of heart transplants, and there was a deadlock when a deputy proposed that a man's mistress be authorized to give permission for a transplant if his wife wasn't available. One of the five priests in Congress put up a fierce fight."

"Only one priest disapproved?" Jane said.

We splurged on desserts and French wine. After dinner I walked Jane to her apartment in Ipanema. "You could rent my apartment if you want," she said. "The owner's not a bad sort. If you give him enough time, he'll fix the odd thing when it breaks."

"I'm content at Nelson Claudio's. I get information as well as maid service."

"I'll send you my address when I get settled. At least you won't have to send me an SOS to dispatch a handsome man to Rio."

IV

Monday at 10 in the morning President Costa e Silva spoke at a celebration marking the fourth anniversary of what he called "the country's bloodless revolution against Communism and corruption." John and I went. We even dressed up — John in jacket and tie; I in a skirt, not jeans. The observance was held at the heavily guarded Laranjeiras

Palace below Santa Teresa, the President's residence when he stayed in Rio.

The square-bodied President looked like a thug, with his dark glasses and slicked-back hair. He reiterated the pledge he'd made when he took office — to humanize and popularize the revolutionary government. "Agitators are seeking blood," he said, "but Brazil's bloodless revolution will continue. We must keep this country free from violence and within democratic ways."

John leaned over and whispered in my ear, "I'm afraid he's speaking from his heart."

As night fell in Rio gasoline bombs were lobbed onto the downtown streets and at bank doors. I was on my way to meet John at the Olimpia when the first bomb went off. I had on the wrong shoes — sandals with two-inch heels — but I managed to run to the bar. "Come quick!" I shouted from the entrance. John got up running and followed me out of the bar. "They're demonstrating at the Ministry of Education," I yelled. "And there's something going on at Cinelândia. I'll take Cinelândia."

"Okay, I'll take the Ministry." As I ran off he called after me, "Don't be a hero, Kate. I mean it."

His words protected me. Several hundred students operating in small groups had blocked commuter traffic in front of the movie houses shouting: "Down with the dictatorship!" I was invincible as the police swung clubs against soft bodies steps away from where I stood.

A gasoline bomb set a Volkswagen Beetle on fire. Within seconds the car was enveloped by flames, so hot they seemed to suck me toward them. The heat tore at my face, singeing my eyelashes. The people standing near me were immobilized. Finally, with great effort, I managed to push my way backward through the crowd, away from the car. It was impossible to turn to run. I reached out and grabbed the arm of a young woman and pulled her along with me. Another car burst into flames several yards away from the first blaze.

Horns blared nonstop. The police arrived with water cannons. They squirted jets of water on the cars and the people. I got doused. My clothes clung to me; water dripped into my shoes. Next the police hurled tear gas, but by then I was out of the dense pack and away.

When I got back to the bureau I found out I had seen more action than John. Mike Evans and I wrote until midnight. John said he would spend the night at the office: "You never know what could come up." I left the bureau intending to take the *bonde* home to Santa Teresa. A cruising taxi changed my mind. At home I fell numb onto my vinyl sofa. I didn't even remove my blouse, brush my teeth, or wash my face.

V

The daily routine of covering the spot news for UPI began to build my confidence. I was paid to report undigested events, with as many deadlines in a day as there were things happening around me. The stories were interesting, bloody, zany. In 1968, Brazil was fed up. It wanted to be France.

French university students gathered in Paris to protest everything: food in the university cafeteria, the U.S. involvement in Vietnam, unequal pay for women, cuts in government spending for higher education, the boring missionary position in sex, traffic congestion, conservative politicians. Brazil read the newspapers, watched TV, and copied.

From their beginning in March, the student protests had been organized under a pretense. As the crowd gathered, manifestos would be distributed deploring university budgets, classroom overcrowding,

109

outdated methods of instruction. Banners, prepared in advance, reinforced the manifestos with their own jejune slogans. The demonstration would coalesce. Within minutes educational concerns would be abandoned. Instead speakers would begin to attack the military regime, the crowd would dutifully break into chants and the true face of the protest would appear. The cry was unmistakable — government repression, in all its perfidy, had to go.

It was a time measured in excitements: youth, truth, death, prison, repression, censorship, dictatorship, torture, the stripping of political rights, expensive hippie fashion, the cult of the beach, long curly hair pressed on an ironing board, soul music from the Motor City, music festivals dominated by protest songs, "happenings," micro-minis, poetry, photography, one-night stands, robbing banks, armed struggle. Walter and his gang thought that things — life — could get better. The situation could "get corrected."

John made the arrangements for my trip to Montevideo to get my work permit. UPI paid for the plane ticket; I paid for the rest.

From the Brazilian Consulate it was a short walk along the city's main thoroughfare to the UPI Montevideo bureau on Avenida 18 de Julio. The UPI reporters there assured me the Uruguayan students had as much passion for politics as the Brazilians, but the Uruguayans were more serious. "None of your Brazilian intoxicated joy, *alegria,* down here," Brian Hayes, the bureau manager, said in a British accent. "The Uruguayans are a sober lot." At lunch Brian suggested I try *puchero*, a popular dish of vegetables and meat cooked in water. "It has everything in it that's loose in the kitchen."

"Sorry to say it," I said as we finished our meal, "Montevideo feels dreary compared to Rio. I wouldn't want to live here."

"Basically Uruguay's flat on its ass. Nobody expects it to be the Switzerland of South America anymore."

110

I sent Jane a postcard in care of her mother in London saying the Uruguayan men were, on average, no better looking than the Brazilians. Uruguayan women were another matter — they didn't come close to the *Brasileiras'* glamour and allure.

When I returned to Rio with my work permit, in a strange way I felt myself coming home.

CHAPTER NINE

Lost in his neck,
Behind his ear,
Kissing, laughing.
She knows only two ways to kiss,
Like a friend or with tears.
She is afraid to sound his name
Because it never existed before.

E. Catherine Lawrence

I

Every exchange John and I had throughout the day was energized by attraction and curiosity. Our courtship was nourished through shared work. Yet there was an unmistakable feeling of postponement between us. John approached me boldly, but he was also on his guard. I knew why I was being cautious. I could only guess at his reasons.

By early April our bureau, our outpost in the samba sun, was caught up in the momentum, the childishness, the seriousness of Brazil's repression. Our stories carried our fondest wish that Brazil would take its place as a giant of respected leadership in the Americas and the world. Therefore our message was urgent, but not to U.S. readers. As James Reston of *The New York Times* had put it, "Americans will do anything for South America except read about it."

Reston's statement, often repeated around the bureau, was only half true in normal times, but the times were not normal. Vietnam was expensive to cover. It crowded our stories off the pages of American newspapers and it used up UPI's 1968 budget.

On April 4, John had stayed late at the bureau. One of the translators, who was also working late, alerted him to the news coming over the wire that Martin Luther King, Jr. had been gunned down. The next morning John assigned Mike Evans and me to report the Brazilian reaction. Brazil received the news with shock. Many Brazilians had heard of King and held him and his principles of non-violence in high esteem. Some radicals, though, thought King should have known that only violence changes society. When John and I met at the Olimpia that evening he said, "Any hothead with a rifle can do a thing like that. King knew it."

II

Every week or so our bureau was expected to produce a "mailer," a one-thousand-word story with photos that wasn't urgent and could be mailed to UPI's headquarters in New York. Our spot news stories rarely exceeded 600 words and were sent by wire. Almost any subject would do for a mailer.

On Saturday, April 13, John and I left Rio to gather material for a mailer. It was the weekend away from the tension in Rio he had promised me. Our destination, Paraty, roughly 150 miles from Rio, was a coastal village founded in the 16th century.

We had two surprises. For one, Avis Car Rental had reserved for us a bright pink stripped-down Jeep with a matching pink canvas sun shade — no metal roof, no doors — very much like the utilitarian Jeeps developed for World War II. The sun shade, with its fringe border made out of heavy pink string, was held in place by four aluminum poles. We eyed the contraption, hesitated, then took it.

"Nice change of pace from student unrest, *n'est-ce pas*?" John said as we drove along the coast road toward Paraty. "We're ready for a bit of time off, don't you think? I'm worried everyone in the bureau's barely hanging on." He was wearing his standard uniform: starched chinos, a blue button-down shirt with the sleeves rolled up, black ox-fords polished to a military spit-shine and black socks. His crew cut had grown out long enough that his luxuriant hair now had a boyish swing when he turned his head. He had changed his horn-rims for silver-rimmed aviator sunglasses. For John, fashion was contrivance, nothing more. He kept a gray suit jacket and a black knit tie in the bureau for those occasions that required formality. He was both well groomed and slapdash.

"What do you know about Paraty?" I asked.

"Prince Dom João de Orleans e Bragança lives there. He's in the *cachaça* business. I bet you don't know who he is."

"I give up."

"He's the great-grandson of Brazil's former emperor, Dom Pedro II, that's who. João's not a bad guy. He actually works for a living because there's no family money. Dom Pedro II was thrown out of Brazil in 1889 when the country became a republic. João grew up in France. In fact, when he was finally let back into Brazil, he became a Marine Air Force pilot during World War II."

"What a fascinating story."

"Everyone knows it." John arched his back for a moment to stretch.

"Tomorrow's Easter," I said.

"Do you go to church?"

"Sometimes. Not regularly. My parents weren't openly religious. My Dad's half Bolivian Catholic, half clipper ship Presbyterian. My mother's family was Mayflower, but they stopped being Puritans and became Episcopalian. Ellen, my stepmother, is Episcopalian, too." I paused to clap my hands over an enormous fly, and missed.

"Bolivian? I don't see any trace of the conquistador in your face."

"I wish you did. My paternal grandmother was born into Bolivia's tiny oligarchy. After Bolivia was defeated in the War of the Pacific, her father didn't see a future in a landlocked country, so he packed up the family and they moved to New York. My grandmother was 10 at the time. My father exploited his exotic parentage when he courted my mother. She loved the idea she was marrying an aristocratic Latin." The fly continued to buzz near my face. I swatted it away. "Tell me about yourself," I said.

"Boring stuff, compared to you. My father was Toronto born and bred like me. My mother immigrated from England. She's still a British subject. I'm just a simple Protestant Canadian boy."

"I want to hear why you were almost a lawyer."

"I did graduate from law school. Top 5 percent of my class — law review, too, for what it's worth. I didn't know what kind of law I wanted to practice, so after graduation I took a temporary job — it was supposed to be for one year — in Malaysia. There was a sign on the bulletin board at my law school looking for someone to help manage a rubber plantation. The plantation was owned by a British company. Experience not required. I jumped at it."

"What'd you do after your year was up?"

"Stayed longer. I was there for nearly three years."

"Why'd you leave?"

"I got restless, for one thing."

"And for another?"

"It's a long story. Let's save that for later."

"You have extraordinary contacts, don't you? I felt your reticence when I asked you about the Grabenz story."

"Reporters don't reveal confidential sources. Nice try."

Our second surprise was that the road into Paraty from the coastal highway was unpaved, one lane and treacherous. *Quaresma* palms and breadfruit trees canopied sharp ruts hardened by the baking sun. In several places where it crossed a stream the road disappeared completely, dissolving into circular muddy ponds surrounded by thick shrubs. It became clear the final leg of our trip was going to take more time than we expected. "No one warned me about this road," John said.

"I hope we don't break our axle."

I hung onto the roll bar as we talked and jostled our way toward Paraty. Just as I had feared, a hidden tree stump buried in mud slammed furiously against our axle. We sputtered to a stop. John got out of the Jeep to take a look. "Nothing's broken that I can see, but I can't see much. I'd need to jack it up to get a good look." He came around to the driver's side of the Jeep. "I'm not eager to do that." He got back in with mud on his shoes and pants, and dirt smudged on his forehead. He pulled me to his chest. "You make me happy, Catherine."

When he kissed me I could taste the dust from the road in our mouths. We kissed again, a lingering, questioning kiss. He brushed my hair away from my face and looked directly into my eyes. "I'd better answer that question you asked before." He released me and leaned a few inches away. "Twelve years ago I defended some British and Canadian women and children in Malaysia. It cost me a lot. It was instinct. I'd do it again. But it went wrong." I tensed. There was a solemn expression on his face.

"Some innocent people got killed. The plantation was under attack by Communist guerrillas who had been recruited from the Chinese population during a war the Brits called 'The Emergency.' It was the guerrillas' policy to leave a lot of dead bodies behind to spread terror. When they came after sundown I picked up a gun and returned their fire but there were civilians between us, Malaysian women and children, fleeing toward our bungalows. I couldn't see them."

I reached for his hand. "It must have been terrible. I'm sorry."

"The guerrillas slipped back into the jungle. I was held responsible for the death of the civilians. The British got me out of my Malaysian

116

jail cell." He let go of my hand and placed it in my lap. "Don't think you want me, Kate. Go home to Boston. Marry the banker."

I turned to him and wiped the smudge from his forehead. "What about the advice you gave me a month ago? Trying journalism?"

"I was wrong."

We stopped talking. I was acutely conscious of my posture. John was conscious of his, I could tell. "We should get the car unstuck," I said. "It's silly to have come this far and not see Paraty."

By this time, all four wheels had sunk into the mud. On our first attempt to back away from the stump, the engine stalled again. Half an hour elapsed before John managed to free the Jeep by engaging the clutch just the right amount to avoid stalling and rocking the car back and forth. Between attempts we kissed again, and again. When the Jeep was finally free, John drove more cautiously than before. A tree limb reached out and dug deeply into the passenger side front fender.

"Wait 'til UPI gets the bill for this damage," John said. "Are you hungry?"

"Yes."

"I am too. I'm looking forward to a big seafood dinner."

In Paraty the threat of tourism was unmistakable. The tiny colonial village had a fine harbor, baroque churches, charming squares. It was being rediscovered by people from São Paulo who were restoring some of the abandoned houses. We found Dom João's house. It was one of the few that faced the sea. He was away. We made notes and John took pictures for our mailer.

That evening we ate cold, spicy shrimp for a first course and sea bass served with black beans and rice for our entrée. We stayed in the town's only lodgings, a converted country house fronting the main square. We presented our passports. John registered us for one room.

In front of the clerk I let nothing show on my face. It was my way of saying yes.

The *pousada* was primitive and spare. On our nightstand was a lamp with no shade. The naked bulb cast a gloomy yellow glow. We turned it off and let the light from the street illuminate our room. We made love on the sagging cot. Our window was open to the street. Loudspeakers strung in trees surrounding the square blasted music and announcements. I couldn't understand a word. The clamor made its statement in our room, but it had nothing to do with us.

"Sex is audio," John said.

"You're saying that because I talked."

"Yes, you did. You told me a story while I was inside you."

"Are you sure?"

"I'm sure. It was amusing. I like holding you."

We slept the sleep of sated lovers, with John's hand covering my breasts. I woke up first. It must have been about 3 in the morning. I moved slightly. John was instantly awake.

"Anything the matter?"

"I can't sleep." I tuned on my side to face him. "Tell me about Malaysia."

"Like what?"

"I don't know. Did you like the food?"

"It got monotonous after a while. A lot of things got monotonous except, of course, when there was political trouble. I followed rubber prices, supervised harvesting. Went to Singapore when I got really bored, but there's not much to do there, either. I read a lot; learned some languages."

"Which ones?"

118

"Malay, for one. Arabic from the plantation bookkeeper. A smattering of Portuguese on a trip to Macao."

He caressed my back. I responded to his touch. We made love again. Afterward he lay on top of me for a long time. Our bodies were wet. A tropical ardor had taken root in him.

Tuesday evening, April 16, at the Olimpia bar, we talked for a long time and drank more than usual.

"I bear a burden from Malaysia, Kate. It was a tragic error." John reached for my hand. "I'm afraid it's made me something of a loner."

I kissed his cheek. "Poets are loners, too."

We stopped talking. We were dependent on the sound of the ice cracking in my vodka and tonic. Our bodies barely touched on the banquette. For a moment we were businesslike. For a moment we were entranced.

CHAPTER TEN

Interviewing.
Every week a sad surprise,
Revolving around a territory that doesn't exist,
A brown and green shading on a paper map.
Where are the mountains?
Where is Mato Grosso? Ceará? Rio de Janeiro?
Where?

E. Catherine Lawrence

I

On the second evening I slept at John's apartment, I examined his books. The selection intrigued me: Machiavelli's *The Prince*, *The Practice of Management* by Peter Drucker, a book on judo in Portuguese, William Blake's *Songs of Experience* (an old edition), T. E. Lawrence's *Seven Pillars of Wisdom*, some novels, including *From Here to Eternity* and Graham Greene's *The Power and the Glory*, several Arabic books, English-French and English-Arabic dictionaries. Had he lived among Arabs before coming to Brazil?

I looked around for other personal statements. Apart from the books, a serious stereo system and an interesting collection of jazz and classical records, the apartment was a blank — no family photos, everything neat and orderly, almost like a hotel room. I wondered whether he had hidden the traces of another woman in anticipation of my spending the night.

By the third week of April we were becoming hardened comrades of the streets. When I was by myself, day or night, I wrote poems. Some prophesied a dark future for Brazil. Some were about John. Others were just terse snatches of overheard conversation.

Sometimes, when I was covering a demonstration, John insisted that I wrap newspapers around my torso under my clothes like the students did, to protect myself from police batons.

"I hate looking fat."

"Do I need to respond?" he said.

By trying to disband the student organizations, the government forced the student leaders into clandestine maneuvers. From underground, they waged turmoil.

Catholic priests entered the fracas on the side of the students. On Sunday, April 21, John, two of our photographers and I attended a mass for student martyrs held at the Church of Candelária downtown. After the mass was over a dozen priests, led by their bishop, locked their arms and led a column of more than 2,000 student worshipers through the main portal into Pio X Square. We walked alongside the procession.

Everyone expected to be met by force. We were prepared for clubs, but instead we were confronted by 50 policemen on horseback, waving naked sabers. The color drained from our faces. For a moment the scene could have been mistaken for a dance performance, a lethal ballet. The swords glinted in the sun. Disbelieving, the marchers backed away from the horses, huddling themselves into smaller targets as they recoiled. I folded my arms tightly across my chest and hunched over, realizing only later that I had been exposing my neck. The sabers tested the air in small circles, then randomly slashed downward.

A saber struck a young man standing next to me, slitting open his shirt. Blood started to soak through. He was delirious with joy. For him dissent was no longer bullhorns and speeches, it was warm and red. He tore open his fashionable shirt, ripping away the buttons. Blood

121

streamed down his suntanned, hairless chest. It was a clean wound just below his clavicle, nasty but not mortal.

He refused his comrades' offers to take him to a hospital. I followed him as he backed away from the crowd. A determined policeman on horseback pursued us right up the steps of the church. I could feel the animal's breath on my back. The student raised his injured arm over his head, fist clenched, in a Che Guevara salute. He was a hero.

I shouted at him, "You need a doctor!"

Students were retreating up the stone steps, trying unsuccessfully to get back inside the church. The shock of the cavalry charge had rendered them mute. John pushed his way to my side and pulled me away from the crush. "That's enough," he said when we finally reached a safe distance. His face glistened with sweat.

"These kids are incredibly brave," I said.

"It's their show, let them be. I hope to God one of our photographers got a shot of this."

We looked around for them. John spotted Luiz before I did. He was dodging the hooves of skittish horses, ducking beneath the unsheathed blades, snapping pictures. "Stay right here, Kate. Don't move." John plunged into the crowd, yelling, "Get the hell out of there, Luiz! That's enough! You've got it! Come on, let's go!"

Heitor, our other photographer covering the scene, rushed up to us. His camera was smashed, its strap cut in two. "First time," he said. "A cop nearly made off with it."

The worshipers ran in every direction as fast as they could. Some fled around the sides of the church into narrow streets. Others retreated toward the entrance. The front of the church had multiple doors but only the main portal was open, not space enough for a crush of panic-stricken people to enter quickly. Some worshipers ended up pressed against the closed doors with no way to move. Finally an officer gave the order for the troops to withdraw. The excited horses were brought under control. Once the cavalry rode off the square emptied quickly. The priests and many of the students disappeared inside the church. John, Luiz, Heitor and I walked in stunned silence the seven blocks back to the bureau.

The wounds were ugly and deep that day, but no one had been hacked to death. Two dozen people were arrested. We thought the drama of a cavalry charge against priests and students would make it to the front pages of the American newspapers. But it didn't. The front pages were given over to the final defense of Khe Sanh in Vietnam.

The Olimpia was closed on Sundays. John and I weren't alone together again until Monday evening. I entered the cool darkness of the bar, eager to be in his company, and made my way toward our secluded table where our kisses could be unobserved and lingering. I felt intrigued, perhaps envious, when I thought about John as a young lawyer thousands of miles away from Canada, responsible for native laborers, relied upon by the English plantation owner. I imagined him at night under mosquito netting, reading his odd assortment of books, drinking a cup of black tea that cooled nearby on a wicker nightstand. Clearly he was holding back much of his story, but I wasn't concerned. The way to satisfy my curiosity, I was sure, was to show him that I could be discreet.

He was waiting for me, but not at our usual table. Two businessmen occupied our place. I felt disappointed that our suitably out-of-the-way table wasn't free. "I have a point to make," I said as I slipped into a chair across from him. He took my hand and kissed my palm gently, then held my fingers to his cheek. The waiter brought our usual drinks. "I keep seeing the irony down here. If I let it, it could get in the way of my reporting. It won't, of course."

"Just the facts, ravishing Catherine. UPI doesn't provide analysis. Our subscribers don't expect it, and we don't have the time. Leave that for the guys who don't file all day long, seven days a week. They have the luxury of really thinking things through. They use us as their starting place. Half the time we're going so fast we don't even write well."

"A sad fact," I said. "There's no time to polish anything."

"It's possible to write gracefully in a hurry. Sometimes we bring it off. Did you have a particular irony in mind?"

"The students, in effect, are demonstrating against themselves. They march against privilege, but without their families' privileges they wouldn't be attending the university in the first place. What would happen if they got what they say they want — a more equal distribution of wealth?"

"Don't kid yourself. It's not just rich kids acting up, there's something deeper going on. There's a dedicated left here. Serious communists . . . If I may change the subject, you worry me, Kate. On the street you don't show any fear."

"I'm too excited to be afraid. It's something I've always wanted — to be on the front lines."

"Careful — that kind of exuberance can become addictive. A healthy amount of fear is what keeps a reporter alive in a dangerous situation."

"Walter says Brazilians feel underprivileged because they've never had a foreign war. Not even a revolution with blood."

"Not true, though guys like Walter Decker like to say it. Their border war with Paraguay was one of the bloodiest in the 19th century. There was hardly a male Paraguayan alive when it finished. Anyway, I mean it, Kate."

"I promise. I won't be foolhardy."

After our drinks we left the Olimpia, lollygagging our way, patently lovers, through the dark streets of Lapa. It was fall; I was shivering slightly. John put his arm around my shoulders while he waited with me for the *bonde*.

As I ascended Santa Teresa hill, I jotted down some notes that later, because of the jerks of the streetcar and its dim light, I found difficult to read:

> Brazil had the misfortune to have Portugal for its colonizer instead of bloody-minded Spain. This tradition formed a country that gained its freedom without a war, abolished slavery without a war, settled boundary disputes with only one big fuss, got rid of presidents without spilling a drop of blood. In Brazil the war is between men and women. It's a battle of wits. Combat ends in bed.

II

Tuesday evening at the Olimpia, I hoped to encourage John to reveal more of his past by prodding him with poems. Although for 10 days I had held back from questioning him about his time in Malaysia, I wanted him to appreciate that I knew there was more. When we sat down at our table, I showed him two poems I had written the previous night. In the first I pictured a striking blue-eyed man wearing a sweat-stained khaki shirt and a brimmed planter's hat directing Malay laborers as they tapped a milky fluid from tended rubber trees hard by the China Sea. It ended with my protagonist in bed with the planter's eager daughter. I managed to work in the fact that the seeds for Malaysia's rubber trees had been stolen from Brazil by an Englishman in the 19th century. The protagonist of my second poem was an Anglo guerrilla fighter dressed in a white caftan and kaffiyeh, galloping a horse away from a desert railroad track where he had planted explosives.

John smiled. "Should I be flattered? Lawrence of Arabia and I have absolutely nothing in common. I guess you've been inspecting my books." He arranged and rearranged the pressed-cardboard coasters on the table. "Let's have another round."

I nodded.

Our waiter brought the drinks. John barely touched his. "You're right," he said, "there's more ... " He brushed my cheek with the back of his hand. "For a change let's get out of here and have a real dinner, someplace nice. You name it."

"All right, but we're not finished talking."

"Agreed."

"How about eating in Copacabana? I hardly have time to go there anymore. I miss the beach."

"I'll take you to one of those restaurants on Avenida Atlântica that has an outside terrace."

John got into the Beetle taxi gracefully, more gracefully than I managed. We arrived at the northern end of Avenida Atlântica, still undecided where to go, when John spotted the Ouro Verde Hotel. Swiss-run, it had the reputation of serving a superior candlelit dinner. The dignified restaurant on the hotel's second floor had no outside terrace, but its large picture windows faced the ocean. We were definitely underdressed in our casual reporter's attire. John ordered lobster thermidor and an expensive Pouilly-Fumé.

"Maybe we should have the local wine," I suggested.

"I've got money."

It was after 10, late to be eating dinner when neither of us had had lunch. We buttered hard rolls and ate them quickly while we waited for our first course, a duck paté. We didn't speak. I looked around the room. The restaurant had only a few patrons, seated at tables distant from ours. The waiter brought the lobster. With its rich cream sauce, it was the most exquisite dish I'd eaten in Brazil. It was served in its shell, which had been expertly split in two, accompanied by rice and squash. The wine was taking the edge off my caution.

"I hoped my poems —"

"Would get me to talk? I know you've been curious. I've taken note of your patience." For a moment he stared out the window. "After the British bargained me out of jail in Malaysia, I was in debt to them. They weren't shy about pointing this out to me. I was invited to become a British asset — regular civil-service status, paid vacations, retirement plan. I wasn't ready to go home to Toronto to practice law, but I also didn't want to be a bureaucrat, even in their outfit, so I said no. The Brits pressed. In the end I agreed to do favors for them on retainer. It seemed only fair under the circumstances. And to tell the truth, a part of me was delighted. I'd gone to Malaysia because I didn't feel disposed to settle down and this arrangement promised to keep me fed in some exotic places."

John's wine glass was nearly empty. He fiddled with the fine stem; our waiter refilled his glass. I refused more. "I was free because the British government stuck its neck out for me. They didn't have to. Mostly I earned a living like a normal Joe but, from time to time, The Service showed up with some errand they wanted me to do."

"You mean MI5, or whatever they call it, owned you?"

"I took my orders from the Secret Intelligence Service, MI6. MI5 deals with internal security. MI6 carries out British espionage abroad. Some engaging chaps there. I liked them. They're very persuasive — God, Queen, the good of the Commonwealth, the good of the free world. And they paid me well. I got sent to Beirut because I was fluent in French and had some Arabic. I had to find employment in the civilian economy. They wanted an agent who couldn't be tied to them. I've saved what they paid me and lived on what I earned from my cover jobs. For special occasions — like tonight — I dip into reserves."

"I didn't see any mementos in your apartment. It was so impersonal . . . so empty. I thought you'd deliberately hidden the traces of a former lover."

"They trained me to cover my tracks. It became a habit. I didn't change anything for you."

"I've always thought of espionage as a sort of gray world where there are necessary lies and cowardly lies. I guess the moral challenge is to know the difference. If you hadn't done this before, why'd they pick you to do favors, whatever that means?"

"I fit their profile in a lot of ways. Commonwealth subject, British mother. Knew some languages that interested them. Trained in law. Knew how to stalk a deer, wait in a duck blind. I'd learned to hunt with my uncle in the Ontario woods. I was good at it. They thought I could learn what they wanted to teach me."

Neither of us said anything for several minutes.

"What kinds of things did you do for the Brits?"

"Sometimes they needed someone watched. I told you I was good at stalking."

"You're being deliberately evasive, aren't you? How long did you work for them?"

"Yes, I'm holding back. Everything I've told you tonight is an official secret. I could be prosecuted for telling you any of it. Let me answer your second question some other time."

"Have you ever told anyone?"

"Never, not even my ex-wife."

"I've been wondering why you weren't married. Was she Brazilian?"

"Renata was German. I met her in Rio a few weeks after I got here. She joined my Portuguese class. She took me to Düsseldorf to meet her family and we got married there. A year later she decided she didn't like Brazil, or me, and went home to Düsseldorf and got divorced. She's married to a German now. An automotive engineer, I think. She left three years ago. It's way in the past."

"If you didn't tell Renata, why tell me?"

"I'd made up my mind before we married I wasn't going to tell her anything about what I'd done. It kept me more isolated than I care to be. It was a mistake I don't want to repeat. I thought I owed you the story. I don't know how to tell you more concretely what I feel for you."

"The other night when you defended the role of a political assassin . . . it must have been a delicate conversation."

"Every conversation I have with you is delicate."

"You've really thrown me."

"I know. Are you upset?"

"More fascinated than upset. You've certainly raised some interesting questions."

Our salad course was served last, European style. The waiter cleared away our plates and brought us cheese and biscuits. I waited until he'd left. "You don't know me very well yet to be taking such a risk."

"I'll take a risk when there's a good reason."

"You should have picked my mother. She's the one who did clandestine things during the war."

"How did that come about? What'd she do?"

"Dad was in the Army in Europe. She wanted to contribute. She packed up my year-old brother and me and moved to Washington so she could do war work. I was only 3. When the war ended, she went back to being a housewife. All she told me, not long before she died, was that she'd worked for the OSS. She died when I was 16. I really miss her."

One floor above street level, I could see the traffic moving along Avenida Atlântica and the mosaic sidewalk that bordered the beach, but beyond that, only black openness suggesting the ocean. John sipped the remainder of his wine, staring into his glass as if it held a cipher. He might have been a survivor of a fire that had consumed his past. He ordered *cafezinhos*. The waiter brought us petit fours with the elegant coffee service.

"It's late," he said, reaching for my hand across the table. He paid the bill and we went out into the humid night.

"Let's walk on the beach," I said. "I want to stick my foot in the water." We crossed the broad avenue and strolled at the edge of the surf, shoes in our hands, careful that a rambunctious wave didn't get us wetter than we wanted to be. The sea was soothing. We walked around fishermen with their lines drifting in the light wind. "You didn't know how I was going to react to your story, did you?"

"I had to find out."

We walked three feet apart. A ship traveling south, its superstructure dressed formally for evening in twinkling lights, slipped out of sight behind one of the small islands scattered on the sea. I thought it might be going to Santos, past Paraty, past our spare hotel room with its window that opened onto the noisy square. We walked into the gentle swells of low tide. I felt turned upside down, keenly aware that I was below the equator.

We continued for perhaps a mile or so, somewhat short of the jutting tongue of land, Ponta do Arpoador, that separated Copacabana from Ipanema. Near the lifeguard's observation tower we crossed the wide beach and walked toward the street.

"Come home with me," he said.

"Not tonight. I need to be by myself. Besides, I haven't got a toothbrush."

"I've got a spare."

"Or clean clothes for tomorrow."

"We'll have to fix that."

We brushed the sand off our feet and put on our shoes. John put me in a taxi reluctantly. He closed the door and blew me a kiss. As the taxi pulled away from the curb, I turned and watched him hail another for himself.

III

The moon illuminated the concrete steps as I walked up to my airy lodging. The house was dark. Perhaps the electricity in Santa Teresa was malfunctioning again. When I stepped into the foyer I heard Nelson Claudio's stereo in the parlor. It was the plaintive sound of Miles Davis's meditation on the moors of Spain. I felt along the wall for the table lamp that usually was left on day and night.

"Hello, Kate," Nelson Claudio called to me from the darkness.

"What's happened to the light?" I asked as I groped for the lamp's metal chain.

"I turned it out." His answer caught me short. I let go of the lamp chain and felt my way to the doorway of the parlor.

"Anything the matter?"

"There's a girl pretending to be asleep in my room."

"Why aren't you with her?"

"Because when I was in bed with Antonia, I couldn't catch my breath. My heart was racing. I wanted to go out with Miles, if it came to that."

"For God's sake, Nelson Claudio, shouldn't you be taking medication or something?"

"Metaphysically racing, Kate. Nothing physical. No need to worry. What happened in the world of confrontation today?" In the darkness I inched my way to the divan and sat down. Miles' somber passages made me feel alone. The castanets in the *Concierto* broke in with small, urgent, staccato accents. The timpani were soft, like a whisper of air.

My eyes were beginning to adjust to the dark when I noticed a figure lying on the floor. I froze.

Nelson Claudio realized that I had detected the recumbent body. "Don't be afraid," he said.

"Hello. I'm sorry. I didn't mean to frighten you. I've had to become incredibly sensitized to security." The voice coming from the floor was a full, clear, female voice.

"Kate, this is Anabela."

"Christ, you did scare me."

"We're just listening to music," Nelson Claudio said.

"Are you hiding?" I asked Anabela.

"I hope I'm hiding successfully."

"Hiding from what?" I immediately thought Anabela must be an agitator, one of those serious student leaders who actually seemed to be making progress in galvanizing public attention. She sounded mature for a student.

"Nelson Claudio tells me you work for UPI. I've met John Wadson. And Mike Evans."

"Can we turn on a light?" I asked.

"Why not?" Anabela said.

I got up, walked over to a table where I knew there was a lamp and turned it on.

Anabela rose from the floor in one athletic bound to shake hands with me. She was tall with long, dark, wavy hair and held herself very erect.

Nelson Claudio said, "They've got one of Anabela's brothers. Now they're looking for her. Anabela came by here because it's easy to get in and out of Santa Teresa undetected. Her oldest brother and I went to the university together."

"DOPS?" I asked.

Anabela nodded.

DOPS was the Department of Political and Social Order. They were plainclothes cops with eyes and ears everywhere; plainclothes cops who would and did pursue the enemies of the state based on the flimsiest of information.

I turned the light off again at Anabela's request. We talked through the night. Anabela, a third-year medical student, vacillated between minimizing the possibility of being caught and advocating provocations that would put her in danger. She was bitter but not afraid. She said her father had told her: "I beg you, finish your medical training in Europe. If you pass into their hands, I don't think I can get you out." As we talked I thought about Anabela's melodic voice someday soothing patients, politics permitting.

"How will you get out of Santa Teresa?" I asked.

"There are more than 60 routes, by mountain trails, by stairs and by road. Not all the routes are known to the cops. Maybe I'll go through Rato Molhado or Fogueteiro."

Rato Molhado (Wet Rat) and Fogueteiro (Rocketeer) were small encampments of shacks, hardly big enough to be classified as *favelas*. They were malodorous places the police didn't enter. They shared Santa Teresa with its middle class and a few wealthy residents who lived in guarded villas. Anabela could stick close to the road that switched back and forth across the top of the mountain, brushing the shanties as it went. On the far side she could take one of the numerous staircases down the mountain to the South Zone, the North Zone or downtown.

Anabela left before daybreak. Just as she was leaving, Antonia, the girl who had been sleeping in Nelson Claudio's bed, entered the parlor dressed for work. I took a shower, slipped on my clothes, drank as much coffee as I could without getting the taste of acid in my mouth and went off to the bureau in a state of somnolence.

When I arrived John was already there, looking fresh and boyish, wearing his usual mufti. We looked at each other across the newsroom. I feared that the glance instantly declared us lovers. Had Mike Evans, sitting next to me, observed our exchange?

I leaned over to Mike: "I spent last night with a student leader."

"I'm not surprised. Should I be? Don't tell our friend Tanner from Salt Lake. Mormons don't do that sort of thing."

"They do."

"They're not supposed to."

"I didn't say I slept with anyone. In fact, the student was a woman. Do you remember interviewing Anabela Palmeira, a medical student?"

"Vividly. She was one of the students who locked the doors of the medical school with the professors inside. That was in retaliation for the police retaining nine medical students. Anabela was their student spokesman. A real looker. They locked the professors inside for 36 hours with only ice cream to eat."

"Anabela spent the night lying on Nelson Claudio's parlor floor. DOPS was after her. The three of us talked all night in the dark."

"Learn anything interesting?"

"I'm always learning something interesting in Rio."

"In the middle of the night, who do you tell your stories to?"

"None of your business."

"Wadson?" He grinned. Mike always had a smile on his face or just beneath the surface. "Just guessing. You'd make a striking couple."

I looked at him with a steady gaze and Mike good-naturedly let the subject drop. I was used to the office paternalism. My male colleagues usually struck an acceptable balance between looking out for me and competing with me for stories. Mike competed less than Ed Tanner and the others because he had a unique specialty — one in which he was in a class by himself — and everyone knew it. He had an amazing gift for finding the ridiculous.

He filed, for example, a droll story from Recife about a mortuary he happened to pass — the Bon Voyage Funeral Home. Another time he wrote about a 75-year-old prostitute who, despite an ample retirement account endowed by her aged patrons, refused to abandon her profession because "she didn't have any hobbies other than love."

I leaned forward so I could rest my head in the crook of my elbow.

Mike patted my shoulder: "Have a nice nap."

When fully awake I had a knack for anticipating crowd movement — I knew how to maneuver through and around a demonstration without getting jostled or worse. That day I was not alert; I might have been injured. Even the journalist's drug of a fast-breaking, life-or-death story could not have overcome my profound fatigue. I sat at my desk all morning and afternoon reading whatever happened to be lying around the bureau. Mechanically, I filed one story on the results of a government-sponsored opinion poll. In a surprising display of candor, the Brazilian military let it be known that half the respondents believed Brazil was worse off now after its first year under the regime of President Arthur da Costa e Silva.

When I got to the Olimpia at 6, I sank onto the banquette and ordered a triple *cafezinho* instead of my usual vodka and tonic. I devoured, by great handfuls, a bowl of peanuts. John arrived 15 minutes late.

"I didn't go to bed last night," I said. "I'm dead."

"You should have come home with me."

"I thought I needed to be alone, but when I got to Nelson Claudio's he was hiding a student leader from the medical school. More than likely DOPS was looking for her. We were up all night. Anabela wanted to talk without any lights on. It was eerie."

"You've had an intense 24 hours."

I slowly nodded my head. "MI6 ... favors ... errands. Am I supposed to believe it?"

"What I've told you isn't an entertainment, Kate."

"I know, but at the same time my imagination is working overtime."

"Isn't that your normal state?"

"By the time you're ready to tell me more, it could turn out to be an anticlimax compared to what I've imagined."

"I doubt it." He said it with a smile.

"Unfair. You've just made me imagine more." John leaned over and we kissed, a long kiss. "I've had a surfeit of surprises and no sleep," I said. "I think you'd better put me in a taxi."

"To where?"

"Home, with you."

The next morning I made do with the clothes I had worn the previous day. I used John's spare toothbrush. That evening I left a few clothes and some essential toiletries at his apartment. I brought him carnations and, because I didn't think he had one, a vase.

CHAPTER ELEVEN

Actually, I was only looking for someone, a man.
It's an old story, isn't it?
I don't mean to bore you.

E. Catherine Lawrence

I

John united so many opposites within himself. He was constantly appraising people, often pursuing gossip with me in private but never at work. On one level he was predictable: His office uniform, his considerateness, his curiosity. He did what he said he was going to do. He was comfortable with his asceticism, which wasn't spiritual — it was just easier not to own too much. All else — his history, his lovemaking, his temerity, his zest for work — seemed extravagant and compelling. I wondered whether his UPI job was another cover. Was he watching someone in Brazil?

John had a maid who came four days a week. Márcia had an easy job. There wasn't much to take care of in his spare quarters. He said that when she felt like it, or when he remembered to leave her extra money, she bought groceries and prepared seafood casseroles awash in *dendê* oil, coconut milk, okra, tomatoes, onions, red peppers and sharp spices — recipes from her native Bahia. She would leave the fragrant food in the refrigerator for him to eat at his convenience.

When I returned to his apartment the first Saturday night after I left some clothes there, I found that she had washed and ironed my blue jeans, a blouse and a brassiere. They were neatly folded and left on top of the dining table. I removed them to a drawer to set the table for dinner — my first domestic act in four months.

138

Giddy with girlish uncertainty, I carefully placed the knives with the cutting edge toward the dinner plates, the way my mother had taught me, and crisscrossed the spoons at the top of the setting, European style. John leaned against the kitchen counter, keeping watch on the *moqueca*, a fish stew Márcia had left, simultaneously leafing through *Manchete*, the slick Brazilian magazine of personality profiles where Nelson Claudio's photo of me with Helena had appeared. While the dinner grew hot on the stove, I cut up oranges for dessert.

Late that night we woke in each other's arms and made love again. Afterward, John turned on his side, adjusted his elbow on the pillow and clicked on the bedside lamp. "Márcia told me last week she's in love with her parish priest. She says Father Alvaro is very handsome and respectful. I'm going to watch her belly. I'd just as soon not have the bother of finding a new maid."

"Before she gets pregnant, I've got a job I'd like her to do," I said. "She told me she knows how to sew. The curtains your landlord furnished are tired, don't you think? Let's have her make new ones."

"Go ahead."

A flying insect buzzed the lamp. John turned it off. I curled inside the curve of his body. We lay in the dark for some minutes. I took his arm off my waist and turned around. "I should tell you my history with Sérgio."

"You don't have to."

"You told me things you didn't have to say."

"I admit I'm curious. You're not the only one who stores up questions."

When I reached the end of the story — how we parted — I said, "I was furious with Sérgio. Brazilians might have changed some of

139

Freud's ideas about what's rational and what isn't. It was hard to forget him in New York, having to walk by all the places we'd been together. The tropics can take the edge off memories."

"Sérgio did what caused him the least exertion — breaking with you. It's quintessential *carioca* behavior in all its glory."

"I should have seen the evidence."

"It's human nature not to."

"But I think you do," I said, "see evidence."

"I try not to fool myself." After a moment, he asked, "Did you ever see Sérgio again?"

"No."

"Do you write to him?"

"No."

II

I assumed John had had serious relationships with other women, and not only with Renata. For the first time I rummaged around in his closet and drawers for clues to his domestic past. I found a clarinet, an old Canadian passport and a picture of a pretty blonde. No letters, no diplomas, no address book, no bank statements.

After dinner I retrieved the photo of the blonde. "Is this Renata?" I asked.

"Where'd you find that?"

"Where you left it." We both smiled.

"You see I don't really cover my tracks. I left a little cache for inquisitive girls to discover."

He put the picture of Renata back in his drawer for a day, then it disappeared.

The streets in downtown Rio were quieter in May than they had been in March and April. The relative calm allowed me to get back to my poems. Virginia Woolf was right: A woman writer needs a room of her own. John's apartment was too small for me to work in.

Nelson Claudio's father had brought me a spare card table from his mistress's apartment. Walter, again, lent me his typewriter along with words of encouragement. "You're a real poet, Kate," he said. "In Greek that's a maker, a doer."

I set the table up in front of my window, which I left open to the night. The evening temperatures in May had dropped to the low 70s. From the back of the house, facing west, I had a view of the lights of nearby houses set into the dark hillside. The muse flitted in and out of the window, bringing me the sullen, rapturous tropics on the breeze.

The front of the house looked down on Santos Dumont, Rio's airport for domestic flights. There was a broad stone terrace where Nelson Claudio and his friends would sit drinking beer and watching the planes take off and land. From time to time I would leave the typewriter to stretch my legs and join them. If he was alone with a girl, I would often find them pressed together.

"Do you know who invented the airplane?" he asked me one night when he didn't have a conquest in his arms.

"Of course."

"No, it wasn't the Wrights. It was a Brazilian — Santos Dumont. He put up a lighter-than-air machine in Paris at the turn of the century and steered it around La Tour Eiffel. And he flew a heavier-than-air machine years before anyone heard of the Wrights."

"You sound like a Soviet, Nelson Claudio. You're a revisionist."

"I can prove my statement."

"Bring me your proof."

"With pleasure."

He did, too, the next evening. He showed me an entry in *Le Petit Larousse* that half-substantiated his statements. Alberto Santos Dumont, Brazilian aeronaut and pioneer in the development of aircraft, was not the first to fly a heavier-than-air machine, but he wasn't far behind.

"Close," I said.

"My dear Catherine, you're too literal-minded and you're wrong."

"My dear Nelson Claudio, you prefer emotion to facts."

I mentioned our discussion to John, who supported Nelson Claudio. He said that in Paris Santos Dumont had actually made the first sustained flight of a heavier-than-air craft before official witnesses. Although the Wright Brothers claimed to have made an earlier flight, there were no observers and, unlike Santos Dumont, they had used a catapult.

Over time Nelson Claudio's waltz of conquest had slackened. I had finally convinced him that, very simply, I was involved elsewhere. He had bowed out gracefully, demanding only one deliberate kiss on our way to a rewarding platonic friendship. Thus he had become my liege landlord, my good and reliable source of information about guerrilla activity on Santa Teresa hill. He saw himself as my protector.

Some people think poems arrive unbidden, like good luck. I think poems are mostly achieved by work. While I labored over a stanza at Santa Teresa, John often would play poker at Charlie Wall's apartment with senior members of the foreign press corps. He was usually a big winner at these games, infuriating especially the ace reporter of *The New York Times*.

As I sat at my writing table stumped over my next line, or my need to find a felicitous form for a poem, I would imagine John sitting around the poker table eating olives and slices of pepperoni, drinking beer and scooping up his winnings, to the dismay of his colleagues. I was coming to understand that John played the whole world as if it were poker, constantly calculating the odds, showing nothing on his face unintentionally. I thought back to the time at the Olimpia when we had discussed Friedrich Grabenz and he had looked surprised. His surprise was genuine but, I was now sure, his decision to let me see it must have been deliberate.

III

On June 6 came the terrible news from California — Bobby Kennedy had been gunned down. I interviewed leading Brazilian intellectuals for reaction:

> One said, "You know, in the Third World, we are more disposed to the Democratic politicians than to the Republican. We prefer their rhetoric — let's say it's better regarded. I am deeply sorry."

> Another said, "Frankly, I blame the Americans for helping put the military in power in Brazil in 1964. President John Kennedy played a part in that. Still, Bobby Kennedy's death is tragic. I have a deep sense of sorrow."

> An iconoclast put it bluntly, "One more Kennedy down the drain. Americans love to pick off their myths, don't they?"

I felt very far from home, looking from a distance at events that affected me deeply. Around the bureau the reporters were grave and silent. Cynical jokes didn't whiz through the air as usual. Fingers seemed weighed down at their black Underwoods. The beat of the keys had the toll of a knell.

On June 15, the war in Rio heated up again. The marchers began to number 10,000 to 20,000. It was a mesmerizing time for the marchers and for me. I loved almost everything about it: its pace, its nonsense, its outrage, working late, overindulging on rich food, the discussions it provoked with Walter and Nelson Claudio, its innocence, its just cause, even its menace. I lived for the smell of tear gas.

John and I kept close to our sources and tried to anticipate the next flare-up. Everyone in the bureau was in full locomotion when we heard water cannon, shouts, cavalry hooves echoing on the pavement below the bureau. Would Brazil explode?

I finally had access to a telephone in Santa Teresa. Nelson Claudio told me his father had initially applied for one so he could more easily talk with his mistress. The Carvalho household had been on a waiting list for four years. At the beginning of May a telephone installer had made the first of several attempts to set up a phone. By the end of the month he was finally successful. Not only was Nelson Claudio's family thrilled to have access to the Bell universe, but so were their phoneless neighbors who hoped that their turns would soon come. "You realize," I said to John, "that as long as I maintain a presence at Nelson Claudio's I have an inside track to what the students are up to and now I can alert you by phone. They're hiding out up there all the time."

"Do they have meetings?"

"Not exactly. They meet outside Rio. I know they have target practice on the beach at Grumari. Anabela, the med student, told me the students throw up Coke bottles and shoot at them with .22s."

John laughed. "Stick to your beat, Brenda Starr."

My three-month trial period with UPI had been up on June 11. The next Monday, the UPI vice president in Buenos Aires notified me I was getting a small raise. John smiled and gave me a thumbs-up sign when he saw me reading Frank Cobb's letter at my desk in the newsroom. I had expected John to tell me himself, in bed, that I had a permanent job.

I wrote to my father and stepmother: "For the foreseeable future, I am staying in Brazil." I told them how much I loved my new career and I was more open about my relationship with John than I'd been in my previous correspondence. John wrote to his family about me. My father wrote back that a Canadian sounded better than a Brazilian. I appreciated his sensitivity in not saying what he could have, that — stereotypes aside — Sérgio was a cad and I should have known it all along.

CHAPTER TWELVE

I had to go, really, you see that.
Above all, I have relatives, blondly handsome.
I saw some photographs of them, one cousin I met in Europe.
I cried when I left for the front
My canteen on my hip.
I wore an automatic rifle and sun cream on my cheeks.

E. Catherine Lawrence

In those winter weeks, the question of where I would sleep became an exciting uncertainty. My nightly dilemma was nearly unbearable and wildly titillating. Every night was open to negotiation and depended on the exigencies of UPI, the privacy I needed for my writing but most especially, I had to admit, the status of my resolve not to make a mistake. In retrospect I thought I had moved into Sérgio's apartment too quickly. With John I wanted to be careful. The chanciness of each night — would I go to his apartment in Leblon or to my lodgings in Santa Teresa — heightened the intensity of the times we were together in bed. Several nights a week, as an exercise in good judgment, I would go to Santa Teresa. I would fall asleep on my convertible bed in a state of tumescence — thinking of John.

At the end of July, Jânio Quadros, who had been the last democratically elected president of Brazil, was taken from his seaside home to the port of Santos, where he was interrogated for three hours by a general from the federal police before being released. In defiance of an order that took away his right to make public statements about politics, the ex-president had held a news conference in which he said the Costa e Silva government "does not work because it is nothing." John left for Santos to interview Quadros and put Ed Tanner, our next most senior man, in charge while he was away.

The following day, a Saturday, I went to the bureau. I hoped John would be coming back soon. When the telephone rang late in the afternoon, I expected it to be him. José answered before I could.

José called over to me: "It's DOPS, *dona* Kate. They want to talk to *seu* John immediately."

"Say he's out of town."

"I did. He wants to talk to you." A shudder went through my body. "He said whoever is on duty."

I was the only reporter in the bureau. I picked up the telephone. "Catherine Lawrence *falando*."

"*A senhora fala Inglês?*"

"*Falo.*"

The caller continued in Portuguese. "We're holding an Argentine national who speaks English and says he knows John Wadson. Come to DOPS headquarters at once. Ask for *delegado* (police chief) Roberto Dutra."

The line went dead. I felt instant panic. I tried to call Ed Tanner but there was no answer at his apartment in Gávea. Mike Evans was still on a waiting list to get a telephone.

"I have to go to DOPS headquarters, José."

One of the translators, an older man, overheard me, turned around and emphatically gestured — no — with his waving forefinger.

"Careful, *dona* Kate," José said.

"For sure," I said.

José walked over to my desk. "Wait for Ed, *dona* Kate. He should be arriving soon. He worked very late last night."

147

"I don't think DOPS was giving me the option. When Ed comes in, tell him where I've gone." I took my purse out of my desk drawer and checked to make sure my press badge was inside. "Tell Ed DOPS is holding an English-speaking Argentine who knows John."

"I think *seu* John would be worried, *dona* Kate. DOPS is no joking matter."

"If I thought I could delay, José, I would. It was stupid of me. I told the DOPS guy my name," I said as I headed for the door. "He's waiting for me."

DOPS headquarters was in Lapa, five blocks from the terminus of the *bonde*. It was a few minutes before 5 p.m. Ed must have been out catching up on household errands or still exhausted. We had all scrambled Friday to cover an appalling riot. A policeman had been killed when an office worker, expressing sympathy with the student activists on the street, threw a typewriter out the window of a tall office building and struck him. Five other people — four students and another policeman — were badly injured in the enormous clash that followed.

As I walked toward Rua da Relação, both the name of the street and the sobriquet by which DOPS headquarters was popularly known, I remembered Anabela's father's caution that once you pass into their hands, "I don't think I can get you out." Did I dare walk inside?

The big gray art deco building was on a corner. Its somber color, squat proportions and lack of transparent windows suggested a fortress. The outside was heavily guarded by military police. Rua da Relação was the place people were brought for their first interrogation under torture. From there prisoners were transferred to even more horrible places — the Army Police headquarters in the North Zone, or to Cobra Island, or Grand Island.

My credentials were checked on the street by three different sets of soldiers. They were checked again inside the front door. As I entered the building, I felt there was no air to breathe. I was kept waiting for an hour in a small, gloomy anteroom that smelled of the perspiration that comes from fear. The room was so quiet I convinced myself I was hearing the beat of my heart in my ears. I sat rigidly, looking straight ahead. Perhaps I was being observed.

Finally a soldier opened the door and told me to follow him. He conducted me down a hallway to another small, musty room furnished only with a battered wooden table that took up much of the floor space and two dented metal chairs. The man who stood before me was tall and dressed in a beautifully tailored navy double-breasted suit, crisp white shirt and striped silk tie. With a graceful sweep of his hand he motioned for me to sit down. He remained standing behind the table.

"I am *delegado* Dutra. We are holding Juan Jorge Fernandez," he said in Portuguese. I recognized his voice from the telephone. "Do you know him?" His dress, manners and modulated voice were a trick, I felt sure.

"No."

"He says he knows John Wadson of UPI, that John Wadson can vouch for him. What can you tell me about this connection?"

"Nothing."

"Fernandez is traveling with an Argentine passport. It's phony. With passports you get what you pay for. His Spanish is accented. I think Fernandez is British."

I tried to appear in control of myself.

"What nationality is John Wadson?"

"I don't think I should be answering questions intended for *senhor* Wadson."

"It's a simple enough question."

"Canadian."

"Where is he?"

"Santos."

"When will he return to Rio?"

"I don't know."

"We are willing to let Fernandez go." I nodded for no reason. "On certain conditions."

Another plainclothesman, not so well dressed, came into the dreary room. He didn't introduce himself. He removed his suit jacket, hung it on a hook behind the door and sat down on the corner of the table, letting his legs dangle over the edge. For what seemed like minutes, neither policeman said a word. They stared at me without emotion. Finally Dutra continued: "We believe Fernandez is a professional agitator and that he came to Rio to help organize the students."

I tried to look impassive as I visualized a paragraph from my own dispatch of the day before:

> The Government has charged that professional agitators are instigating the disorders. It seemed evident that non-students were participating in the rioting.

I nodded again at *delegado* Dutra. I shifted my posture, waiting. Was my poker face working?

"Fernandez picked a stupid place to shoot his mouth off. He didn't know it but he was talking to a police informer at the Casa Simpatia. He says he's a tourist and was simply having an orange juice when a stranger joined his table."

The other cop broke in: "Fernandez can't be very bright, selecting an outside café and choosing to spill his guts to a total stranger. Our informant called us right away. Fernandez likes to brag. We went straight to the Leme Palace Hotel to pick him up."

"Why am I here, *Delegado*?" I dared to get to the point.

"Fernandez wants a neutral party to handle the money transaction. I accepted his terms. He asked for John Wadson."

"I will telephone *senhor* Wadson and have him get in touch with you, *Delegado*." I started to get up to leave.

"Fernandez is willing to talk with you in *senhor* Wadson's absence. You can appreciate *senhor* Fernandez is anxious to be on his way. Come with me." The *delegado* smiled politely.

I wanted to say I preferred to wait where I was, but I followed Dutra out of the room. The second cop didn't move off the corner of the desk. Out in the hallway, again I had the feeling that it was hard to breathe. Dutra led me to another anteroom.

A disheveled man who looked to be in his late 40s, with dirty blond hair and pale blue eyes, was sitting in a chair with his hands folded on his lap. If this was Fernandez, he looked like an Anglo-Saxon. Perhaps he was Anglo-Argentine.

"You can speak for 10 minutes," Dutra said.

I paused, waiting for Dutra to leave the room, but he didn't. He leaned into the corner, watching. The man in the chair got up and shook hands with me.

"I am Juan Fernandez," he said in British-accented English. "Who are you?"

"Catherine Lawrence."

"Do you know John Wadson?"

"I work for him. I'm with UPI. John is in Santos."

"You're American?"

"Yes."

"Perhaps you could perform a small service? I know John would want to help. Old favors, you understand." He paused. "*Bab Edriss*." He looked straight into my eyes. "*Bab Edriss*."

Bab Edriss, whatever it meant, was obviously important to Fernandez, so I memorized the words. I nodded. Fernandez spoke in a low tone. I had no idea whether *delegado* Dutra understood English, or how well.

"I've got 10,000 U.S. dollars in the safe at my hotel. The police will let me leave Brazil if I pay them off." Fernandez moved closer to me. He smelled awful. "If I let one of these cops go to the hotel and get the money, what's to say he won't just skip with it? I could rot here. There's an elaborate payoff system afoot. I hoped John could go to the hotel, get the money and bring it to me." Fernandez tapped his rib cage and winced. "This is not a comfortable place."

I planned to go back to the bureau and telephone John before I did anything. "I'll see what I can do," I said.

"Thank you." He took a folded piece of paper from his hip pocket and handed it to me. I scanned it quickly. It authorized the Leme Palace Hotel to give me the contents of Juan Jorge Fernandez's safe deposit box. My name had been typewritten on the document. I was stunned.

Delegado Dutra didn't give me the chance to leave the building on my own. He walked me to a plain black sedan idling at the entrance and opened the rear door for me. The *delegado* took the passenger seat in front. A soldier drove. I felt desperate not being able to contact the bureau. I wondered if the manager at the Leme Palace would give me the money. The sun had set; it was dark as we headed south in the winter evening. The Leme Palace seemed an unlikely hotel for a revolutionary to use as his base. It was a new luxury hotel that attracted the jet set.

As soon as we entered the lobby I turned to the *delegado* and said, "I have to use the ladies' room." I prayed someone who could get a message to the bureau would be using the facilities. No one was in the pastel, frilly ladies' room, and there was no telephone. I washed my hands, used the toilet and washed my hands again. No one entered. I splashed water on my face, stared at myself in the mirror. Perhaps Dutra had stopped anyone from entering while I was inside.

When I finally came out, Dutra took my arm and led me to the hotel manager's office. I shook hands with the manager and gave him Fernandez's authorization. The manager left the room, returned with three document-sized manila envelopes and handed them to me. The *delegado* told the manager to leave us alone in his office. "Count the money," he said after the manager left.

I sat at the manager's desk. Dutra watched while I counted 9,879 U.S. dollars, which included several $500 bills. Dutra called the manager back into the room and I signed a receipt. Dutra took charge of returning the money to the envelopes. He held onto them.

We drove north through the dark streets, heading back downtown.

Fernandez was in the same anteroom when we returned. He looked much worse than he had two hours earlier. Dutra handed the envelopes to me. I placed them in Fernandez's lap.

"Is it all here?" Fernandez's voice sounded hoarse.

"I don't know," I said. "There's 9,879 dollars."

"That's correct." His posture on the wooden chair became more erect.

Dutra left the room when the plainclothesman I had seen earlier in the day entered. "Well, well, *señor* Fernandez," the cop said in Spanish. His voice was menacing. "This will take a bit of time."

"I was told I'd be free to leave when you got the money," Fernandez said in Spanish.

"There are many benefactors to be taken care of, *señor* Fernandez. Many patriots."

The cop took one of the envelopes out of Fernandez's hand, counted out $1,500, separated it into three piles and slipped the money

153

into separate trouser pockets. Fernandez looked worried. He glanced at me. I shook my head slightly. I wanted to get out of the room, out of DOPS headquarters, but I wasn't sure how. I looked at my watch. The cop regarded me checking the time. It was 9:20, four hours since I first entered DOPS headquarters.

"I hope the *senhora* is not in a big hurry, though it is Saturday night. Did the *senhora* have plans?" The cop left the room. We were alone a few seconds.

"What's next?" I asked Fernandez.

"I'm not sure. I think we stay here and pay off cops. Nobody trusts anybody with this much money."

"We?" The word was barely out of my mouth when Dutra re-entered with another cop, one I hadn't seen before. They each took a share equal to the first cop's. I wondered if the *delegado* was going to buy expensive clothes with his money. They left without a word.

Throughout the next several hours other cops came and went, each taking from the pile on the table an amount of money that must have been carefully negotiated. Around midnight a uniformed policeman brought each of us a ham sandwich and a Coke. I took two bites and gagged. I drank the soda, grateful for once that, to accommodate local taste, Brazilian Coca-Cola was sweeter than American Coke. Perhaps I was getting more calories. I'd had nothing to eat since breakfast.

When I asked, I was shown to a bathroom that smelled of the effusions of whatever can be released by a human body. During the periods when Fernandez and I were left alone in the anteroom, we barely spoke. Once, when I started to speak very softly, Fernandez put his finger to his lips. By 4 in the morning all the money was gone except a $100 bill. Dutra returned. "Had a pleasant evening?" he asked in English (so he did understand!) as if we had been to a fabulous party. "We are leaving for the airport very soon."

"I want *señorita* Lawrence to accompany me to the airport," Fernandez said in Spanish.

"I must leave, now," I said. "Right now." I didn't try to hide my surprise and panic.

"You are free to go," Dutra said politely. "The last hundred dollars is for you. Services rendered."

"No thank you," I said. I turned to Fernandez: "Use it for your safe trip home, *señor* Fernandez." I exaggerated the words "safe trip home" for effect.

"Please, you must accompany me to the airport," he said. His eyes burned into mine.

Dutra opened the door of the stuffy anteroom. "This way." He escorted us to the main entrance and out onto the street, where a black panel van was waiting with a soldier at the wheel. Dutra sat in front with the soldier; Fernandez and I sat in back. We were driven through downtown on our way, I prayed, to Galeão International Airport.

Fernandez whispered: "Make sure you see me actually get on the plane for Buenos Aires and that it takes off before you leave." I nodded. "Tell John hello from Lord William."

As the van pulled up to the curb, two uniformed policemen were waiting. Dutra and the two cops walked us through the airport terminal directly to a Varig gate. I saw a gate number but there was no sign indicating where the plane sitting on the tarmac was going.

Fernandez realized this. The waiting plane could be making an internal stop before going on to Buenos Aires. If the plane stopped in São Paulo, Fernandez could be re-arrested there. I looked around frantically for a sign.

"Go to your flight," the *delegado* said. He handed Fernandez his passport and a voucher that didn't look like a regular airline ticket.

"Where is this plane going?"

"Buenos Aires."

A woman passenger approached the gate, holding the hand of a young boy. I decided to take a chance and test Dutra's word. Summoning my limited Spanish I asked, "Do you know if I can change *cruzeiros* for *pesos* at the Buenos Aires airport on Sunday?"

"I plan to do it myself when we arrive," she answered in Spanish and smiled. Fernandez, looking somewhat relieved, followed the woman and the boy through the gate, across the tarmac and onto the plane.

"Can I take you somewhere?" Dutra asked.

"No thank you, *Delegado*."

The three cops departed, leaving me at the gate. Other passengers walked through the gate to board the plane. I overheard them speaking Spanish. I asked an older man his destination.

"Buenos Aires. Do you need a ride downtown from Ezeiza Airport? My sister is meeting me. We can take you."

The gate agent assured me the flight made only one stop on the way to Buenos Aires — in Montevideo, Uruguay. It appeared safe to leave, but I had promised Fernandez to wait for the plane to take off.

Lord William? Was Fernandez titled? A British peer with lots of money who used it to instigate leftist revolutions in South America? Or was he a colleague of John's from The Service?

At last the plane's door closed. The aircraft lumbered from the apron toward the runway. I felt dirty in ways I didn't think would easily wash off. I found a telephone and called Ed at home. It was 6:45 in the morning. He answered sleepily.

"Meet me at the bureau, Ed."

"Jesus, are you all right? Where are you?"

"Right now at Galeão. Basically I'm okay."

"I'm on my way."

My taxi pulled up at the *Jornal do Brasil* building a few seconds before Ed's. I must have looked gray. I knew I stank. We took the elevator to the sixth floor and entered the newsroom before I said a word.

"You must be crazy. You actually went to DOPS headquarters?"

"I didn't think I had the choice of saying no." I told Ed what had happened, though I withheld what I thought must be code words meant for John alone.

"You look beat," Ed said.

"I'm wiped out."

"I'll get in touch with John." I could tell Ed was nervous. "Go home and get some sleep. Don't worry."

Dona Rita and Nelson Claudio were asleep when I arrived in Santa Teresa. I took a long, long shower, washed my hair, brushed my teeth, ate two oranges and some cold leftover spinach omelet I found in the refrigerator and fell into bed. I telephoned Ed around 3 in the afternoon. "Did you reach John?" I asked.

"Not yet. I've been trying all day. Did he call you?"

"I've been dead asleep. He might have. The phone's in the living room and right now I'm the only one here."

"Are you really okay? You told me the whole story, I hope. They didn't touch you?"

"Not physically. It's a hell of an experience being at DOPS."

Ed finally reached John in Santos Sunday evening, and I spoke to him briefly half an hour later. Monday, at midday, he returned to Rio. When he entered the bureau I fell in step behind him, followed him into his office and shut the door. "You bastard," I said half in anger and half in relief at seeing him. He shut the door, dropped his briefcase on his desk, took me in his arms and held me. He kissed my hair.

"Poor darling. You look exhausted. I'm sorry. How does Cabo Frio sound? We'll leave after lunch."

"Do I have to spend the rest of my life looking over my shoulder? Who is Lord William?"

"What are you talking about?"

"Lord William."

John let go of me. "Where'd you hear that name?"

"Fernandez whispered it to me in the car when DOPS took us to Galeão. He said 'say hello to John from Lord William.'"

"Jesus! Ed didn't tell me that."

"I didn't tell him. When *delegado* Dutra called from DOPS he asked for you, specifically. He settled for me because I spoke English. Fernandez settled for me because I worked for you. Fernandez — Lord William — mentioned something else. *Bab Edrus*? He definitely said *Bab* something. The second word was hard to catch. He said 'old favors, you understand. *Bab Edrus*.'"

"Why didn't you tell me when I rang you last night? I would have come right back to Rio."

"I didn't think it was something I should discuss on the phone."

"Come on, Kate." He opened the door of his office without another word. I followed him through the newsroom to the elevator. When we reached the street we headed toward the Olimpia. His face was set.

"*Dois cafezinhos, por favor,*" he called to our waiter as we headed to our table.

The bar was completely empty at 2 in the afternoon. John sat on the banquette next to me. "Lord William is William Reed, and he works

158

for MI6. Or he did. I knew him in Beirut. He was the senior field officer there for years, in charge of day-to-day stuff. Bab Edriss is a main street in downtown Beirut. Reed had a private income from his family, claimed he never cashed his paychecks. Behind his back people called him Lord William. He knew it. I think he enjoyed the appellation. I have no idea what he's doing traveling on an Argentine passport, getting mixed up in Brazilian politics. William was an idealist. Funny, impractical guy. Not the type one imagines when one conjures a spy. That's why he was effective."

"How do they look, then? Dashing like you?"

"William Reed could actually trip over his own feet. He can be absent-minded."

"He wasn't absent-minded Saturday night."

"Oh, when there's danger, there's nobody better. I guess it's not completely astounding that in his retirement he'd be involved with students. He has skills they would do well to learn. I'm sure he sees their plight very differently from the way they do."

"What do you mean?"

"The students down here like to think of themselves as leftists. William's been around long enough to discount their cant. I doubt that he sees the 20-year-old Maoists at Federal University as potential soldiers on the communist side. He may be using his money to help a few of them get a first-class education in England. It would be like him to do something like that. It's a damn shame DOPS got their hands on ten grand of his money. I don't believe for one minute William blabbed to a police informant while he was downtown drinking an orange juice. DOPS got their tip somewhere else."

"Do you really owe him a favor?"

"No. If anything, he owed me one." John smiled for the first time. "It's bloody awful what you went through. If it's any consolation, you probably saved William. A misstep on your part could have gotten him tortured or killed. It's just bad luck I wasn't in the bureau. I usually am on Saturdays."

I waited for him to say more. When he didn't, I asked, "What did you do in Beirut? How long were you there?"

"I was assistant manager at the Bristol in Beirut. It's a famous hotel — super-deluxe category. I was there for two years. Then I got a job with the Beirut office of BOAC. I was British Overseas Airways Corporation's public relations manager. An airline, like a hotel, is good cover for watching. A friendly word from the MI6 boys and it was arranged. I had access to all sorts of information and rumors. We used to invite the senior members of the major press organizations for a fancy French dinner at Lucullus the first Wednesday of every month. It was always fun. The UPI guy knew a lot.

"Lebanon sits right on the edge of the Arabian world. It's at the mercy of outsiders who are feuding with the West. After five years I'd had enough. I talked with MI6 about where I'd go next, and we settled on Rio. The Service was worried about communism in the Caribbean and South America and they thought having someone with my skills available there could be useful, especially if I got a job that gave me a good reason to travel. I liked the idea of Rio, partly because of its reputation, partly because I already knew some Portuguese. MI6 agreed to help me get started in Brazil. After that, I'd have to find work on my own."

"You mean MI6 got you your job at UPI?"

"No, I got it myself."

"I guess you're still working for them."

"I don't have any assignment at the moment, but if they asked me to do something, I might."

John rented a car and at 4 in the afternoon we drove to Cabo Frio and did nothing for two days except lounge on the beach. John was completely solicitous of my every wish. His secret world had been flung in my face. He didn't belittle my anxiety. I tried to stop reliving my frightening night, but the dry odor of fear I had encountered at DOPS clung to my nostrils.

After our trip, when I returned to Santa Teresa, I found the clothes and the shoes I had worn to DOPS in a pile on the floor. I couldn't stand the sight of them. I stuffed everything in a sack and put them at the bottom of John's closet intending to give them to Márcia. The next day I found that Márcia had washed and ironed the blouse, the khaki skirt, even my underpants and my brassiere. I gave her the clothes to keep on condition that she never wear them in my presence. She looked baffled but agreed. I went to the closet and got out the shoes I'd worn and gave her those as well.

"These also, *dona* Kate? You want your shoes to disappear from your sight?" I told her I did.

CHAPTER THIRTEEN

The plot to assassinate whom?
A meeting at the Casablanca café.
Jaidi, myself and a small battalion with solutions.
We hold hands and schedule his death by hair tonic poison.
The plot to assassinate whom?
Oh, you know, that madman.

E. Catherine Lawrence

I

The breeze on Santa Teresa hill was quite cool in July and early August. I wore a sweater as I wrote in front of the open window. I wrote poems about Beirut in the voice of a female character, a young woman from a bourgeois background not unlike my own. I hoped that by imagining Rajaa I could better understand myself.

Anabela dropped by at odd hours. She would come to my room and we would talk about the political situation, her decision to specialize in neurology, the fact that John and I were becoming a team both in and out of the office and yet, in some ways, I didn't really know him.

"Getting to know a man takes a lifetime," she said, smiling. "My parents are still working out their relationship after 30 years. They argue constantly, but also let each other know they love each other on a daily basis." Anabela paused, reflecting, I thought, on an interesting home life. "Changing subjects, Kate, there's a rumor the government is going to ban street demonstrations. We're talking about how to respond. We have to be ready."

162

II

Sometimes when I slept at John's apartment we would make love, take a brief nap, whisper desultory thoughts and make love again. One August night he awoke at 2 a.m. in an expansive mood. He turned on his back and folded his arms behind his head. "Ready for another mailer?" he asked. "I have an idea. When Juscelino Kubitschek was president he used to visit the Javaé and Karajá Indians on Bananal Island. It's in the southwestern Amazon basin, basically the middle of nowhere. Juscelino built an airport and a hotel there — the Hotel Juscelino Kubitschek — so tourists could watch Indians put on performances in a temporary village. Rich American matrons would go to get a look at genitals."

"Sounds interesting," I said. "Let's go."

"You haven't heard the amusing part. The hotel wasn't a palace, but it put on a show of elegance. All the china, flatware and towels were monogrammed JK. When the military government took over, they didn't want any reminders of Juscelino, but they didn't want to throw away all that expensive china. Take a guess what they changed the name to."

"How about Javaé Karajá — same initials? It works."

"Nope, they picked John Kennedy — Hotel John Kennedy. Brilliant and practical, don't you think?"

"I can see the headline for the mailer — 'Brazil's Military Avoids Waste.'"

"I love it! I'll use it!"

"What about pictures?" I said. "It sounds like a good picture story."

"Oh, I've thought of that. I'll take Luiz along. I'll share a room with him. You can have your own room. That'll really confuse the office gossip mill."

163

"You're not serious?"

He laughed. "I'm teasing. I'll take the pictures. A few good shots should do. The problem with my idea is that going to Bananal means I'd be out of touch with the bureau if something big breaks. There aren't phones out there. The government could decide to put on another show of force. My instinct is that both sides are quits for a while, but things could explode."

"I'll ask Nelson Claudio to check with his student sources. He can usually find out what they have planned a few days before they try something."

John turned over on his side. "We'd only be gone two days," he said. "Ed can mind the store." He pulled me to him. "I'm sleepy. Let's talk about Bananal in the morning."

III

I agreed with John that the story of the Hotel John Kennedy could provide a welcome bit of amusement in the face of the grim news that had been coming from the jungle. Just as I joined UPI, Brazil's Attorney General, Jader Figueiredo, had released a devastating 21-volume report documenting the massacres, enslavement, torture and systematic poisoning of Brazil's indigenous population. We had been so busy with the demonstrations in Rio that John used a stringer in Brasília to follow-up on Figueiredo's revelations. Hardly a month went by without the Rio and São Paulo newspapers carrying a story on the near-extinction of the Indians by land-grabbing white men.

Nelson Claudio checked with his sources and reported back to me: "Nothing's going to happen for a while. Go to Bananal and have fun. My uncle went last year and he said the Indians put on some pretty interesting displays for tourists."

"Like what?" I asked.

"Dance. Sing. They'll take you fishing, hunting, let you watch magic ceremonies, spit in a pot of manioc. Clothes on, clothes off, you name it."

"It sounds like play-acting," I said.

"It's probably as close as white people are going to get to the real thing. I wish I were going with you. It's terrible, though, what's happening to our Indians. There's no excuse."

When I relayed Nelson Claudio's report to John, he said, "Okay, we're going to Bananal. I'll speak to Ed."

Thursday morning we left Rio by air shuttle to Brasília. From there the Brazilian Air Force would fly us 340 miles northwest to Bananal Island, a service the Air Force provided for journalists and distinguished guests. Since we had to go through the capital, John had arranged for an interview with an official of FUNAI, the government's National Indian Foundation. The Figueiredo Report had detailed a catalogue of atrocities against the Indians by the very government officials who were supposed to protect them. It was a delicate balancing act for the military to admit neglect and wrongdoing by prior populist governments in the hope that, by taking the posture of protectors of the Indians, they could legitimize their authoritarian rule.

"Their tactic isn't working," John had said the night before we left. "The military thought they'd get credit for exposing the abuses, but instead they're catching hell at the U.N. over charges of genocide. The truth is the military government is committed to rapid development in the Amazon and the Indians are in the way. It's a duplicitous game."

Our government contact, Lt. Colonel Raimundo Arantes, stood up to greet us from behind a large mahogany desk. He looked decrepit. His dried-out skin hung in folds over the lower half of his face. I hypothesized that his features had drooped in response to numbing

165

bureaucratic routine and pat answers. He offered us coffee. We had already had our fill and declined.

"In a month the rains will come and the land will be transformed into water," the lieutenant colonel said. "Life won't return to the forest in all its variety for six months." He spoke slowly, as if summoning weighty memories and images. "Bananal is especially beautiful in the dry season. Along the river, white sandy beaches appear. What's dangerous isn't the jaguar or the maned wolf, it's the struggle between the Stone Age and commerce. If the Indians don't own the land outright, at least they should have the right to live unharmed on lands they've inhabited for centuries." He paused to look directly at us. "Perhaps you think the Indians are bloodthirsty warriors with poisoned arrows? They aren't, though they can become that when they are pushed. The Indians are in the way of the cattle ranchers, the farmers, the gold and diamond prospectors. It takes a lot of nerve to make a fortune in the Brazilian jungle.

"For the businessmen, Indians are worse than useless. They occupy government-protected land and they resist work. The Indians would rather die than be enslaved. So what do the land grabbers do? You know the answer — they massacre the Indians. Torture them. The misery is immense. They use planes and bomb them or shoot them from the air with machine guns. They give them poisoned candy. It's all in the Figueiredo Report."

Arantes paused and cocked his head as if he were staring in at his own story. "When the Service for the Protection of the Indians was founded it had the highest ideals, but over time some S.P.I. agents became complicit in crimes. That's why, last year, the S.P.I. was dissolved and replaced by FUNAI. The S.P.I. agent gets lonely at his station, he drinks to pass the time and too many looked the other way when terrible things were happening to the Indians. Some officials were more than derelict in their duties. They were corrupt. They helped

166

the ranchers in their persecution and exploitation. As I think you know, more than a hundred S.P.I. employees have been charged with crimes."

Arantes slumped in his chair and peered at the clutter of paper and files on his desk. He had put a human face on the military that I wasn't expecting. Were there others like him? I had prejudged a source. John and I looked at each other, trying to conceal our surprise. Lt. Colonel Arantes, retired from his jungle outpost, but still a member of the military that ruled Brazil without generosity, was not retired from his passionate concern for the Indians.

"The record of Indian massacres stretches for 400 years," Arantes continued. "It's a lamentable story and it's not over."

"How many Indians are there in Brazil today?" I asked.

"Once there were maybe five or six million. Now only 200,000 or so are left. No one really knows. No doubt there are still uncontacted tribes. How can you count what you cannot readily see?"

Arantes answered each of our questions with no apparent attempt at concealment. Each answer was a sad snapshot from the jungle.

Bounded on the west by the broad green waters of the Araguaia River and on the east by the narrow black waters of the Javaés, Bananal is the largest river island in the world, about the size of Belgium. The white, two-story Hotel John Kennedy was located on the banks of the Araguaia in the southern part of the island — indigenous land. Beyond the perimeter of the hotel, the struggle between man and the elements, between the white man and the Indian, was hidden in an endless labyrinth of rain forest and wetlands.

I wanted to do a mailer on Arantes. "Good idea," John said. "You do that and I'll write one on the touristic goings-on at our lovely, custom-built Indian village."

167

After dinner we went to our room and made notes. I sat at the dressing table. John sat in a leatherette arm chair. The room reverberated with the cacophony of the jungle after dark. John finished first and busied himself reading a magazine until I finished writing.

"Outside is one of the most poisonous and pestilential territories on earth," he said. "The Indians smoke to keep the bugs away. They've read your Surgeon General's report, of course, but they'd rather risk cancer than mosquito bites."

"I had no idea the jungle was so noisy at night. I hope I can sleep with all this racket."

"You can hear howler monkeys from two miles away. Sorry about the twin beds. It's all they had. We'll have to put up with them for two nights in the line of duty. One night here would have been enough. The headline should be: 'Tacky and Humid.'"

"I noticed there were some board games down in the lobby."

"No thanks."

"Well then, let's talk," I said. "Isn't this a good occasion? I didn't press you to tell me what you were doing in Beirut with Sir William. Don't you think it's time? I've been patient enough. You're going to tell me sooner or later — why not now?"

He shifted his weight to lean an elbow on the arm of the chair. For a few moments he said nothing. "I could credibly tell you I picked up rumors in Beirut — intelligence — and stop there. But I really want you to know more. Frankly, William's little trip to Rio has tipped my hand. I've always been intending to tell you, but in my own good time."

"If I'm not up to coming to terms with your past, we might as well find out now." I took his hand and led him to sit on one of the beds. I sat on the other bed directly across from him, face to face. There was barely room for our knees.

168

"I've held back a lot about what I was trained for. The Service taught me a number of skills. Among them, they trained me to be a sniper."

"I thought MI6 was interested in your language skills."

"They were, but they wanted me to have the full range of their training. Every army has snipers, so do police forces. You told me you had an ancestor who was a sharpshooter."

"I did. I'm impressed that you remembered. What about your glasses? I'm surprised they wanted you."

"I take them off and adjust the sight for my myopia."

"Are you good at it?"

"Very good — at what really counts. The most important part is knowing how to get in position and wait for the right moment. I learned a lot about that part hunting in Ontario. The first time they sent me out on a training exercise, I got within a hundred yards of my instructors without being spotted. That may not mean anything to you, but a lot of their trainees never learn to do it. With a 10-power scope, even from 500 yards away, I could watch one of my instructors take a deep breath. It's not like hunting deer. It took me a while to get used to it. I was taught how to camouflage myself with a ghillie suit made out of twigs to blend in with the surroundings, to close one eye for a minute or so before moving from light into darkness, how to elude packs of dogs and that if you keep still at night and blend with the background, you are totally invisible."

I reached across the space between us, took John's right hand in both of mine and examined it. "Your hand seems so ordinary."

"It is." He smiled. "No discernible stigmata. The real challenge for a sniper is to deal with the loneliness and stay focused and reliable. It's an entirely private struggle. Either you learn to control your emotions or you get out. The fact is I was better at hitting a target half a mile away than at some of the other things they wanted to teach me — like interrogation."

"But you're a reporter!"

"I'm a good listener, but I have no stomach for the ugly ways of getting people to talk."

He stood up and stepped over me to reach the foot of the bed. He put his hands on his hips and arched his back to stretch. His expression was impassive, professional. I didn't move. He resumed his position on the bed across from me.

"Is that the whole story? You never put your sniping skills to use?" I gently touched his thigh. I wanted him to know it was safe to continue. I waited for his response.

"I've chased a few fanatics around."

"Where?"

"Beirut. Around Lebanon. I wasn't sure you wanted to hear."

"While you were working at the Hotel Bristol? Go on. I'm ready."

"The Brits had their eye on one particular fanatic who came to Beirut looking for money to raise an army for a holy war against non-believers. He said he was the Mahdi. MI6 called him to my attention."

"What's a Mahdi?"

"In Sunni Islam the Mahdi is supposed to show up at the end of time to restore justice on earth and establish universal belief. Britain had had trouble several times in the past from fanatics claiming to be the Mahdi. A Sudanese named Muhammad Ahmad declared he was the Mahdi and led a war of liberation against the Egyptians. He was finally defeated at Omdurman by an Anglo-Egyptian army under Lord Kitchener. That's how Britain got control over the Sudan. The Brits were on the alert for the next guy who said he was the Mahdi. One showed up in Beirut in 1957 — another Ahmad. Ahmad Riad was one of my assignments."

"Is that meant to be a euphemism?"

"If you like. The trouble with Arabs is that they run everything, their lives, their governments — every daily decision, large and small — from a reservoir of excess feelings. There's no gray in the Moslem world."

We had come to this juncture in our conversation so naturally, I hardly had time to steady my nerves. I heard myself ask: "Did it happen in Bab Edriss?"

"Downtown? No. The Service made the decision that Ahmad Riad was too dangerous to ignore. Up to 1956 Lebanon had been the most pro-Western among the Arab nations. Its forte was making money. Their politics was mainly talk. But things changed. There was a battle over how much foreign oil companies should pay Lebanon for pipeline rights. The conflict got to be so bitter it was driving Lebanon into the Soviet camp. Not only that, but Egyptian and Syrian agents were busy instigating the overthrow of the Lebanese government. Eventually British and French installations in Beirut were bombed. Ahmad Riad was clever. He found ways to exploit every circumstance to attract fanatic followers. MI6 made the political decision Riad's assassination should serve as a warning. William made the tactical decision to do it during the '57 Pan-Arab Games that were played in Beirut. 'Lebanon has a chance to get to the finals,' William said. 'People will be obsessed with soccer. Riad will never suspect he's being hunted.'"

"And you . . ?" I asked. "What was your part?"

"I chose the time and place."

"You make it sound easy."

John shrugged. "Relatively speaking, it was. I took my shot as Riad was strolling along the Corniche, Beirut's seaside promenade. It was about 3 in the morning. I'd been following him for days without my rifle. I knew he liked to walk alone by the sea very late at night."

171

"Is there more, John? Did you shoot anyone else?"

"Yes. Another fanatic. An Egyptian. He was dangerous like Riad, instigating anti-Western riots and bombings. It was a more difficult assignment because he knew Riad had been taken out. This guy used to tell his followers to approach him with caution because his 'thousand-sided flame seared and burned those who were not obedient to his spoken words.'"

"Sounds like the door to Ali Baba's treasure, obeying the words 'open sesame.'"

"Only in this case the treasure was Soviet Kalashnikov rifles."

John got up and walked to the window. "That's the story, Kate. It may be my imagination, but I think things are a bit quieter outside." He turned to face me. "Are we still friends?"

"Of course. But it isn't easy for me to take this in."

John looked relieved. "Take your time with it. Get some sleep."

John drifted off quickly in his separate bed. I stared into the darkness of the room listening to the howler monkeys, to strange buzzing sounds, cicadas, high bird trills. I lay awake most of the night thinking about his revelation and about how Sir William had come out of his past into my life. By dawn it had become cooler; I climbed into John's bed. He opened his arms to me and I fell asleep.

We woke at 8, bathed in sweat. We rinsed off separately in the small shower, then dressed and ate breakfast in near silence.

"I'll prowl around the compound today," John said. "I probably should go out on one of those nature walks they've organized. Want to come?"

"I think I'll stay here and work on my Arantes piece."

"Is there something I should be saying?" he asked.

I shook my head no. "I just want to be alone for a while."

Before he went off, he put his arm around my waist and kissed me. I went back to our room but I couldn't write. I fell asleep and woke in time for lunch. When I got to the dining room, John was waiting for me. "What do you want me to say, Kate?"

"There's no need to say anything. I'm working things out in my own way."

"I'm here to help you."

John took pictures in the afternoon. I read ancient magazines in the lobby. An exotic river fish was on the dinner menu. I didn't like its pungent smell and I wasn't hungry. John finished his plate and mine. We ordered flan for dessert and went back to the room together. "You've been distant all day, Kate. I don't know how to behave. Can I touch you? I don't know where I stand."

"I'm sorry, John. I've been so absorbed in my own thoughts, I didn't realize how it was affecting you."

"You're unhappy with me."

"Actually, I'm learning about myself. I'm excited by your story, maybe even a little bit envious. I've always known I wanted adventure, but it turns out I'm not the Kate Lawrence I thought I knew. I'm not sure how to reconcile these feelings."

"Write about them. You like to work things out in poems."

"I hardly know what to think. You've taken me outside of all my reference points." I smiled. "Including this trip to the jungle."

"I need to be able to be open with you, Catherine."

We undressed and lay naked on our twin beds. John reached across the narrow space that divided us and massaged my hand and forearm.

"Hard day writing?" he asked.

"I hardly wrote a word."

The jungle announced itself all night. I lay awake. What had I been invited to? John obviously had a taste for a life far removed

173

from my world. I worried about the psychological residue left by his experiences. Eventually I fell into fitful sleep. The early dawn came alive when the *arara*, a jungle parrot, began its relentless squawking.

Over our morning coffee I said, "I was awake most of the night thinking."

He rested his hand on my thigh. "Friends?"

"Yes, John, we are. Have you got your story about the hotel and the Indians?"

He nodded. "I think I have more of an ecological piece than about Indian song and dance. From talking with some of the hotel employees, I get the idea the military is planning to abandon the hotel and let it fall into ruin. It's lucky we got here when we did."

When we returned to Rio, Ed said that the streets had been quiet.

CHAPTER FOURTEEN

Around here these things
Are usually determined by coroner's
Inquest, seldom
By the man who pulled the trigger.

E. Catherine Lawrence

I

I told myself John had been an irregular soldier in a shadowy outfit — not the sort of army my father, grandfather and earlier forebears had served in with honor from the American Revolution through World War II. What would it mean to marry a man who volunteers for secret hostile encounters outside of war? Do I sit home worrying? Will I have to be involved? My mother married an educator, and then one day she was married to a soldier who carried a gun and killed people. In her own way she went off to help fight the war. Thoughts, images and daydreams of John preoccupied me, but I wasn't ready to ask him further questions.

In August, just as Anabela predicted, the government announced a ban on street manifestations. To test the ban, the students scheduled a midweek demonstration in Cinelândia where Rio's grand movie theaters were clustered. In the face of a show of force that included 13 light tanks, 40 armored cars and half-tracks, 8 Jeeps mounted with machine guns, 1,500 infantrymen and state policemen, over 50 DOPS police in plainclothes swinging blackjacks and another 500 state police armed with rifles, the students didn't appear. The soldiers napped in the sun or lounged on their tanks, flirting with girls. The DOPS police milled around excitedly in the crowd of office workers and vagrants, arresting passersby at random. After three hours, DOPS had arrested dozens of people for no reason at all.

The very next day, 200 high school and university students showed up for a lightning-quick lunchtime demonstration downtown. They were armed with pocketfuls of glass marbles which they threw on the pavement, impeding the horses from chasing them. Spectators hooted and whistled their approval from high up in the surrounding office buildings. The students waved back, shouted their anti-military slogans and quickly lost themselves in the lunch-hour throngs before any arrests could be made.

John had assigned Mike Evans and me to cover the story. Mike was in his element, chuckling over his typewriter as he wrote. "Marbles! I love it," he proclaimed against the steady rhythm of his typing. "Those kids are geniuses. I'm going to say that in my article."

Three weeks after our return from the jungle, I showed John clippings of my Arantes story sent to me by my father in Boston and by Jane in Hong Kong. I wondered if my former colleagues at Macmillan, or Sérgio, had seen my bylined mailer.

Monday, September 2, in the fleeting twilight of Rio's spring, John and I left the bureau together. We no longer bothered with the pretense that our evenings were spent apart. Instead of going to the Olimpia as usual, we walked 12 blocks to Central do Brasil, the downtown railroad station on Avenida Presidente Vargas, and took a commuter train to Santa Cruz, a distant suburb.

John needed to check on the whereabouts of José, our legman. He had been missing in action for four days — the first such lapse in his near-perfect, three-year attendance record. Without José there was no one to monitor our telephones for a functioning line and no one to roam the city carrying our urgent messages. The only way to get in touch with him was to travel to where he lived.

The train to Santa Cruz was crowded with scrawny odd-job laborers and domestic workers in shapeless, faded cotton dresses. The animated passengers gabbed and flirted. We didn't get seats until half an hour after the train pulled out of downtown Rio. "It's not going to be easy to find José's house," John said. "The suburban towns around Rio are foul places — really they're just dormitory quarters with stalls that sell cheap clothes and *cachaça*. But they're better than living in a *favela*. José's doing well to live out in Santa Cruz."

An hour later we got off the train in a swarm of people. John asked directions. Well-meaning residents didn't agree on what route we should take. When we got off the paved roads the place stank of multicolored garbage strewn about. We looked for street signs and house numbers in the maze of packed dirt alleys. They didn't exist. The inhabitants, it seemed, were too poor to receive mail or uninitiated visitors.

José's dwelling, indistinguishable from the others, was a tiny hovel made of cinderblocks and corrugated sheet metal. When he opened the door, he was disheveled and red-eyed. *"Seu* John! *Dona* Kate!"

"What's wrong, José? It's not like you to be absent from work." John said.

"Did you come so far to tell me my job is gone? I already know it."

Looking over José's shoulder, I could see his entire abode: a lumpy, unmade double bed, a tiny refrigerator, a small TV with several empty shot glasses sitting on top and a scarred plastic table surrounded by three chairs. The illumination in the room came from two lamps with red shades; one lamp sat on the table, the other rested on the floor near the TV. I could see a sink in the corner of the room.

"Are you sick?" John asked.

"It's very complicated, *seu* John. Maria Lilia has gone out of her head. I'm waiting for her to come to her senses. When she comes back, I'll throw her out for good."

"For God's sake, man, don't let Maria Lilia jeopardize your job. I'm telling you as a friend, not as your employer."

"I'm not fired? I just want to know for sure who Maria Lilia ran off with." José looked sheepish. "It might have been that shit Benedito. Maria Lilia's sister said she saw them together in a bar holding hands."

"I want you in the bureau tomorrow morning, José. Work's piling up."

"I can't say 100 percent." José looked woebegone but it was obvious our visit was having an effect.

"He'll be there tomorrow morning bright and early," John said after we bade José goodbye.

Retracing our steps to the train platform wasn't easy in the dark. Here and there, naked light bulbs on primitive standards offered minimal illumination. The dirt alleys were bustling. Shoppers carried string bags of produce. Naked toddlers squatted to play. Teenage boys kicked miniature soccer balls and shouted as they made goals in semi-collapsed cardboard boxes. We were at the end of Rio's suburbs, 30 miles west of the city, not far from the coast, a place where only God survived without hard work. In downtown Rio the paddy wagons, nicknamed "the Mother's Heart" because everyone knew there was always room for one more, collected protesters itching for revolution, while outlying Santa Cruz was a place of scavenging after dreams.

As we approached the train platform, I noticed how empty it had become. Wispy clouds dimmed a gibbous moon. A lone couple leaned against each other, petting. My mind careened from our talk with José to my first febrile days as a reporter when everything was new, my reve-latory discussions with Nelson Claudio and to my first interviews with Brazilian men. They had answered my questions in feigned amaze-ment. "But how can such a pretty girl know so much?" I should have been incensed; instead I had allowed myself to be charmed. We stepped onto the train platform. "Brazilian fathers are terrified when their virgin daughters venture forth into the world," I said. "Every-body's on the prowl, including the daughters, and denying it."

"There's a lot riding on their virginity," John said, "and a whole country of Brazilian males ready to relieve them of their burden. What brought that up?"

"I was thinking of Nelson Claudio's lecture on restoring virginity —"

A loud crack cut me off. Something went flying. Another crack. It took me a few seconds to realize it was not a backfiring car but a gunshot. I felt my face flush. Another gunshot rebounded to our left. I fell onto the rough concrete platform, skinning my elbows and hands. John's chest was over me, pushing my head lower. We were completely exposed. From the corner of my eye I could see our nearest cover, a small kiosk papered with broadsides, some 40 feet away. My hands burned. I could feel John moving, cautiously.

"There are trees behind us," he shouted. "Run!"

I was halfway to the trees when I realized John wasn't running beside me. I stopped and turned back. He waved at me to get down. I could just see the gunman on the other side of the tracks, but I couldn't make out his face. He was dressed in white pants and a light-colored shirt.

John dropped into a shooter's crouch. In silhouette it looked like he was taking aim. The gunman hunched down and took several strides backward, weaving from side to side, watching us. He moved steadily

179

back, holding his pistol in both hands, and vanished into the darkness. I was frozen on the platform. John stood up and hurried over to me. He took my arm, pulled me to my feet and we moved, half-walking, half-jogging toward the trees.

"You were supposed to keep running." He was angry the way a parent is angry with a child who runs carelessly into the street. I looked across the tracks to where the gunman had stood. He wasn't there.

"It looked like you were holding a gun, ready to fire. Since when do you carry one?"

"I don't have a gun and you know it." He held out his empty hands. "I hoped the guy would think I did. He'd have nailed us if he got closer."

We squatted behind a scrubby tree. I peered around the trunk. Stretched along the platform were five very dim vapor lamps on wooden standards. Everything surrounding me was magnified — the movement of the air, the shadows, the buzz in the overhead electric wires, the chatter of cicadas in the shrubs. I had felt something graze the side of my head. It felt like a bee sting. I reached up and felt my scalp. It was sticky. I touched my shirt. It was sticky, too. I felt light-headed. John ran his fingers lightly over my scalp, my shoulders and my arms. "Christ, you're bleeding. Are you hit, Kate? There's something in your hair ... feels like a piece of concrete."

"I don't feel anything. It must have grazed me."

"You've got to get looked at immediately."

"I'm okay. Really. I'd tell you if I wasn't."

"Scalp wounds always bleed a lot, even if it's nothing serious. Can you hold on till we get to Rio? I doubt José knows a doctor out here."

"Where's the guy now?"

"I'm not sure. No one's crossed the tracks. We could go back to José's place so I could take a good look ..."

180

My jeans and my feet felt sticky. The insides of my sandals were slippery with blood. John took off his cotton jacket and his shirt, wrapped his shirt turban-style around my head as tightly as he could manage and put his jacket back on. The pressure on my head felt good.

"I must look a little strange."

"Like Carmen Miranda."

"Let's go home," I said.

John took my purse off my shoulder and slung it over his. "You're unflappable."

"I'm faking. Feel my hands." John took them in his and rubbed them. "Do you see the guy?" I asked. "I don't."

"I think he's gone," John said.

When the train pulled in, a couple in flaunty clothes ran past us onto the platform. We made our dash.

The train was three cars long, half its rush-hour length, pulled by a diesel engine. The first two cars were completely blacked out. Something must have gone wrong with the train's electrical system. Only the last car had any illumination, and that was dim. We ran past the dark cars. I caught the smell of decaying vegetables through the open windows and heard voices cutting the warm night with gaiety.

There were only a handful of people in the last car, and they didn't seem to be having the same good time as the passengers in the dark. The train began to move. The couple, young mulattoes, had jumped onto the dark, boisterous car next to ours. A few moments later our car door opened and they entered. The man's manner let the world know, without any doubt, that he owned it. He wore a zoot suit. He looked like a *malandro*, the Rio archetype of a strutting hustler, a parasite. "Maybe we were mistaken for them." I nodded at the couple.

"Could be." John sat poised on the seat beside me, ready for anything. His breathing was fast and shallow. He took my hand; his was as damp and clammy as mine.

"What's a hoodlum like that doing way out here where working families live? We're nowhere near Caxias." Caxias was the capital of suburban crime, a place of cunning and alienation where the professional killers of Rio lived unmolested. "Let's ask. It must be a story."

"Leave it alone, Kate. These guys deal drugs." I stood up. John grasped my arm firmly and held on. "You're still running on adrenaline."

The train swayed; I lost my balance. I sat down abruptly, half on my seat, half on John's lap. My turban was beginning to slip down my forehead. John adjusted it. "Tight enough?"

I nodded and tapped the side of my head lightly. "I'll probably have a goose egg." I shifted in my seat. "You presented quite a target on the platform."

"What else could I do? It was a bluff. It was either going to work or it wasn't."

"Why'd you face him square on?"

"It's the way I was taught. You're a bigger target but you're less likely to get killed if you're hit. A bullet in the side can tear hell out of several vital organs. Lucky he didn't have a rifle."

It was nearly 9 p.m., late to find medical attention. I glanced at the *malandro*. He looked amused. His hand moved up his woman's thigh. Every few minutes John gently touched my turban. "I think the bleeding stopped," he said.

My clothes felt uncomfortably stiff. John was keeping something back from me, and he knew that I knew it. After some minutes listening to the clatter of the train, I said: "That guy wasn't shooting at us by mistake. I think he knew you."

"You need to see a doctor. You could have a concussion."

"You're avoiding what I said."

182

"I'm not going to discuss this now, Kate. I don't think we should waste time when we get back taking a taxi out to Leblon."

"If I had a concussion, wouldn't I be slurring my speech, or vomiting? Actually, I'm hungry. I'd rather have a good meal than go to an emergency room."

"Fear makes you hungry? I have the opposite reaction. The Hotel Gloria's near the station. We'll take a room. I'll look at your head in decent light. We'll make plans after that."

II

The train crawled back to Rio. John held my hand, massaged the small of my back, rested his hand on my thigh, adjusted my tourniquet, kissed my cheek, kissed my fingers. As we approached the outskirts of the city he said, "Rio's a place where people's interests can collide in funny ways."

From the station we took a taxi the few blocks to the Hotel Gloria. Fortunately the hotel entrance was deserted, though brightly lit. "I'll go to the gift shop and wait for you," I said. "I don't think the reception desk should see me."

"Okay. We need a few things."

After he joined me in the gift shop, he picked out a very expensive, blue-and-white-striped, button-down shirt for me and a plain blue button-down for himself. I added a bottle of rubbing alcohol, a tube of French shampoo, two toothbrushes and toothpaste. Two matching bathing suits, a woman's and a man's, colorful and brief, the type tourists would purchase in a convention hotel, were displayed on a counter. John gathered them up to add to our purchases.

"The *senhora* was in an accident?" the clerk asked. "Traffic on the Aterro is dangerous night and day. You must speak to the front desk. They will find you a doctor, even at night."

"I banged my head on the dash," I said. "Nothing serious. I just need to get cleaned up. Thank you for your concern."

Our large room on the seventh floor, at the front of the hotel, had somewhat worn furniture and a faded carpet. It was comfortable, not luxurious. I opened the window and gazed out at Guanabara Bay. Sugar Loaf Mountain plunged into the bay to my right. To my left, I could see the jut of land and runway lights of Santos Dumont. "Let's order dinner from room service," I said.

From the bathroom I heard John order steak, rare, French fries, hearts of palm salad and rice pudding. I took off my bloody clothes and piled them on the blue-and-cream tile floor, but left the makeshift tourniquet around my head. "Let's have a look," John said as he entered the bathroom. He unwound the turban. My long auburn hair was matted with dried blood. I touched the spot where it felt tender. It was sticky and there was a lump. He made me crane my neck this way and that under the bathroom light while he carefully picked cement chips from my hair. "It's just superficial, but it bled a lot. Are you dizzy? Nauseous?"

"No."

I turned on the shower over the bathtub. John held onto my arm as I stepped inside. After I was clean, I gathered my clothes off the floor and threw them in the tub with half the tube of shampoo. "You shouldn't lean over," John said from the doorway. "You could faint. Better let me do it."

It took six rinses to get the water to come out clear instead of reddish brown. He hung everything on the shower curtain bar. My shirt, my blue jeans, bra, even my panties were blotched with russet stains. I soaked some toilet paper with alcohol and John dabbed it on my raw elbows.

"Ouch!"

"Blow." I blew on one arm, John the other. I used the tiny scissors in his pen knife to trim two of my fingernails that had torn.

I was naked, watching John swab the insides of my bloodstained sandals, when I heard a knock on the door. I put a towel on the toilet seat and sat down to wait. It was one thing for me to be cool under fire, but if John didn't tell me what he knew about the shooter, I was going to leave him. I was convinced they knew each other.

When the waiter left, John opened the bathroom door and signaled me to come out. I wrapped a large bath towel around my waist, sarong-style. John handed me my new shirt. A bottle of champagne rested in an ice bucket on a rolling dining table covered in white linen. I sat down on a small upholstered chair drawn up to the table; John pulled over a desk chair. I began eating a French fry. John uncorked the champagne, poured a taste and took a sip. "Not bad. It's imported. You shouldn't be drinking alcohol right now, but I couldn't resist ordering champagne. I don't think one small glass will hurt you."

"I wish there was a way to keep it from going flat," I said. "Put the cork back. I'll drink it tomorrow for breakfast with orange juice." I dug into my steak.

John picked at his food for several minutes. "I recognized the guy who was shooting at us."

I put down my fork. "Someone you wrote a story about?"

"Someone I worked for. We had a falling out. He fired me. I'd been watching him for MI6."

"Good God, does he follow you?"

"If he does, it's news to me. I'm not in hiding. If he wants to find me, he can do it more easily than following me to Santa Cruz. I'm sure it was a coincidence. Marcos likes to walk around with a pistol under his shirt. He's a real cowboy — half Brazilian, half Lebanese. I've got no idea what he was doing in Santa Cruz."

"I thought you were a reporter since you left Beirut."

"Except for six months in the food business. Marcos had a contract with Pan Am to supply in-flight meals at Galeão. The crews used to tell us our food was much better than what they got in Santiago or BA or Caracas. MI6 wanted me to watch him because he was sending money to Cypriot terrorists. They had traced the funds through Beirut to Marcos in Brazil. The Service wanted to know where he got the money. It couldn't all be coming from his catering business. The wealthy Maronite Christian community in São Paulo was one possibility. They could afford it."

"You just walked through his door and asked for a job?"

"The Service facilitated the introductions. It wasn't hard to sell him on my experience at the Bristol. He liked it that I spoke French and passable Arabic, so he was willing to put up with my lousy Portuguese. After I'd made myself indispensable, he gave me the title of Operations Manager. Every few days, in the North Zone, we had short blackouts — a few minutes at most. The kitchen learned to work around the outages. But one day there was a major blackout. It lasted nearly four hours. When they got the beef out of the fridge for the Miami flight, it was still cool, but not cold. There were a few green spots on the meat. I told the chef to trim the green spots off before he cooked it. Over the Atlantic everybody on the flight got violently sick. It was the end of Marcos' contract with Pan Am."

"Jesus, John. Didn't you know better? It's funny and it's not."

"It's a famous story now. I smelled the beef and it didn't smell bad to me."

"Your chef should have said something."

"He should have, but he didn't. Marcos was really sore. When he fired me, he was waving a gun. He'd trusted me. When he thought about it, he might realize that he had a disgruntled former employee

186

who knew about his unusual money transactions. I disappeared to Cabo Frio and let him settle down. The electricity blackout, the green spots on the meat, the sick passengers — the whole famous story — it wasn't exactly what MI6 had in mind. I did get some useful intelligence on his São Paulo contacts. I could have gotten a lot more if I hadn't been sacked."

"Apparently he hasn't settled down," I said.

"I think he did at first, but I can think of a reason why he might have gotten stirred up again. The Service used what I gave them to start connecting the dots to terrorists overseas. They'd been busy rolling up his network. Marcos could suspect the information came from me."

"Do you think he realized you were spying on him?"

"Maybe."

"What about the Brazilian military government? Do they know about you? Could Marcos have been tipped off by a corrupt officer?"

"Certainly not. No Brazilian has any reason to think of me as anything other than the UPI news director. Besides you, there's only one person in Brazil who knows about my connection with The Service."

John picked up the champagne bottle, hesitated, and put it down without pouring. I was feeling relieved. I wanted facts and John had revealed enough of what he knew to satisfy me.

"I wasn't going to be patient this time," I said.

He nodded. "I didn't want you to be."

"I'd like to take a walk," I said.

"Alone or with me?"

I didn't answer right away. John got up and went to the window. "Nice view."

"Let's have a swim," I said. "We've got the suits."

"You really feel up to it? You haven't finished your dinner."

I dropped the towel from around my waist, took off the shirt and kissed him for a full minute. I put on the green and blue bikini. John stripped fast and put on his European-style trunks. While he took a moment to arrange himself so his erection wouldn't show, I kissed his shoulder. "We'd better walk down the back stairs," I said. "It's a bit obvious."

At that late hour the pool was deserted. It was surrounded by tropical gardens; floodlights in the palm trees cast glamorous shadows. I sat by the edge of the pool and dangled my feet in the water. It was cool, delicious. I felt giddy. John went to the board, dove in and swam underwater to me. He scooped me up and carried me into the water until I was submerged to the top of my breasts. The hair on his chest felt delicate against my skin.

"Want to see my butterfly stroke?" I said. "I won a butterfly competition when I was 11 at summer camp on Lake Winnipesaukee, New Hampshire."

"Let's see, Miss Winnipesaukee." We kept our voices low so they wouldn't carry to the open windows of the guest rooms that faced the pool. I took off with a display of energy meant to impress and swam half the length of the amoeba-shaped pool, but I didn't have the stamina to finish. When I stopped, John surfaced by my side. "It's bleeding again," he said.

"Do you see any piranhas?" I wrapped my legs around his waist. A waiter appeared and asked if we wanted something to drink. John ordered two *Guaranás*.

"You should tell the police what happened," I said.

"Kate, you've been in Brazil long enough to know that's not the way things work here. Mind if I do some laps?"

John pushed off and swam about a dozen laps while I floated on my back, keeping my head out of the water. The waiter brought our drinks and set the tray down on the concrete lip of the pool. I waded over to the tray, told the waiter our room number and carried the glasses back to John. "A toast to Pan Am," I said, "and to Rio's unreliable power plants."

"A toast to your thick skull, Edwina Catherine Lawrence."

We finished our drinks, returned the glasses to the tray and floated, holding hands, until our feet sank to the bottom of the pool. My feet landed on his, reminding me how, when I was 5 years old, I used to love to stand on my father's feet while we waltzed. I leaned against John. "Dance with me," I said.

We attempted a box step in waist-deep water, but we couldn't keep our balance. We dried off by the edge of our private pool. The air was humid and warm. "Next time I order steak, I'm going to check for green spots," I said.

An hour later we lay sweaty on the bed, its pastel flowered bedspread kicked onto the floor. John stroked the curve of my hip. "Marcos isn't going to do it again," he said. He sat up abruptly and put both his feet on the rose-colored carpet. "Should I turn on the air conditioning, Kate?"

"Actually, I like the open window." He lay down again on his back and I rested against him with my head on his shoulder, my leg between his. "How do you propose to stop him?"

"You got hurt tonight. It could easily have turned out much worse. Before Marcos gets it in his head to shoot at me again, I'm going to put a stop to it."

I squirmed in his arms. His words were electrifying. I rolled off him and turned on my side. He turned too, as he always did, to hold me with my buttocks against his loins, his arm tucked around my breasts. He was asleep, or pretending to be, almost immediately.

I'm reckless, I thought. I am available for danger the way some women are available for any passing man. I tried to stay motionless while I asked myself what kind of person loving John made me. After a few minutes I lifted his arm off of me, turned and looked at him. In a wide-awake voice he answered my gaze: "You can't work it all out tonight, Kate."

I leaned over and kissed his eyelids. In the liminal minutes before I fell asleep I was conscious only of John's body, his smell and the moonlight that swept across our room from the eastern sky.

CHAPTER FIFTEEN

Let's marry on horseback
At the Police Academy,
With an apple split in two,
Half for the marrying magistrate
And half for the horse.

E. Catherine Lawrence

I

When I was 16 and my mother was dying of cancer — in her last days, a time of twilight at the edge of consciousness and fitful, drugged sleep — she told me she was having a continuous, rapturous dream of making love with an unknown man.

In the days following our night at the Hotel Gloria, I was having a recurring, voluptuous dream of my own. Sometimes I thought I knew the man, though I couldn't name him. Sometimes I thought he might be John. I had the dream whether I slept in John's arms in Leblon or on my makeshift bed in Santa Teresa after an evening of hard work on my poetry. When I awoke in the middle of the night, I tried to push the dream aside.

Was my dream, as my mother's had been, a way to deal with an impending calamity? I found it hard to admit that I was aroused by danger. We could have been killed on that train platform. Did John really mean to kill Marcos? I imagined John looking at Marcos through the sights of a rifle. Where did he keep a gun? I hadn't found one in his apartment.

Drowsy, lying awake, I let my mind wander. I thought about being a reporter, a paid observer for whom every second was a deadline, punctual in a country set to no clock. I didn't see Brazil's promised technological future, I saw its sex. I saw men's passion in the dusk, lechery replacing industry, bits of glorious coasts under the stars. I thought about the big lie of the country. The reckless search for diversion that ended in promiscuity. Restitching virginity. A couple drinking the clear watery milk of a green coconut on a beach at midnight, sharing the straw, each seducing the other. "Beloved one, *meu bem.* The sand is soft." The woman taking the risk.

In Rio the quality of the atmosphere teases with possibilities, but in the end disappoints. The soft air beckons to beauty, to romance without pain, to resolution, to excitement just beyond reach. You own the day; the day does not own you. Each day begins with excited renewal, the fresh restorative morning coffee with warm milk, the finger banana, the papaya with its tiny, bitter, black seeds. You begin with hope: The phone will work. Simple promises will be kept. An opportunity for fame will stride forward. Gumption is what you want from Rio de Janeiro. Propaganda and boldfaced lies are what you get.

Brazil is a private club. By half past 11 in the morning, its members — the conspirators of the day — have met. They darken your path, confuse your messages, send you on wild goose chases to see someone who couldn't help you even if you found him. By late afternoon the traffic moves in, trapping you in the post you are guarding. Things are never what they seem. You begin to think you understand at your peril. Two men spread the word that they are enemies; they turn out to be accomplices.

Brazil is a spider's web.

II

Just as John had predicted, José was back at work on Tuesday, September 3, glum, but present. On Thursday, José told us that Maria

192

Lilia had returned. "She figured out she was better off with me than with Benedito. She's lucky I took her back."

The next day Nelson Claudio gave me devastating news. Anabela had "disappeared," the familiar euphemism everybody used when someone was presumed to have been arrested but there were no witnesses.

"Let's not think the worst right now," I said, feeling as though I'd been punched in the stomach.

"I'm seeing her brother tonight. The family is desperate. They think DOPS took her."

"She's always been able to outwit them."

"She took risks."

Nelson Claudio and I hugged each other and cried. "Tell me if there's anything, anything I can do," I said.

If DOPS really had taken her, there was nothing we could do for Anabela. In the midst of all the tumult in September, our fear for her hovered over our daily activities.

Little by little, DOPS' method of inquiry was becoming known: professionally administered torture. Torture with a doctor present to make sure the prisoner stayed alive to give information, torture with a good guy and a bad guy to reinforce hope and despair, torture that employed a psychoanalyst to rove from room to room, where electrodes were being applied to students, trade unionists, and by late 1968, a few Brazilian journalists.

The psychoanalyst's job was to maximize the success of the torture. He probed for weaknesses. I imagined him saying: "I think you should let the prisoner rest for 10 minutes, then ask him such and such. The prisoner is breaking down. If he doesn't confess, shock him again. Ask him again about his mother. About his childhood masturbation.

You're making progress. Your prisoner is, at most, a day away from telling you everything you want to know."

Some of the psychoanalysts employed by DOPS had been trained by the Instituto Brasileiro de Psicanálise, a respected institute of psychoanalysis in Brazil. Years later we learned that important members of the Institute had helped the military oppressors find psychoanalysts who were willing to cooperate with them.

III

John didn't mention Marcos again; neither did I. He was giving me a metaphorical lesson in poker. I refrained from pressing him for details. At night in his bed, our bodies intertwined as usual, I fretted about what might be happening between us. It wasn't difficult for me to admit that I was thrilled by John's presence, by his touch. When he first told me about Malaysia he had said, "Don't think you want me, Catherine. Go home to Boston." Had that been good advice? I prayed it wasn't, that we weren't hiding a conclusion from ourselves we didn't want to reach.

John made two trips out of town to interview opposition politicians who were willing to talk to him off the record. Both times he was gone longer than I expected. I counted the minutes until he returned. When he got back from his second trip, he said: "Let's take a long weekend away from the bureau." I was ready to get away from all the clamor in the street, my monkish writing schedule.

John wanted to take me to the landmark Hotel Quitandinha, built in the 1940s on a grand scale as a gambling casino and resort in Petrópolis, a quaint town in the mountains 40 miles from Rio. In 1946, just as the elaborate Normandy-style hotel complex was ready to open its doors to Rio's café society, international high rollers and movie stars, the government issued a decree ending gambling in Brazil. The project failed at once. Sixteen years later, with the roulette wheels still stored away just in case, the Quitandinha became a condominium apartment house supposedly for members only, although a phone call from John got us accommodations.

On a glorious spring weekend, we rented a car and drove to Petrópolis, the retreat where Emperor Dom Pedro II spent his summers away from Rio's heat. The road wound through tropical forest, pasture, fields of tall sugar-cane that resembled corn ready to be cut. Orange and banana trees grew near the road until we reached higher elevations. Hairpin turns, some without guard rails, were set into the faces of small mountains. I put my hand in John's lap until the road became too challenging for distraction. "We won't live to make love again if you keep that up." John patted my hand as I withdrew it.

At the hotel we hardly bothered to inspect our beautifully furnished suite. John, already naked, caressed me as I hurried to undress. We pulled the bedspread off the large bed and fulfilled what we had both been aching to do during the drive up the mountains — affirming our good will through our sexual urgency, then lingering under the warm water in the commodious shower, kissing. "You told me one of your little stories," he said as we soaped each other.

"I don't remember what I said. Was it silly?"

"It was."

Roses and blue and white hydrangeas erupted from tended gardens on our walk to explore the Quitandinha's grounds.

"Isn't the Portuguese name for Impatiens delightful?" I said.

"What is it?"

"They call them Mary without shame, *Maria-sem-vergonha*, because they grow wild everywhere."

We rounded the hotel's chatty aviary, the aromatic stables, the land-scaped lake. John stopped and looked at me. "Marcos has gone into hiding. I can't find him." He waited for me to respond.

"Go on," I said. "So where does that leave us?"

"I've been afraid of getting you into something you shouldn't have to handle, Kate. Weeks ago I came very close to quitting with you, but I couldn't bear the idea."

"I was afraid, too, John. Maybe I still am."

"There's probably more risk in covering civil unrest than in my work for MI6. Sorry . . . Finish your thought."

"I have a mix of feelings, John."

"I know. I'd be alarmed if you didn't."

"Not about you. I've already made up my mind." We had been sauntering along the lake, stopping now and then to watch a pedal boat scoot across the water. "In a way I envy your connection with MI6," I said. "It's exciting. But . . . it makes me feel queasy."

"You mean dirty?"

"A little scared, a little dirty, I guess. I wish you'd quit."

He let go of my hand and turned to face me. "Don't worry about Marcos, Kate." He had on his poker face. I put on mine. He took my hand again and smiled. "I'm told Margaridas has the best food in Petrópolis. Let's have a leisurely dinner. The best wine available."

Despite our worries, John and I had been feeling optimistic when we packed for the weekend. I had brought a red silk halter dress I had never worn for him. He had packed the fashionable blue blazer and paisley necktie he had bought in London. At dinner he astonished me by slipping a wedding band with a single row of round diamonds

196

on my right hand. "When we marry you switch it to your left hand, Brazilian style."

"I've been afraid to let myself tell you, John. I love you . . . Yes."

The hall outside our hotel suite was wide with gleaming white walls and dark brown wainscoting. John picked me up and carried me over the threshold. I had packed a sexy white nightgown. I put it on just so he could take it off. Before we went to bed we stepped out onto the wooden balcony that adjoined our bedroom. The air was still and cool. In the moonlight I could see the outline of the vast formal gardens.

Sunday morning we played tennis. John was quick and agile with a powerful serve I could barely return, but enough out of practice that he often double-faulted or shot out of bounds. I played a patient and ultimately winning game by just trying to return the ball while waiting for his mistakes. "You would have beaten me if you'd been more cautious," I said.

"I don't have to be cautious in tennis."

We visited the cathedral to see the tombs of Dom Pedro II and his empress, *dona* Teresa Christina, and joined an animated crowd of tourists to gaze at the Brazilian crown jewels. I was more absorbed with my own diamond band.

I slipped my hand into his lap again on the drive back to Rio. John downshifted on a switchback turn: "Going back to the very beginning, Kate, to Malaysia . . . I didn't ask to join."

"You didn't say no, either."

"It's not that easy to turn them down. In my place you'd do the same, I bet. But I'm not going stay with them much longer."

I didn't respond.

"I have new responsibilities now."

CHAPTER SIXTEEN

Then comes winter and it's time
For a husband's circle and
Let the arms fall where they may.
That damp cold chill that
Fills the ribs with sex and
Can only be warmed against
A sweating man under covers.

E. Catherine Lawrence

I

When we got back to Rio, our lives were both the same and quite different. We announced our engagement to our colleagues at the bureau to a round of applause. Mike Evans offered, with a big smile and a sly wink, to contact UPI headquarters to ask about their anti-nepotism policy. José returned from lunch with an engagement present of Brazilian champagne. It was too sweet to drink, but we appreciated the gesture that we knew he could barely afford. Ed Tanner had only a few weeks left before he himself got married in Salt Lake City. We talked about the intricacies of planning a wedding. "It's one giant headache," Ed said. "I'll really miss Rio. I wish I could convince Shirlene to move here."

John and I began leaving the bureau earlier than usual so we could look for a two-bedroom apartment in Leblon, our preferred Rio neighborhood. We hoped to find a beachfront apartment on Avenida Delfim Moreira, the prestigious, reasonably quiet street of four-story apartment buildings that bordered the sea. John said we could afford it.

I tried to maintain my writing schedule, which meant spending several nights a week at Nelson Claudio's. The discipline was wearing thin. Staying there did have one advantage — it kept me in touch with the student activists. "I only met John Wadson once, briefly," Nelson Claudio said when I interrupted his game of solitaire to tell him John and I were getting married, "but I liked him." He jumped up to embrace me. "Congratulations, Kate. All the best. Are you pregnant?"

"Oh, for Christ's sake —"

"Just kidding. Even if you were, so what, there's a cure."

"If the wedding is in Rio," I said, "you have to take the pictures. I wouldn't trust anyone else."

"It will be my pleasure. I'm really happy for you. Any pre-marriage jitters?"

"A few."

"For that I have no advice."

"I'm surprised, Nelson Claudio. You're always so full of advice."

"Not about marriage. I never get involved in anything I can't easily get out of."

Late at night, my evening's writing finished, Nelson Claudio and I would discuss what the activists were plotting. An underground group had pulled off a bank robbery in the suburbs. People were shocked at their brazenness. "Other groups are planning more robberies," he said. "They need cash to keep going."

John and I vacillated over whether to have our wedding in Boston or Rio. Both sets of parents saw advantages and disadvantages to either option. They left the decision up to us. Finally we decided on a January wedding in Rio so our parents could escape the worst of the North American winter.

I introduced John to Walter, Eva, Jaime and Ana Maria. We went out for a Chinese meal together. Afterward, at David Jr.'s apartment, we talked politics while Walter picked at his guitar. "The soul speaks in different languages," Walter said. "If there's a God for the U.S., it's Apollo. Brazil's God is Dionysus. Apollo works harder, but Dionysus has more fun."

"Who's Canada's God?" Jaime asked.

"A slightly boring God, no doubt," John said. "Let me think. It's probably Ceres, Goddess of Agriculture."

"Yeah, Ceres like cereal." Walter let loose a series of exuberant arpeggios.

On the way home to John's ultra-neat and clean apartment, I commented on the squalor of David Jr.'s bachelor abode.

"I wasn't going to mention it, but how did you manage to live in that mess?" he asked.

"I'm not sure myself. Thank God it's behind me."

A week later John brought his high-school clarinet to David Jr.'s apartment and he and Walter improvised. John was a better player than he had led me to believe.

Dona Rita invited John to dinner. She set out her best china and table linens and fixed a delicious dinner of pork with a fiery sauce, squash and my favorite dessert, *doce de leite*, a sweet pudding made by laboriously stirring a boiling mixture of sugar and milk. After dinner John and Nelson Claudio discussed the student comings and goings on Santa Teresa hill while we watched the shimmering parade of lights in the sky from the airplanes landing at Santos Dumont. Nelson Claudio gave me a discreet thumbs-up sign when John and I were about to leave.

One night, on a whim, we again stayed at the Hotel Gloria. We wanted to swim in the deserted pool, very late, surrounded by floodlit palms. We succeeded in waltzing, my feet on top of his, in the shallow

200

water. "It's for keeps down here, Catherine. There's no divorce under Brazilian law."

The drier months of winter drew to a close in relative political calm. I was making my peace with John's covert career through the daily business of living with him. When he had said on our way back from Petrópolis he wasn't going stay with The Service much longer, I took him at his word.

He proposed we write a mailer about one of Brazil's large plantations. "They're like little countries, fiefdoms really, with their own rules and eccentricities. The military government has gone out of its way to court the owners."

"Sérgio told me his favorite cousin owns one of the largest *fazendas* in the state of São Paulo. He made me want to meet the owner — he sounded like a fascinating eccentric."

"I'm game. What does he produce on his *fazenda* and how do we find him?"

"Coffee, mainly. And I believe some cattle. I don't know where it is exactly, but I remember the name — Fazenda Maraíba. I think Sérgio and his cousin have the same paternal last name — Barbosa."

"I'll find him. We'll do the story, Kate."

Many nights my resolve to write weakened and I went to Leblon with John, or we went to the movies, or out to a late, unhurried dinner in Copacabana or Ipanema, or to a party at Charlie Wall's apartment. Twice we attended huge parties at David Sr.'s.

John had one routine that was more inviolate than my writing schedule. Three times a week, for precisely 11 minutes, he did the Royal Canadian Air Force exercises. It was a habit he had established as a teenager. Chart 3-B was geared to his age group of 35 to 39 but he performed at Chart 5-D+, maintaining a level of stamina, speed and flexibility thought suitable for "Flying Crew" aged 25 to 29. He performed the last exercise of each session by running one mile along the mosaic sidewalk bordering Leblon beach, timing himself to make sure he finished in less than the recommended 6 minutes, 45 seconds. When it rained heavily, he would substitute an indoor high-stepping, 400-count run in place. Throughout the busy weeks while we planned our wedding, looked for an apartment and covered the political situation, he never slacked off.

<h2 style="text-align:center">II</h2>

On the last Saturday in September, I continued our search for a larger apartment while John went to the bureau. I saw several with the right amount of space but they didn't face the Atlantic Ocean and neither of us was ready to forgo that requirement. At noon, wearing my bikini underneath my jeans, I headed to Copacabana to meet Walter at his apartment, hoping he hadn't already left for the beach.

As I walked along Avenida Nossa Senhora de Copacabana, breathing in diesel from the avenue's never-ending stream of buses, I was acutely aware that Copacabana was a cement fortress set against the tropics. It was completely unnatural and ramshackle, with more inhabitants per square mile than was good for it. The lines of a poem I had shown John echoed in my mind:

> Lovers, I thought,
> Setting out in the concrete city.

Walter was working on a new composition when I arrived at the apartment. He shoved aside his pad of music notation paper to welcome me. He was wearing a shirt over a bathing suit. "Kate, not working today? No skirmishes?"

"I needed a day off. I thought we could spend some time together at the beach. John'll meet us for dinner."

"Certainly, certainly. What do you think of the military's ban on demonstrations? I wouldn't call it a success, would you?"

"Hardly. It's a new game now. Cat and mouse."

"I really think the lightning raids downtown are getting under their skin," Walter said. He wandered off to the kitchen to find Coca-Colas and came back with two warm cans. I sipped mine slowly. Walter poured his Coke into a glass. As usual, he stirred it vigorously with a tablespoon before he took a sip. "Where are Eva and Ana Maria and Jaime?" I asked.

"At the beach, waiting for me, but I'm not in a hurry. Do you remember Antonioni's film *Blow-Up*? The scene at the end where they play a game of tennis without a ball? Antonioni showed us we don't need a ball to have a tennis match. It will become obvious who the winner is without it. In the same way, the students don't need to assemble to demonstrate. They merely need to announce their intention to rally. Let the cops and the military make their preparations, drive their light tanks through the streets to show their force. Let them mill around Cinelândia, waiting in a high state of excitement. But if nobody shows up for an announced rally, or if 100 students pounce unexpectedly and leave so quickly the police can do nothing, then we make our point at no cost."

"I don't think anything is accomplished by these 10-minute rampages," I said.

"Chaos, baby. Brazilians are artists of chaos. In this, only the Russians are our equals."

The truth was, Walter's heart was no longer in street nonsense. He was a serious musician. In the past months he had dedicated himself to composing songs and to polishing the intimate singing style he used to deliver his complaining but optimistic lyrics. He went back into the kitchen to get another Coke. When he returned, I pointed out to him that if chaos did come, he and everybody he knew could buy a plane ticket and leave. "There's no final curtain for people with education," I said. "What if the social compact between rich and poor breaks down and there's class warfare with guns? Believe me, that will be a bigger problem for Brazil than whether there's a military government in power or not."

Walter smiled as if to say, I take your point. I took the final sip of my warm Coke, stood up, stretched and suggested we go to the beach. I wanted to break away from the gloom of Brazil's politics, from the apartment's dark, dirty living room and reset our conversation along the path of my real concerns. "Do you mind if we sit by ourselves on the beach?" I hesitated. "You know, Walter, I value your intelligence and your friendship."

His expression turned irrepressibly kind. "Why didn't you say so before, baby? Of course we can sit alone."

We wandered several blocks along Avenida Atlântica before we took off our sandals and walked onto the beach. The sun was still nearly straight overhead. On our way I had asked Walter about his music.

"I recorded the last two songs for my album yesterday. The record will be out before the end of the year." Walter dropped his towel on the sand. "How about this spot?"

"Fine." We sat down. "I'm impressed. Congratulations. You're a real innovator. The record is going to take off. I'm sure of it. You're a star." I took off my jeans and shirt and sat next to him.

"You never know what will happen. Eva says she likes the new songs I just cut. What about you, Kate? Do you have new poems for me to see?"

"A few, yes. I do all my writing at Nelson Claudio's. I need my private space. I'm a magpie, always collecting stuff and turning it into poems," I said.

"If life weren't an excuse for imagining, there would be no point to it."

"You see my problem, Walter?"

"I do, baby. You can't fix it. You know that. People who are constantly using their imaginations live apart. It's a small price to pay."

"I could spend hours alone in a dark closet and thoroughly entertain myself," I said. "I wouldn't be bored for a second. John, on the other hand, is a man of action. We're very different."

"The real work's unconscious, Kate. Anyway, private space is essential. Once my record is released, I plan to get an apartment of my own in Ipanema."

"Alone?"

"With Eva. She puts up with me."

"She shouldn't."

"She's Brazilian, baby. In all seriousness, you seem to be saying one thing and thinking another. You have such a troubled expression."

Concerns about John's past and how it might affect our life together must have been showing on my face. I was about to deflect the conversation from that forbidden territory when we both noticed a young woman dressed in street clothes walking slowly, with a slumped posture, toward us. She stood out, a forlorn figure, among the bikini-clad sunbathers. She waved to us. The slant of the sun made it difficult to see. Walter leapt up, dashed over to her and embraced her warmly. It was Anabela. I hadn't known Anabela and Walter were friends, but it didn't surprise me. They walked back to me hand in hand. I jumped up to embrace her. "My God, Anabela, it's a miracle seeing you like this. Are you all right?"

205

"I can't believe you got out," Walter said. *"Tudo bem, querida?"* Walter caressed her shoulder. *"Tudo bem?* Everybody's been frantic worrying about you."

Anabela looked at us with a blank expression. It alarmed me. What had she been subjected to in prison? How could I, or anyone, truly comfort her? I felt inadequate. "John and I have been trying to get information about you through our UPI sources. You were constantly on our minds. It was impossible to find out anything."

"I know how that goes," she said.

Walter turned to me and said, "I had no idea you knew Anabela."

"We're friends through Nelson Claudio." I spread out a towel for her. "Please join us," I said.

"I'm supposed to meet my brother. I can't stay long." Anabela's face was pasty and gaunt; the whites of her eyes were streaked with red veins. She sat down, hugged her legs to her chest and stared vacantly at the sea. "It's as bad as they say ... when you're inside ... you're cut off with your isolation and your pain. My family is doing everything they can think of to help me."

I took Anabela's hand gingerly. I was almost afraid to touch her. I could only guess at her injuries. "Nelson Claudio didn't tell me you had been released." I said.

"He didn't know. When I got out, my family immediately took me away to the mountains. To a sort of health sanitarium."

Walter looked more anguished than I had ever seen him. He stared at the sand and shook his head slowly. "I don't know what to say."

"Don't worry," Anabela said. "Everybody has the same reaction. What's there to say? My fear is it's all for nothing. We're wasting our energy. That's what I think about. I don't sleep. Day and night are the same for me."

Had she been raped in prison? Prodded with electricity? The reported tortures were too terrible to contemplate. How did she get out? There might never be a right time to ask. "You impressed everybody, Anabela," I said, "you were so good at evading DOPS. I didn't think it would really happen. Is there anything I can do? Or John? Anything you need? You can reach me any time through UPI."

"I'm okay, really." She nodded her head slightly. "I have to go. My brother will worry if I don't join him pretty soon." Anabela got up and we stood up, too. We both embraced her.

"Take care of yourself, Anabela," Walter said. He was having trouble speaking. I could feel the tears in my eyes. "Rest if you can," he said.

She reached out and touched his arm. "I'm determined to recover. My nerve damage will heal. It just takes time."

"You're comforting us, Anabela," I said. "It should be the other way around."

"I heard about throwing marbles to stop the horses when I was inside. It made me laugh. It was ingenious."

Anabela walked away from us with her head down, looking at her feet. We watched her until she disappeared on the crowded beach. Then we sank onto the sand. Neither of us spoke.

Finally Walter said, "I'm not sure what I would have told them if it had been me. Anabela's not out of danger. The military could issue a new warrant for her arrest anytime they feel like it."

I didn't know how one recovered from being tortured. Was there a prescribed treatment? I was overwhelmed imagining what Anabela must have gone through. It made me tremble. "What would happen," I asked Walter, "if you had been tortured by DOPS. Five years from now Brazil has a democratically elected government. The military has been hung out to dry. Everybody is as content as they can be, considering that there's still plenty of poverty. One day you go to a party in Copacabana and the hostess introduces you to one of your torturers. What would you do?"

"After I broke a glass in his face?"

"Suppose the torturer sincerely believed he was a patriot, doing something that was ugly but necessary, like a surgeon does ugly things that are necessary."

"There's no way I could or would forgive. It's a good reason not to be a Christian."

"You realize, Walter, it could happen. We all know there are doctors who collaborate with DOPS right now."

"No forgiveness for the people with blood on their hands. It has to be a precondition before the dictatorship is allowed to disappear. In the future, what happens to our ex-torturers? Shit, what happens today? Torturers go home in the evening after a day at Cobra Island or at the First Battalion of Army Police in Tijuca, or wherever it is they perform their dirty business, and play with their children. How many showers does it take to wash away the stench? I understand in Uruguay every member of the police has to have tortured at least one person. It's their bond and their protection in case questions are ever asked."

"How would you feel toward someone hired by a democratic government who assassinates a bad person ... like a torturer or the person who orders torture?"

"He'd have my sincere thanks, though I couldn't do such a thing myself."

A vendor stopped to sell *Guaraná* to a group of teenagers sitting nearby.

"Want one?" Walter asked.

"No thanks. Do you think Eva and Jaime are still waiting for you? I feel guilty keeping you from them."

"No need to worry, Kate. I'm very unpredictable these days because of working on my album."

We got up and walked toward the sidewalk. "I'm shaken by Anabela," I said. "She's remarkable . . . "

"I'm shaken, too," Walter said. We embraced and held each other for a while. "We didn't finish our conversation about privacy," he said.

"I can solve the space problem. We're looking for a larger apartment, but finding private time just to think, to let random ideas take over, that's not so easy."

"In Brazil's current situation, emotional space is a luxury."

"Dinner at Jangadeiros?" I said in a shaky voice. "John's planning to join us." Walter nodded. We embraced again. "Eight-thirty?"

I hailed a taxi to Leblon. I had yearned to share my burden. In the final moments of my conversation with Walter, he had unknowingly offered me some solace. Jumbled thoughts filled my mind: I wished John had never seen the announcement of a job opening in Malaysia. I wanted to recall his bullets to his gun. I wanted all the torturers in Brazil to get a taste of their own medicine. With luck and time, I hoped Anabela would heal and be whole again. I wished for that.

I asked the taxi to drop me on Avenida Delfim Moreira because I had one last apartment I wanted to see. This one faced the ocean. It had two large bedrooms and one very small one, big enough for a child. John had said, "I want you to have my babies, Kate," in a way that did not need an answer. I told the agent we would take the apartment.

As I dressed for dinner, I knew in my bones it was pointless to obsess about John's past. I had taken the effective action. He would keep his promise to leave MI6. He had even told me he was relieved, finally, to confront the break he knew he would have to face sooner or

209

later. Jane had it right in her letter, the one in which she said she was planning to attend our wedding:

> A perfect man doesn't exist. So far, I have to say that my experience is in loveless love. The reverse, real love, must be sublime.

III

"We have a problem to work on, Kate," John had said as we lay in bed, sleepless, two nights later. "What should I do next? There are opportunities all around us. I don't see myself growing old at UPI."

"You said you were finished ... "

"Don't worry, Kate, I am. I don't feel like going home. Do you?"

"Not yet," I said.

CHAPTER SEVENTEEN

Back at the office,
In the city of dreams,
First light shines through an open window
Making the bleached newspaper too white to read.
A porter collects yesterday's coffee cups,
The morning prattle picks up speed.
Choices, I think, will be interesting again
After our night of temptation.

E. Catherine Lawrence

I

John struggled to prevent our bureau from being overwhelmed by the pace of political events. We all sacrificed sleep. It seemed every time we could catch our breath, guerrillas robbed another bank or there was another demonstration and we were again scrambling, reporting nonstop. Terrorists set off a series of bombs. Priests preached rebellion. Police and military presence on the streets increased. Indira Gandhi arrived in Rio to begin a three-week tour of South America and the Caribbean. She left Brazil, fortunately, without incident. Queen Elizabeth of England was expected in four weeks. "I asked Frank Cobb for more money to run the bureau," John said over drinks at the Olimpia. "He knows we're stretched thin. I told him I think the Brazilian story is only going to get bigger."

"Did he buy it?" I asked.

"What I got from him was a discourse on his own problems. He didn't really want to hear about mine. To quote him, 'The Argentine story is darker than yours, Wadson. At least Brazil's still got a Congress that meets. I've been complaining to New York for years about getting short-changed.'" John leaned back on the banquette and smiled. "Frank's expected to run South America within budget and he does, but I'm not giving up."

At the end of the first week in October, John went to São Paulo for two days to supervise the bureau's coverage of the assassination of a U.S. Army captain, C.R. Chandler, who had been studying Portuguese at the University of São Paulo. The police found a note near his body that said his death was "punishment for a Vietnam war criminal." The captain was survived by his wife and four children. His 9-year-old son witnessed his father's being struck by machine-gun fire coming from two automobiles. John was drained when he got back from São Paulo. He was disturbed and saddened by Chandler's killing. We all wondered why he had been singled out.

Over a late supper of ham and cheese sandwiches at John's apartment I said, "Walter and I talked on the beach about whether it was ever going to be possible to forgive Brazil's military torturers. He said never. I asked him if he would feel the same way about a person who killed a torturer, and he said he'd thank him but he could never do it."

"You're not drawing a parallel with killing Chandler —"

"Good God, no. Whatever group was behind killing Chandler has some desperate ideas about how to fix the world."

"I hope they catch the bastards," he said.

"I wasn't thinking of Chandler, John. I was thinking of you. What you've told me is a heavy burden, and I can't talk to anyone about it."

"You can talk to me."

"I know."

John was so busy he had to leave the details of renting the apartment to me. It wasn't simply a matter of signing a lease, as it would have been in New York. I had to obtain letters of reference and gather all sorts of notarized documents.

The spring buds on Rio's *ipê* trees burgeoned into masses of purple and yellow flowers. John and I moved into our new apartment facing the Leblon beach when the blossoms were at their peak. On the day I packed the last of my things in Santa Teresa, *dona* Rita was terribly sad. "Leblon isn't that far away, *dona* Rita. We'll still see each other."

"I'll miss the strong coffee you make for me when I'm suffering one of my migraines. Nelson Claudio is a good son, but you know yourself, Kate, he can be impossible. You're a good influence on him." She patted my hand, kissed me and left me alone to finish.

I took a last look around my Santa Teresa sanctuary, recalling its evening view of the lights of houses cascading down the hillside. I thought with satisfaction of the nights at my desk when I peered into the darkness from my wide-open window, feeling the muse flirtatious one moment, aloof the next. I would miss this room, filled as it was with my private excitement and inescapable frustration.

When there was a lull in breaking news, John and I wanted to shut the world out and play house. He painted our bedroom pastel yellow, the same color as my favorite baroque building in Rio, and he stained the scuffed wood floor in the corridor. We went furniture shopping and bought an expensive Italian black leather sofa, a glass cocktail table, a new double bed and bookshelves.

We invited friends to dinner. John bought a case of vintage white Burgundy. I planned the menus and Márcia cooked her spicy Bahian

213

shrimp dishes. One evening, over a pot of simmering *vatapá*, she confided she was no longer having romantic thoughts about her priest and had been to confession.

II

The political stage was set for the black month of December 1968 by the military's responses to a provocation that, in mature countries, would have been viewed as amusing. Even an archangel would not have predicted such perfervid activity, empowered though he be to move through walls, observe people in their unguarded moments, peer into the generals' base hearts and report back to God.

A 32-year-old newspaperman, Marcio Moreira Alves, had been elected to Congress in 1966 on the strength of his widely read column in *Correio da Manhã* in which he frequently assailed the armed forces. On September 2 he had made a speech on the floor of the Chamber of Deputies urging people to stay away from the annual military parade on September 7 — Brazil's Independence Day — as an act of protest. He compounded that affront in October when he advised Brazilian mothers not to let their daughters go out with military men, and then had the impudence to deny that he had intended to insult the military.

Bachelor officers complained of social snubs by young women. Dangerous feelings of persecution filled the hearts of captains who felt the armed forces were not getting enough recognition for their service to the nation. (An Army captain earned about the same salary as a young girl who knew shorthand — $175 a month.) The dignity of Brazil had been endangered by the intemperate remarks of this one man. The military seized upon Moreira Alves' affronts to the honor of Brazil as a test case and demanded that Congress hand over the deputy for military trial. Vexation in Rio de Janeiro and elsewhere in Brazil mounted.

By the end of October tensions were high.   President Arthur da Costa e Silva conferred with his top military advisers about "national security measures."   A 22-year-old medical student, a classmate and friend of Anabela, was shot to death in a police raid. The next day the police used water hoses to break up an attack by 3,000 students on the offices of the newspaper, *O Globo*.   Three days later the police raided an active cell of the Maoist Communist party in suburban Rio, confiscating 80 dynamite sticks and detonators.

Throughout October, a series of newspaper stories, notably in *Correio da Manhã*, had been exposing attempts by radicals in the Air Force high command to revamp the Para-SAR (Air Force Parachute Search and Rescue) unit into a team of terrorists to suppress opposition to the government. Senior Air Force officers intended to order the Para-SAR to kidnap 40 political leaders and other "inconvenient persons," take them by plane over the Atlantic and drop them in the sea. They had targeted two former Presidents, Juscelino Kubitschek and Janio Quadros, the outspoken liberal archbishop of Recife, D. Hélder Câmara and the former governor of Guanabara State, Carlos Lacerda. Among the more incredible scripts of horror discussed by the high command was a plan to blow up the gasworks adjacent to downtown Rio during the evening rush hour. This provocation, with deaths estimated at 100,000, was to be blamed on communists. The plot had been exposed by Captain Sérgio Ribeiro Miranda de Carvalho, who had become a pariah in the armed forces by standing alone against the use of his unit for "illegal purposes."

Everyone in Rio and throughout Brazil was shocked by these revelations.   Our bureau was trying to catch up with a story that other reporters had broken. I spoke to Walter and contacted Nelson Claudio and my student sources to get reactions. Walter said he wanted to discount the story because "Brazilians like to dream up amazing things, but then they get distracted and don't really do them. Still, I don't put any crime past our generals."

III

In the midst of this agitation, on November 4, the second prominent woman to visit Rio that spring, Queen Elizabeth II, arrived with Prince Philip aboard the royal yacht Britannia. Mist robbed the royals of a clear view of the city. Nevertheless, as their yacht entered the harbor, a fleet of pleasure boats from Rio's yacht clubs gave them a rousing welcome and a 21-gun salute.

I had been a serious fan of Elizabeth, the Princess. As an 11-year-old I had savored a book about her upbringing. I had thought Elizabeth was perfect. Her biography occupied a special place on my bookshelf, along with another favorite book about a radiant girl from Belgium who became a nun and went to live in Africa.

Technically the Queen arrived in Rio twice. After her tribute at sea, she stayed in Rio for only 10 minutes, time enough to hurry through Galeão Airport to board a Royal Air Force jet for a one day visit to Brasília. On her return to Rio she used the resplendent Britannia, anchored in Guanabara Bay, as her floating palace.

I covered the fast-paced ceremony in which the Queen placed a wreath before the tomb of Brazil's unknown soldier of World War II. The press was excluded afterward when she and Prince Philip attended a Remembrance Day service at Christ Church, the Anglican church John and I had chosen for our wedding.

Before I had a chance to sum up her visit in my story, the Queen had flown away to Santiago de Chile. What remained were the words of the Governor of Pernambuco, a northern state, who had praised the Queen as "a living example of a group of countries linked by their democratic spirit and powerful tradition of dignity." The royal saleslady's production, carefully choreographed to boost English exports, was a success. It seemed to me the Governor's words had drifted southward and settled on Guanabara State, where they were taken to heart. Rio calmed down after the Queen's visit. The *cariocas* returned to their usual weekend pastimes — sun, soccer and concocting dreams.

Tuesday evening, November 19, John and I were invited to a reception at the British Ambassador's residence. John couldn't attend because he had to leave for Santos to interview the first black to be elected mayor of a major Brazilian city. Still captivated by the Queen, I went to the reception alone.

The British Embassy diplomatic staff looked relieved that their royal charges had passed out of their hands without major mishap. I settled myself with a vodka and tonic and was just learning from the pregnant wife of the British First Secretary that the Queen's toilet seat aboard the Britannia was covered in finest pigskin when I caught sight of Sérgio talking with a plumpish blonde. She had hold of his arm, attempting to direct him around the crowded room, as some wives do to make themselves important.

He was supremely elegant, his posture easy and erect. There was the familiar flash of his smile, drawing his listeners in with its quick brilliance. His expression was one I knew well — it promised to unravel mysteries. It had stopped my heart the night we met. I couldn't take my eyes off him. How did I look? I hastily checked my drinking glass and noticed lipstick. Did I have any left on my mouth? I had debated whether to get really dressed up for the party. Reporters in Brazil often went to elegant affairs in very casual attire. Our casualness was our conceit. It announced that we, the country's brainy elite, the fourth estate, had our own rules for style.

In honor of my girlhood fascination with Princess Elizabeth, I had decided to dress up. I wore a sophisticated, off-one-shoulder black dress, new Italian-designed high heels and the present Sérgio had given me for Christmas in 1965, a gold-link bracelet from Tiffany. I looked past the wife of the British First Secretary to study Sérgio. "Are you all right?" she asked.

"Oh . . . yes, I am. I just saw someone I knew in New York."

She followed my stare. "He's handsome. He looks Spanish."

"He's Brazilian. His father's family came from Spain."

"Not Portugal? That's unusual here. I'll let you catch up."

The diplomat's wife moved away to join a group mostly of women. I stood alone, rooted to the floor with no idea which way to move. Out the front door? Or to Sérgio's side? The woman with Sérgio continued to hold onto his arm expertly, with just enough pressure to prompt him toward a group that looked conversationally promising. I took a sip of my vodka. Sérgio looked in my direction just as a tall, well-knit man with sandy-colored hair came up to me and introduced himself. "James Ralph," he said in a modulated British voice. "You were just talking with my wife, Meredith."

"Kate Lawrence. How do you do? Meredith was telling me the royal secrets of the Britannia."

"Oh dear, she hadn't ought to do that." He smiled. "Are they safe with you?"

"I'm afraid not. I'm a journalist."

"I know you're not Reuters, I think I know everybody in that shop."

"UPI," I said.

"You covered the Queen's visit?"

"When we were allowed to. You don't give the press much of a chance close up."

"On the Queen's next visit, call me. I'll see to it you get to the front of the line."

We both smiled, knowing it was unlikely she would ever return to Brazil.

Sérgio uncoupled himself from the plumpish blonde. He was walking toward me. My knees were actually shaking. "Hello, beautiful young lady." He greeted me with a kiss on each cheek.

"Hello, Sérgio." James Ralph and Sérgio exchanged introductions and pleasantries that seemed to go on forever. Finally, James Ralph wandered off to join his wife.

Sérgio looked at my wrist, noticing his gift, and smiled. "We could have a late supper. Let me think where. Can you meet me in the lobby of the Copacabana Palace at 10?"

"I'm not sure I should, Sérgio. Or that I want to."

"I'd very much like to talk to you, Kate."

"I gave you every chance a year ago."

"We must be a classic case of could have been, Catherine. It's useless to search for excuses."

"I'm going home now," I said. I gave him the standard Brazilian light kiss on each cheek.

"I'll wait for you at 10," he said.

I didn't answer as I turned to leave. I didn't know what answer I should give.

Sérgio was waiting for me in the lobby when I arrived at the hotel.

"I was afraid you wouldn't come. You look really wonderful. The beach suits you. You are the most beautiful girl in Rio." He winked. "Are you hungry? We can have dinner here in the hotel or wherever you like."

"Food is the farthest thing from my mind."

219

"What would you like to do, then?"

"Talk. Have a drink. The bar here is fine."

As we entered the Copacabana Palace bar, Sérgio put his arm around my waist the way he used to when we walked into restaurants in New York. We sat down facing each other at a small round table. "I read your bylined story from Brasília about Lt. Colonel Arantes. I didn't know you had become a journalist. I was surprised and very impressed. I hope you haven't stopped writing poetry."

"I haven't." I let my index finger trace the rim of my glass for a few moments. "I can't pretend, Sérgio. I'm angry —"

"I apologize, Catherine, deeply. I was under pressure. I don't think I've had one happy day since the last time I was with you in New York. You have every reason to be angry with me."

His apology astonished me. I didn't want to imagine in his presence what might have happened if he had offered it before I went to Brazil. I tried to control my emotions. He leaned forward and kissed the tears in my eyes. He gave me his handkerchief.

"Have you been recalled to Brazil?" I said.

"I'm home on vacation, Kate. I'm still assigned to Geneva. Maybe for another year or so before I'm transferred. Of course, it's enough for me to think one thing and my ministry decides the opposite. I wasn't going to leave Rio without seeing you. UPI's in the *Jornal do Brasil* building. I looked it up."

"I'm glad we met by accident at the reception instead."

He removed his wallet from his breast pocket and took out a picture. It had been taken by a roving photographer on New Year's Eve 1965 in New York showing the two of us toasting each other over a restaurant table strewn with confetti and streamers. We were smiling. Our eyes sparkled. A happy, glamorous couple.

"I always carry this picture with me."

"I'm getting married in two months in Rio. My fiancé hired me at UPI."

"Smart man. Congratulations. You deserve your happiness."

"Funny, that's exactly what Paulo said to me when I told him you and I were getting married. I am happy, Sérgio. I hope the woman on your arm at the reception makes you happy. You looked like a couple."

"She's the niece of our ambassador to Italy. Poor thing, she loves Coca-Cola. I remember her as a young girl, weighing 10 kilos less, before she discovered the flavor of paradise. My arrival seems to have signaled Celeste to go on a diet."

"I brought you a poem. I wrote it when I was first learning my way around Rio. I had just visited a *favela*." I took the published version of *Macumba* out of my purse and gave it to him.

"Should I read it now?"

"Save it for when you get back to Geneva." I wiped my eyes with his handkerchief.

People were staring at us — a handsome, felicitous man, a tearful young woman. Sérgio suggested we go upstairs to his room. I didn't refuse. He sat on the edge of the bed. I sat in a nearby chair facing him, ramrod straight. "My mother wanted me to stay with her," he said, "but her apartment is small and her endless well-meaning intrusions into my life are just too much." He looked around the well-appointed room. Neither of us spoke. Finally he said, "Before you left New York, I wrote you long-winded letters I never mailed." He stood up, came to my side, reached for my hand and held it. "Do you want me to say it straight out? Yes, I feel diminished by my behavior in New York."

My mind no longer functioned. It would have been unbearable to be fully cognizant of everything we said, every kiss we exchanged. Sérgio wanted to take me to bed. I didn't let him. We held each other. Talked. He insisted on reading my poem, the last few lines aloud:

221

Carnival, carnival-madness, a mulatto I didn't
Know handing out checks for costumes. The President
Of the Republic wanted to please his children.
But my roof needs attention, I am away off from Feira de Santana.
My husband is dead and far from me. The money
We saved for ice cream is gone, too. I wonder
If somebody will return his shoes.

"You're disappointed with the Brazilian reality, but so is everybody. The price of living is a little bit higher for you, I've always thought that."

"I'm not sure I'd write the same poem today."

"All my posturing in New York has brought us to this," he whispered. "I love you too much to be your friend. My wish for you is that you use your talents wisely."

"Did you really intend to marry me?"

"From the beginning, Catarina," he said using his pet name for me, the Portuguese translation for Catherine.

The morning light claimed us. Sérgio ordered coffee from room service. We said goodbye at the doorway of his room at 6. I felt his gaze as I walked to the elevator. I didn't look back. I was afraid he would blow a kiss off his open palm or give his ear lobe a small tug signaling, as in the past, our bond. I never said one word to him in Portuguese, my new language.

IV

The humming heat of the late-spring morning felt comforting on my skin. I walked partway home, then hailed a taxi. I felt dazed. Weirdly relieved. To myself, I pleaded temporary insanity. At home I took a shower and put on my reporter's uniform. Going upstairs with Sérgio was stupid. I should have left him at the bar.

Once, when we were having a fight about whether he was committed to our relationship, Sérgio left me a note on the dining-room table: "I could not be any more free from you than I am from the Queen of England." Later, that same day, he recanted. I never forgot the line. How ironic — it was the Queen's visit that brought us together and obliged us to say adieu a second time.

I arrived at the office two hours late. Mike Evans looked at his watch when I flopped down at my desk, next to his. After our rousing and sentimental sendoff party for Ed Tanner, John had announced that, when he was out of the bureau, Mike was in charge. "Aha, when the cat's away," he said. "You're late."

He assigned me to sample the public's reaction to Friday's election of mayors. Only two artificial parties had been permitted to enter candidates. President Costa e Silva was in Rio at Laranjeiras Palace, studying the still-incomplete returns. I went out on the street to interview voters. I treated each boring detail of the pro forma story as if it were a buoy in swirling white water. How and what was I going to tell John about meeting Sérgio?

At 3, earlier than expected, John rushed into the newsroom. I walked into his office and we kissed casually behind his closed door. "This Para-SAR scandal is incredible. I think I may have stumbled onto a good background source." He slammed his fist into his palm, the way he did when he was excitedly sizing up a situation. "I'm interviewing an Army colonel in an hour. He's working on a manifesto about returning the government to civilian control that he says certain military leaders are ready to support. I'm going to ask him about the Para-SAR. Anything going on here I should know about?"

"Nothing out of the ordinary at the bureau," I said. "I went to the reception at the British Embassy. Sérgio was there." John stopped pacing immediately and turned to study my face closely. For a moment, I hesitated. "It was pretty emotional for me. For Sérgio, too."

"You were bound to run into each other sooner or later ... Didn't you think you would? I've been expecting you to tidy up that relationship one day."

"We had drinks at the Copacabana Palace. I went to his room." John gave me a questioning look and waited. "We heard each other out ... talked all night."

"You're a damn fool. Did you sleep with him?"

"I feel guilty, John, even though nothing happened. I desperately wish you hadn't gone to Santos."

"You didn't use the best judgment, Catherine. I knew Sérgio was in Rio."

I leaned against John's desk in stunned amazement. "How did you know that?"

"Contacts. I keep in touch."

"When did that start?"

"Since you showed me your poem about João."

I was infuriated and flattered at the same time. Even before we were romantically involved, he had been investigating me.

"I understand Sérgio's planning to marry the niece of an ambassador in April," John said.

A flicker of a smile crossed my face as I imagined the plump blonde who loved Coca-Cola having to give up the "flavor of paradise." "You know I love you, John. When Sérgio ended it in New York, I didn't completely accept it. Some things take time."

"I went through my fair share of emotions with Renata. I said and did things I shouldn't have. But it was a cleaner parting than yours was with Sérgio."

"If I could have Sérgio on a silver platter, no strings attached, I wouldn't."

"I know that." He stretched out his arms to me. I went to him, leaned against his body and put my hands inside his back pockets. We kissed. "I love you, John. You can't imagine how much."

"Yes . . . I can."

He called me at home later in the evening to say he was still working on the Para-SAR story and that I should have dinner on my own. "Don't worry about me," I said, "I'm thrashing with a new poem."

"I'm sorry I didn't have much time to spend with you this afternoon, Kate."

"I'm missing you, John. Come home as soon as you can."

I didn't say that I was berating myself for being a tropical butterfly, as desultory as the strays who bunked in David Jr.'s apartment. I struggled with my writing until John came home. I fixed fried-egg sandwiches. We were both exhausted but not sleepy. "A short walk on the beach before bed?" he asked. When we stepped outside, it started to drizzle. We ignored it, crossed the beach and strolled at the edge of the surf until it began to rain in earnest.

On Saturday Anabela and I met at a rustic seafood restaurant in Barra da Tijuca, an unpopulated area of unspoiled beaches south of Leblon. Physically Anabela had mostly recovered from her torture. "I'm sleeping very little, Kate. My dreams are terrifying, as you would expect, so I sit in a chair all night. Sometimes I take a sleeping pill, but the narcotic makes my dreams even more menacing."

It wasn't safe anymore for Anabela to attend lectures at the medical school. She was careful where she went, and when. Sometimes she stayed with her grandmother, other times with friends. She abandoned completely her parents' apartment in Gávea. If she went out in the evening, her boyfriend, a doctor, or one of her brothers accompanied her. Clandestinely she kept up with the student activists. She studied French. "Hélio thinks we should get married," she said. "How can I? He's just beginning to establish a cardiology practice in Rio. I live on the run, out of a suitcase."

"Do you give any credence to the Para-SAR story, Anabela?"

"Of course it's true. And their plan to blow up the *gasômetro* wasn't only a talking scenario. The radical high command had worked out the specifics. They even chose Friday as the best day because the bus station is nearby and it would be crowded. We've got to be prepared . . . at least with intelligence."

Shocking as the Para-SAR allegations were, they felt remote. I needed to talk to Anabela about my own story. I told her about running into Sérgio at the reception while John was away, spending the night in his hotel room. I recounted what had happened in New York. "When John got back from Santos, I told him about meeting Sérgio at the reception but not about still being furious with Sérgio and, at the same time, in some irrational part of me, forgiving him. When you've loved someone like Sérgio, when it ends, it doesn't just end all of a sudden."

"I've never known a woman friend who was spellbound over a man to be completely rational," Anabela said. "And I include myself. At bottom, Kate, which would you rather have, passion or trust?"

"That's easy, Anabela. With John I have both."

My talk with Anabela was therapeutic. I heard myself say some hard-won truths. When I saw John that evening, he could sense I was all right again. I made sure to tell him I appreciated his trust, his understanding and his forbearance.

CHAPTER EIGHTEEN

"Well, you see, Excellency,
The people like it," said one of the President's advisors.
"The people have bad taste," replied the Brazilian President.
"Carnival is anachronous, predatory, thievish!"
"Excellency, be realistic,
You can't elevate the people's taste!"
"The people are caricatures of themselves."
The President watched the steady rain for some moments.
"Where is their vision? I ask you!"
"Just be glad the people haven't thought about dressing
Like guerillas. Think, Excellency,
If they looked forward instead of back . . ."

Secret societies sprang up to dance samba.
Rotating lookouts were hired, vigilant
For the Special Samba Police.

E. Catherine Lawrence

I

As the end of the year approached, John and I turned inward. Our attention was on our life together, but around us the Brazilian political situation was heading for a turning point. In our self-absorption we looked on with detachment, seeing the military as both thugs and buffoons. We weren't Brazilian and therefore were not stakeholders — we could keep some distance from the fracas. Of course, I now know that, as a result of the events of December 1968, lives would be lost, dear friends forced into exile and an entire generation of Brazilians grow to middle age without ever having voted in a democratic election.

After years of doing without, John was discovering that he quite enjoyed domesticity. A few weeks after we had moved into our apartment, he surprised me when he speculated about buying it. "Three months ago you said we had to figure out which way our lives were going next. We might not even stay in Brazil. Aren't you getting ahead of yourself?" I asked him.

"Someday we might go back to Canada or the U.S., but my instinct tells me we should stay in Brazil for a while — make a reputation here before we head off. Or maybe invest in a business. I'm just playing with ideas."

"Brazil could be heading into a civil war."

"I don't think so. Military governments don't last forever. Things will change, I think for the better."

The military had strengthened its hand in October when it arrested 1,240 students at a clandestine meeting at a farm on the outskirts of São Paulo. It continued to hold 71 of them, including all the leaders who could direct organized subversion. At the beginning of December, the government's ban against street demonstrations was in full force in Rio. The military could now return its attention to the most serious crisis it had faced since wresting power from President João Goulart in 1964 — the series of insults to its honor sparked by Deputy Moreira Alves' call for a boycott of the Independence Day parade and his subsequent "dating speech." The Attorney General had asked the Supreme Court to try him on charges of violating national security. After two months of deliberation, in a session that extended into the evening, Congress defied the Court's recommendation that Moreira Alves' parliamentary immunity be waived so he could stand trial. The Moreira Alves affair was no longer a joke.

The next day, Friday, December 13, four days into a heat wave with no breeze anywhere in the city, special police patrols were on the streets. The President spent the day at Laranjeiras Palace in conferences with the commander of the Rio military area and Ministers of the Army, Navy and Air Force.

That evening, without warning, President Costa e Silva positively closed the door on democracy in Brazil when he assumed emergency powers, ordered an indeterminate recess of Congress and established one-man rule. The Minister of Justice announced a new special act — "Institutional Act Number Five" — giving the President powers to declare a state of siege, annul the mandates and political rights of legislators and suspend the right to habeas corpus in cases of "political crimes." The Army had been placed on full alert.

John and I were having dinner in Ipanema when the Minister made the announcement in a nationwide television broadcast. Within minutes, people in an agitated state began congregating at the restaurant, wanting to share their outrage with their friends and neighbors. John and I interviewed several of them before we jumped into a taxi to get to the bureau. "If we were raising teenagers in this atmosphere, I'd be worried every time they set foot out the door," I said as our taxi sped downtown. When we were near the Hotel Gloria I told the driver to leave me at Cinelândia. John looked at me. "A demonstration might organize there," I said.

"Listen to yourself, Kate. You worry about raising teenagers here —"

"I know how to take care of myself. Our children wouldn't be spectators, they'd be involved."

The taxi stopped for a light at the intersection of Avenida Rio Branco and Senador Dantas. John and I kissed quickly before I jumped out of the cab. As I walked toward the big movie houses I saw police fanned out everywhere. I was 100 feet away from former President Kubitschek when he was taken into custody as he left the Teatro Municipal. A group of Army officers cleared a path and took him. He

229

looked astounded as he was marched toward a black sedan idling at the curb.

The government sent military censors to all the newspapers, television and radio stations. When I arrived at the bureau at 11 p.m., John was arguing with a pimple-faced Army captain in the newsroom.

Everyone who worked for UPI, regardless of shift, was in the bureau. They came as soon as they heard, or heard about, the Justice Minister's broadcast. The atmosphere was frenetic. I went to my desk and began writing. Out of the corner of my eye I noticed the captain turn on his heel and leave. Mike was typing rapidly at the desk next to mine. "He probably went to get reinforcements," Mike said without pausing. "What've you got, Kate?"

"They arrested Kubitschek. I wheedled it out of one of the soldiers that they were taking him to the Third Infantry Regiment."

"I'm not surprised. Kubitschek's been on their purge list from day one."

Saturday, December 14, Brazilians watched to see how far the President would go. During the previous night, dozens of opponents of the Costa e Silva government had been arrested. At 9 a.m. I went to Moreira Alves' home. The maid said she hadn't seen him for several days and didn't know where he was.

Throughout the day we expected military censors to arrive at the bureau at any minute. We transmitted to New York the list of prominent people the military was holding for questioning. Hundreds of people were jailed. We worked all day Saturday without a censor and held our breath.

Sunday, everything changed. Two army captains walked into the newsroom at 7 in the morning and imposed censorship on all our dispatches. The rules affecting foreign correspondents required military clearance for any comment made about the armed forces. Regulations also barred reports on the censorship arrangements themselves, differences among the armed forces or between the military and civilians and details of political arrests.

John walked calmly into his office, casually closed his door and attempted to telephone the story to New York. He was dictating the lead paragraph when the connection was broken.

Mike Evans went to Galeão Airport and handed a startled American tourist a large envelope containing our dispatches. He asked her to contact UPI when her flight arrived at John F. Kennedy Airport.

The *Jornal do Brasil* building was quiet because the *Jornal* had stopped printing to protest the arrest of its publisher. The newspapers that did publish Sunday editions concerned themselves with stories about animals and soccer games. A headline in *Correio da Manhã* declared:

Rich Cat Dies of Heart Attack in Chicago

Radio and television stations broadcast only popular music. The business of pleasure went on as usual Sunday. The beaches were crowded and lustful in the blazing hot sun. The tension in the bureau dissipated somewhat when one of the staff translators told John our censors could barely comprehend English. We went to the corners of the newsroom and laughed among ourselves. I was transported by the hijinks of love, the seducing December heat, the outrageous acts of the military, the energy that came from circumventing their hold over us. Everything was exciting, the way life can seem before a war is old. The seditious news was kept off the streets in Brazil, but it appeared outside the country via the foreign press.

Our censors came and went in eight-hour shifts throughout the day and night. Every word was checked before it could be transmitted.

There wasn't a minute we were unguarded. John hired couriers to fly to Buenos Aires with our dispatches so our news could be relayed by wire from Argentina to New York. Monday night I negotiated for nearly two hours with a dour censor to let a toothless story pass directly through the ether to UPI in New York.

I continued to try to find Deputy Marcio Moreira Alves. His maid stopped answering the door. No one knew if he had been arrested, was in hiding, or had been smuggled out of the country. On Monday, in an address to the graduating class of the Army Staff College, President Costa e Silva made it plain that the military did not accept criticism and abuse covered by "cowardly immunity."

For everyone except the nation's journalists and those 200 or so who had been arrested without judicial proceedings, life went on as usual. *Jornal do Brasil* resumed publication in censored form Tuesday. In the usual little weather box on its front page, the paper reported:

> Weather black. Temperature suffocating. The air is unbreathable. The country is swept by strong winds.

Although the armed forces were on a state of alert, there were no troops in the streets. Back in the United States, the Johnson administration decided not to lecture the Brazilians, fearing that condescending statements from Washington would not improve the situation and might even harden it.

Five days into the crisis the government presented, apparently, its first rationale for seizing extraordinary powers. An unsigned article in *Diário de Notícias*, a newspaper close to the military, said the President had assumed virtual one-man rule to thwart a plot by unnamed "national oligarchs" to keep Brazil underdeveloped. We hoped our laughs behind the backs of our censors in the newsroom — "the clowns" — were discreet.

232

The government detailed a diplomat to give daily briefings to the foreign press at half past 4 in the afternoon. On Tuesday, John and I took a taxi to Itamaraty Palace, the elegant chancellery of the Ministry of External Relations, to hear what he had to say at his first briefing. It was a hot afternoon though the humidity had fallen to 80 percent, unusual for December, when the humidity commonly lingered in the 90s. Fernando Galvão stepped to the podium and announced that the current issue of *Time* was being withheld from distribution because it contained an article critical of the political changes. The foreign press corps shared nods of dismay and walked out.

Complete censorship lasted for one week, then it was eased. It was understood, however, that the local newspapers and broadcast stations had agreed to censor themselves. When our censors departed at 6 o'clock Friday evening, looking fatigued, no others arrived to replace them. At 8, Mike went downstairs to *Jornal do Brasil* and was told that there had been no censors in their newsroom since late afternoon. When Mike reported back the good news, José beamed. He had become the censors' slave, serving them endless cups of coffee and glasses of mineral water. The UPI staff spontaneously converged in the center of the newsroom and cheered. Mike smashed the blue pencils our censors had left behind. We were still wary, though. Were they really gone?

Saturday morning, with Christmas only four days away, I tumbled out of bed early, had coffee with John and kissed him goodbye when he left for the bureau. I went through his armoire and dresser drawers, hoping their contents might suggest what I could buy him for Christmas. A silk ascot? A new double-breasted blazer? A dressing gown in case we decided to take a trip to Boston or Toronto? John hadn't even had time for his Royal Canadian exercises since Costa e Silva had proclaimed his Fifth Institutional Act. Perhaps he would like a pedometer? A Swiss chronograph?

I took a taxi to Copacabana to shop. The interior streets were festooned with tinsel Christmas decorations that looked cheap and incongruous in the tropical sun. A year earlier, just after I had arrived in Rio, I was so overwhelmed with other impressions I had barely noticed the holiday decorations. I went to a chic record store. Walter's record, just released, was prominently displayed. I bought one for us and several more as Christmas presents for my UPI colleagues. Walter had invited us to the party given in his honor by his record company, but John had told the entire staff to cancel all their social engagements until the censors left the bureau so we couldn't attend. I asked the hip salesman if Walter's record was selling well. "Steadily. He's the real thing — a musician's musician."

Former President Kubitschek also had a recording on sale in which he sang the serenades he loved from his home state of Minas Gerais. I had it gift-wrapped for John. At Roditi on Avenida Atlântica, known for its fine jewelry, I bought John an elegant waterproof chronograph.

On the way home I stopped by David Jr.'s apartment, hoping to say hello to Walter and Eva. I thought Walter would be pleased to see I had purchased a half dozen of his records. No one was home. I hoped that, in the wake of his success, they were out looking for a sanitary place to live.

Sunday morning early, I rinsed and stacked the dishes we had lazily left dirty after dinner. John was stretched out in bed, naked, sound asleep in the morning heat. I turned on the radio. Walter had telephoned John at the bureau to say his record was being played on several popular stations. When I tried to find a music station I heard instead a live broadcast from Rome. Pope Paul VI was delivering his customary noon address to the crowd in St. Peter's Square:

234

We open the window and instinctively our eyes, thoughts and heart go skyward, unable to escape from the spell of amazement and expectation of the launching of the Apollo 8 toward the moon with three men aboard prepared for the celestial exploration of the silent and silvery planet of our earth.

The moon would never again seem so far away, so unreachable and mysterious after Apollo 8's circumlunar trip. Later we learned *The New York Times* had reported that, while the Pope spoke from the balcony of his private study on the top floor of St. Peter's Basilica, a group of 150 people, mostly youths, demonstrated against the Brazilian government in the square below.

Monday evening, John and I sat thigh to thigh on the banquette at the Olimpia, drinking beer and eating ham-and-white-cheese sandwiches. "Happy birthday, darling," John said. "I bet you thought I forgot." He took a black velvet jewel box out of his pocket. Inside was a beautiful double strand of pearls. "Happy 29, dearest Catherine. You're catching up to me."

"I did think you'd forgotten. I nearly forgot myself. The pearls are beautiful. Thank you, my love. I'll wear them to Christmas dinner."

II

Tuesday, the day before Christmas, I took the day off. John said he would work until 3. I had a date to meet Walter and Jaime for lunch in Copacabana at an outside café. I was on my way out the door when Steve, a young reporter, newly transferred to us from UPI's Los Angeles bureau, telephoned: "Is John home?" he asked. "He said he was going home early."

"He's not here yet," I said. "He probably went out for lunch."

"A guy was here looking for him. I think he may be one of John's sources. He didn't give his name. Just said he'd be back later. I'm leaving now for the day. It's very quiet around here. I'll drop a note on John's desk."

"What did the guy look like?" I asked.

"Not Brazilian. He spoke English with a thick accent, like a native French speaker. He didn't look like a Frenchman, though."

"I have no idea who that could be. I'm rushing off to a lunch date. Merry Christmas." I hurried out the door to meet Walter and Jaime.

Chaos wasn't working out as Walter had imagined or hoped. "The Dark Ages are here," he said over our lunch at an outdoor restaurant. "No one will know anything anymore. We'll lose a whole generation."

I noticed a group of some 30 demonstrators in bathing trunks — surfers — marching along the sand close to the sidewalk. They held up white cotton banners with green and blue letters. I caught the word "Fascist." It was a risky thing to do. I got up, quickly kissed Walter and Jaime goodbye and ran across the street.

"Don't bother, baby," Walter called after me. "It's all meaningless now."

The marchers picked their way through the sunbathers, chanting:

Power for the people

Freedom for the press

Down with Institutional Act Number Five

For 15 minutes it might have been one of the most relaxed demonstrations in the history of protest. Then, out of nowhere, the police Shock Battalion arrived in a large open truck. The police jumped from the back, swinging their batons, rounding up more than a dozen of the tanned demonstrators who didn't have time to lose themselves among the beach crowd. I felt a blow in the middle of my back and found myself being hustled along with the surfers to a paddy wagon that had just arrived. A policeman shoved me roughly inside. My shoulder hit a metal stud. I fumbled in my purse for my press identification and passport. They weren't inside. I realized I must have left them in the purse I carried to work. While the door was still open, I thought of shouting out that I was a journalist, then reconsidered. It could make my situation worse. What should I do?

The right to habeas corpus had been suspended and the press had been the target of recent arrests. Had Walter and Jaime seen me taken? I thought not. They had finished lunch and were about to leave for a tai chi class when I dashed off. John would never suspect I was in police custody. He knew only that I was having lunch with Walter. Copacabana Beach was an unlikely place for a demonstration and arrests.

At home I had boasted, to John's dismay, that I could maneuver around and through a crowd of demonstrators. "March right through the middle if need be, get my story and exit without a scratch." Others in the press corps might get caught, detained, roughed up, but not me. I could avoid attention anytime I chose by taking the precaution of dressing inconspicuously, slumping my shoulders forward and looking down at my feet. Instantly I would become as unobtrusive as cinders on a path. I had invented my disappearing walk in New York for late-night jaunts through dicey neighborhoods. It was one piece of a reporter's streetcraft John hadn't needed to teach me.

But this time I had on a very short sundress. It would be no protection against the harsh physical conditions I was about to encounter. I remembered again the caution of Anabela's father: "If you pass into their hands, I don't think I can get you out."

237

Would they let me talk to the American Consul? Put me on a plane and expel me from the country? Torture me? Rape me? God, if only I'd worn jeans and a long-sleeved shirt, had my passport with me. If only Walter or Jaime had seen me taken. I was "disappeared." Now the frightening euphemism applied to me.

Inside the paddy wagon were several young men and women in street clothes mixed in with the barefoot surfers. They looked defiant, ready to do battle. Should I tell my fellow prisoners who I was? I kept quiet. We were taken to Botafogo, to the baroque gray castle that served as the headquarters for the Shock Battalion. Across the street was the British Ambassador's residence and next to that the residence of the American Ambassador. As we were led out of the wagon, I thought of making a run for it.

The interior of the castle smelled dry and lifeless, exactly like DOPS headquarters. I thought of Lord William. He knew the ropes, knew how to stay in control. But what the cops wanted from him was money. They would want my body. I was dressed for the occasion.

I looked at my watch. It was half past 3 p.m. Maybe I would be out in a few hours. When would John realize I was missing? No one had read me my rights. Shouldn't I be given a dime and told I could make one phone call? If ever the difference between my justice system and Brazil's military despotism was perfectly clear, it was now.

We sat in a large holding area on three long metal benches. I had only a small space to sit. The walls were olive green, covered in grime; the cement floor was cracked and slimy. There was an overpowering stench of urine mixed with sweat. "Are you okay?" I whispered to the detainees sitting on either side of me. They nodded. I tried not to call attention to myself. We were being watched.

Two young men in bathing trunks sitting on the floor moved closer to me. One had sandy-colored hair bleached by the sun; the other was dark-haired with a deep, copper tan. They looked like serious surfers. "I saw you were hit by a police club. Are you all right?" the dark one asked under his breath.

"For the moment I am. Thanks for asking. I'm scared about what might be coming next."

"You're not Brazilian?" he said when he heard my accent. "From the States?"

"Yes, but I live here."

"With your family?"

"I work for UPI." The instant I said it, I was sorry. "They're arresting journalists," I said. "I don't want them to know."

"Not foreign journalists," the surfer with the fair hair said. "You have your passport?"

I shook my head no.

"I don't think honestly you'll have a problem," the dark one said.

"It was stupid of me not to carry it."

"The Shock Battalion keeps order on the streets. It doesn't have the social controlling function like DOPS. Stay calm."

"Does anyone know you were taken?" the student to my right on the bench asked.

"I don't think so. There's a small chance two friends saw what happened."

"This place doesn't have the legends like DOPS headquarters, or the Army Police, or the Federal Police headquarters downtown," the light-haired surfer said.

I tried not to stare at my watch. I'd been sitting on the metal bench for more than four hours. Sometimes I spoke with my fellow prisoners; sometimes I let myself get lost in my fear. A guard opened the door and put a tray of glasses filled with a clear fluid on the floor. "Do you want some?" the fair-haired surfer asked me.

"No, thank you." I smiled at his kindness.

The police were interrogating people one by one. A rumor circulated that two dispositions were possible: Either release or being put "at the disposal of justice," which meant staying in prison. I willed myself to fixate on a small barred window high over the door, not on my watch. I was already experiencing a kind of torture. I couldn't speak to anyone outside the room. The fear and suspense were taking their toll. My back throbbed where I'd been hit with the baton. My scraped shoulder looked angry and red.

At seven minutes past midnight, three policemen with semiautomatic weapons on their hips entered the detention area. Eleven people were left sitting on the benches. All were young men wearing bathing trunks except me. There was no way to find out what happened to the people who had not returned. One of the policemen picked out four of us, including me, and herded us out of the holding area. We were led through rank corridors. Where were we going? I could hear muffled noises from behind closed doors. We gave each other apprehensive looks. One of the young men whispered something. A policeman told him to shut up. Suddenly we were at the main entrance to the castle. Would we be transported somewhere else? A policeman opened the door: "You're free to go," he said. "Christmas amnesty."

The three policemen departed down a corridor and left us standing at the entrance. We half-walked, half-jogged out of the gray building. We didn't stop until we had crossed the street and reached the end of the block. An *ipê* tree in full bloom peeked over the fence of the British Ambassador's residence. We silently embraced each other. What could we say?

I got into a taxi and went to Leblon. I was filthy and bruised. My legs were stiff. John rushed me into a hot bath and brought me a glass of Scotch. He knelt down next to the bathtub and helped me wash. "You're a brave kid."

"I shouldn't have run across the street to the demonstration. Walter even yelled 'don't bother.' I didn't need to get close."

While I soaked in the bathtub and finished the Scotch, John phoned all the people he had contacted when he realized I was missing. He came back to the bathroom, carried me to bed and held me. The phone rang. He got up to answer it. "That was Walter calling from a pay phone. He sends his love. When you didn't answer the phone at 7:30, I stopped by his apartment on the way home to ask if he had seen you. I hope when Walter moves, he gets a telephone."

After a while we got up and went to the kitchen. It was nearly 3 in the morning. John made scrambled eggs and toast. We went back to bed and slept entwined in each other's limbs.

Christmas day we stayed in bed until noon. I gave John the chronograph, the record of Kubitschek's serenades and Walter's record. He gave me a floor-length, red silk robe. "Let's try the watch out underwater," he said. He put it on and we got into the bathtub together. Every few minutes, we checked to make sure it was still running.

"A close call yesterday, Catherine."

I nodded.

We went out to Christmas dinner at the Ouro Verde Hotel with Charlie Wall and his wife, Emily. I wore my fabulous birthday pearls and a scarf to cover the bruises on my shoulder. Everybody ordered the hotel's special Christmas meal: pheasant stuffed with chanterelle mushrooms.

We had come through.

CHAPTER NINETEEN

I am looking for him,
But not in other faces.
Really looking,
Because I cannot support this feeling.

E. Catherine Lawrence

I

John and I had planned that I would take a few days off after Christmas to attend to a list of wedding arrangements and chores around our new apartment. On Saturday we were going to fly to Bauru, 150 miles northwest of São Paulo, to visit Fazenda Maraíba. John had finally succeeded in setting up an interview with Sérgio's cousin, Jorge Antônio Barbosa, who owned the enormous coffee and cattle *fazenda*.

Our parents, John's two sisters, my brother Jeff and his wife, Linda, and friends from around the world would be starting to arrive in Rio in three weeks. The day after Christmas John went to the bureau as usual. He called me at noon to say he had tracked down Mrs. John J. Malloy, the sister of Moreira Alves, in Cambridge, Massachusetts. "She says Marcio's in Buenos Aires. I'm putting it on the wire now — 'Marcio Moreira Alves, a member of the dissolved Brazilian Chamber of Deputies, has escaped safely from Brazil to Buenos Aires, according to his sister, who lives in the United States.' I'll probably be late tonight, Kate. How's the list of chores coming?"

"I'm slogging through them."

"Kisses till later, darling."

I waited to have dinner with John but eventually ate alone. I went to bed and read. Around 10 p.m. I phoned the bureau. No one answered.

John must be off following a lead — maybe one having to do with the man with the French accent who had come by the bureau.

I called the bureau at 11 p.m. and again at midnight. Still no answer. Why hadn't he called? I kept hoping he was just out of the office on a story, but I couldn't shake the feeling that he had been "disappeared." If DOPS had taken him, wouldn't he be freed in the Christmas amnesty? Maybe amnesty had expired on Christmas day. Maybe there was no amnesty from DOPS. Maybe he had been in an accident. I began to think again about the man with a French accent who had been asking for John. Maybe he wasn't a news source. Could it have been Marcos? They spoke French in Lebanon. By now it was past 1 a.m.

I convinced myself I was becoming paranoid and tried to make myself stop theorizing. I wrote down a priority list of contacts: The American and Canadian Embassies, Charlie Wall, Walter, Nelson Claudio, Anabela, Fernando Galvão (the government's press spokesman), the traffic police, hospitals. Mike Evans still didn't have a telephone. I considered taking a taxi to his apartment to ask if he knew where John was, but I didn't want to leave my phone unattended in case John called. I telephoned the bureau every 30 minutes until half past 7. No answer. José and a skeleton staff should have been there by now.

I tried to calm myself by taking a shower. I had just turned off the water when Mike Evans called at quarter to 8. Dripping wet, I answered the phone. "I'm coming right over, Kate. I'll be there as fast as traffic will let me."

"Where's John? Tell me, Mike."

"I'm leaving right now."

"Where are you?"

"The bureau."

"Just tell me … "

243

"See you in about 20 minutes, Kate."

Mike rang off and I began to cry. John must have been hurt. If he was in a hospital, he would need his toiletries, pajamas, a robe. I hurriedly started to pack a suitcase. I'd stay with him. I threw in a change of clothes for myself. While I was packing I thought about what I would do if, instead of lying injured in a hospital, he had been disappeared. I would swallow my fear and revulsion and go see *delegado* Dutra. DOPS had the files. Dutra could find out which military or police organization was holding him. All the most terrible places came to my mind — places where detainees had a 50-50 chance of disappearing forever. Trying to suppress these thoughts, I put the suitcase by the door, ready.

I started to count how many times I paced through every room in our apartment, but after 50, I stopped. Mike's trip from downtown to Leblon took exactly 27 minutes and 10 seconds. When he knocked, I jumped to open the door. Mike embraced me immediately. Charlie Wall was with him. He also held me close. They led me into the living room and sat me down on the sofa.

"There's no way I can make this easy, Kate," Mike said. "I wish to God I could." He took my hand and held it. "When José came in this morning, he found John dead in the elevator. He was shot through the chest. His pockets were empty. That beautiful stopwatch you gave him was gone. It looks like a robbery."

I ran to our bedroom, shut the door and screamed. I climbed into our bed and breathed in the smell of our sheets for a long time. I went to John's drawers, pulled out his sweaters and buried my face in them. I opened his closet, put on his navy blazer and returned to our bed. I sobbed, I don't know for how long. I listened for the phone. Surely someone was going to call any minute and tell me it was a mistake. It wasn't John who was dead.

244

In a crying daze, I walked to the front door. Mike and Charlie were still talking in the living room. They hurried over to me. I mumbled that I needed air and rushed out. I couldn't wait for the elevator. I staggered down four flights of stairs and kept going. I have no idea how long I walked, or where. When I got back to the apartment Mike and Charlie were there, waiting for me. I collapsed in their arms. I dimly remember my doctor's merciful injection.

II

I must have slept for nearly 24 hours. I woke up dimly aware of voices coming from the living room. It was 10 o'clock in the morning. I was still wearing John's blazer. I got out of bed and listened at the door. "It's too pat," I heard Charlie say. "I'm looking for another explanation. I think we've been set up. Was John working on something that would get the military riled?"

"The Para-SAR horror, but so is everybody."

"If that's what got him killed, the police can't touch it. There wasn't another woman? Nothing like that going on?"

"Absolutely not," Mike said. "From the day she walked into the bureau, he only had eyes for Kate. It was obvious to everyone. John was careful. He always had a plan ... even in the thick of a demonstration, he knew where the exits were."

"He took bigger risks than I would," Charlie said. "Sometimes he made me think he'd died once already and wasn't afraid of doing it again."

I leaned against the door frame. I had to get hold of myself. My legs trembled. After several minutes, I walked into the living room. Charlie and Mike stopped talking when I entered. Their faces were anguished. Mike was pacing. Charlie sat erect on the front edge of our black leather sofa. He had two cigarettes going at once, one in an ashtray and another between his fingers.

Our living room looked spare and uncomfortable. Why hadn't we bought that rug and the lamps we needed? I wandered over to the bookshelf and stared at a silver-framed photograph John had asked a passerby to snap of us, arm-in-arm, at Paraty. I still clung to the intense feeling that someone would phone or knock on the door and tell me it was all a mistake — it didn't happen.

Mike embraced me. We held each other for a long time, sobbing. "I loved the guy, too, Kate," he said. "We all looked up to him." I sank onto the sofa. Mike sat down next to me and held my hand. I sobbed so much, the trembling spread from my arms to my legs. I couldn't stop it. Charlie told me to take deep, slow breaths. I tried. It did help. "We don't have much to go on," Mike said.

"I overheard you guys talking," I said.

I began to feel angry. I thought to myself: robbery, bullshit! It was the guy who came by the bureau. The guy Steve talked to. Mike and Charlie haven't got a clue. Nobody does. Nobody I know, anyway. Nobody I can talk to. I wanted to telephone Harold Wilson, the British Prime Minister, and ask him to put me in touch with MI6.

I went into the small bedroom, my private writing place, which I had hoped one day to use as our child's room. I had to keep John's secrets. I willed my brain not to go crazy. The phone rang. I rushed to the living room to answer it. Someone was bringing me a message — John wasn't dead. Instead it was a police detective calling from the UPI bureau to say he was on his way to see me. I wandered out of the living room, lingering just beyond the doorway, listening. "Robbery doesn't make sense," Mike said to Charlie. "Why would a robber be looking for a victim at night in the Jornal do Brasil building? If he was looking for a tourist wearing jewelry in Copacabana — I can imagine that. But what else could it be?"

Charlie said, "Maybe he was trying to get into the building to steal from an office and John surprised him."

I came back into the living room.

Charlie put his arm around me: "We have to look at every angle, Kate. Was John working on something we don't know about?"

I shook my head. "Not that I know."

"If he'd gotten close to some radical student group . . . it could have landed him on a government hit list."

"What the hell difference does it make now?" I said. I walked to the window. Hot spots of morning sunlight passed through the tilted window blinds onto the floor. Through the slats I stared at a narrow strip of sparkling ocean. Then I turned to look at a pile of books and newspapers that lay scattered on the coffee table. I could hear John's voice: "A bit messy, don't you think?" I felt his presence in the room with us. "Help me," I said under my breath.

Mike joined me at the window: "I spoke to two reporters from *Jornal do Brasil* who were working late. They didn't realize anybody else was still in the building. They left around 8:30. José came in and found him at 6:30 a.m."

The detective arrived and asked me if John had any enemies.

"Only the enemies any reporter might have," I said.

He had more routine questions. I told him that I had called the bureau at 10 p.m. and John hadn't picked up the phone. None of my other answers seemed to help. Finally, the detective left. Mike and Charlie departed a short time later. Márcia hovered in the kitchen, crying. She brought me cups of tea, which I didn't drink. I poured myself a Scotch and drank it down like cough medicine. Charlie and his wife and Mike came back in the early evening. Emily Wall took me into the bedroom and helped me pick out a change of clothes. Colleagues from the bureau began appearing. José came. They tried to comfort me with stories about John. Some were funny. Everyone said they would miss the best boss they'd had, or ever hoped to have.

III

My doctor injected a second round of sedatives that gave me another day to collect my thoughts before I had to begin functioning again. Márcia prepared bland food that I tried to eat. I went to the beach alone at dusk and threw the wedding band John would have worn into the Atlantic Ocean for Iemanjá, goddess of the sea. The next morning, full of regret, I went back to the spot and waded into the water to look for the ring. It was gone.

My father and stepmother, Ellen, arrived 48 hours after I got the news. John's father and his older sister arrived shortly afterward. Friends from the different compartments of our lives sat in our living room talking softly. They wanted to stay with me; I wanted to be alone. They left me reluctantly. Whenever the phone rang, the mad feeling would overcome me that John was ringing back. He had found a way.

The Canadian Embassy helped with the Brazilian legal formalities and the death certificate. John had given me a key to his safe deposit box. I emptied it into a suitcase without looking at anything. I insisted that Walter take two brand-new button-down shirts and, foolishly, John's neckties. Only later did I laugh, trying to imagine Walter in a four-in-hand. Márcia was grateful for John's remaining clothes, which she gave to her four brothers. I kept John's high school clarinet, the blue shirt he had bought at the Hotel Gloria gift shop the night I was wounded in Santa Cruz and his books, of course.

There was a funeral at Christ Church. It should have been our wedding. Friends and colleagues made all the arrangements. During

248

the service, my father and John's flanked me on the pew. John's mother had been too distraught to make the journey. Mr. Wadson would take John's ashes home to her in Toronto. Reverend Frank Reynolds, the minister who was to have married us, embraced me at the door of the church after the funeral: "Catherine, God helps all those who mourn."

I mumbled that I was well beyond God's comfort.

I stood on the step just outside the church entrance with my parents and John's father and sister, and gratefully received our friends' expressions of sympathy.

Walter and Eva, Jaime and Ana Maria, embraced me wordlessly. Our tears spoke for themselves. I introduced them to my family and to John's. Nelson Claudio put his arms around me. We hugged for a long time. I sobbed on his shoulder. "Where's Anabela?" I asked.

"This morning DOPS arrested one of her colleagues at the medical school. She knew she was next. Before she went underground, she asked me to give you her love and her deepest sympathies."

"Where is she?"

"No one knows." Nelson Claudio held me. "The situation here isn't leading anywhere. No one knows what to do. I've got a possibility for some work in New York. I think I'll go. I might as well hear Miles Davis play live."

"John loved Miles, too. Maybe one day we'll go hear him together in New York."

A tall man came up to me. For a moment, I didn't recognize him. "James Ralph," he said, "from the British Embassy. I just wanted to say how sorry we are. You have our condolences. When I met you at our embassy party the other week I wasn't aware you were John's fiancée. I've known him since before he came to Rio."

In my bewilderment and grief I simply nodded my head. "Thank you," I said. It wasn't until the next day that I realized James Ralph must have been John's MI6 contact. Telling me he had known John before he came to Rio was a signal. Did he want to find out whether I knew enough to recognize his remark as an invitation? Was he worried for me? Did he want to warn me? Was he the one person I could talk to?

Mike and Charlie continued to pursue their suspicions. Steve told them about the guy who came to the bureau looking for John, but that information led them nowhere. I didn't offer any clues that would expose John's MI6 secrets. As I expected, they didn't find any. John had been well trained.

Three days after the funeral I went to the British Embassy and asked for James Ralph. His office was well appointed. He used an ivory-colored cigarette holder. A servant brought coffee. "I'm glad you've come, Kate. I counted John as a friend. How are you getting on?"

I took a deep breath. "I miss John terribly. He's dead and the sun still comes up. It's just so sad. I'm trying to put the pieces in place. Just for my own sake."

"I well understand. Have the police come to any conclusion?"

"They say it was a robbery. John always carried a lot of cash. And his watch was gone. A lovely chronograph I had just given him for Christmas."

"Do you think they're right?"

We held each other's gaze. "No," I said. "My reporter colleagues don't either, but I don't think they'll find anything that can help."

For what seemed like a full minute we looked at each other without saying a word. I broke the silence: "John never mentioned your name to me. Did you know him in Beirut?"

"Precisely. I was posted there when he was at the Bristol. Marvelous place. First-class hotel. He did a brilliant job."

"He was good at whatever he did," I said, "even when no one would notice."

"John was a real professional. He had many admirers."

"I'm glad to hear you say that."

"I hope it will give you some comfort. You know, Kate, untangling what's happened — it's like a bell you can't unring."

"I want to desperately."

I paused, debating if I dare take a risk. "One night in Santa Cruz ... Do you know the town?"

"I do indeed. Sad place, really. Dangerous, too. A suburb to avoid, wouldn't you say?" His penetrating gaze silenced me. "You have my full sympathy, my dear."

When we said goodbye, James Ralph asked: "Are you going home?"

"Yes, to Boston. At least for a while. I plan to keep busy. I'm finding out it's a mistake not to. It just makes me sadder when I sit still."

It was settled between us. If James Ralph had his suspicions about why John was killed, he wasn't going to tell me. And I had let him see I would keep John's covert life firmly to myself.

After 10 days my father and Ellen left Rio. I stayed on another two weeks to tie up loose ends, to say goodbye to dear friends. I had completely forgotten our appointment at Fazenda Maraíba to interview Jorge Antônio Barbosa. Embarrassed, I telephoned to apologize. I didn't feel ready to say that John was dead. In some totally crazy way, I still didn't believe it. "I'm calling on behalf of John Wadson at UPI,"

I said. "There has been a crisis at the bureau and he sincerely regrets he was not able to keep his appointment with you. He hopes it didn't inconvenience you."

"Not at all," *senhor* Barbosa said in English. "You don't mind if I practice my English, do you?"

"Please do," I said, switching languages.

"I was a little surprised Mr. Wadson wanted to write about Fazenda Maraíba. There are life-and-death stories to choose among these days. I'm the first to recognize that growing coffee and grazing cattle don't carry urgency. When should I expect your visit? Does Mr. Wadson play poker? I play every Wednesday night with good friends. Mr. Wadson is welcome to join us."

"John plays," I said. "He's quite good. At least that's what his fellow players have told me. They're all journalists."

"Oh dear, journalists are experts at bluffing." He laughed. "I withdraw my invitation to play."

"Someone from our bureau will be in touch with you soon," I said. "I regret it won't be me." Sérgio was right. I would have liked to meet his cousin.

I went to the Olimpia alone at 6 and drank John's drink, draft beer. Our waiter refused to count my coasters to calculate the bill.

On my last day in Brazil, I went to the bureau one final time. Early in the morning a landslide in downtown Rio had destroyed a *favela*. Mike Evans' story epitomized my feelings:

> Rio de Janeiro, Jan. 21, (UPI)—Civil authorities searched with heavy earthmoving machinery today in a canyon near the center of Rio de Janeiro for victims of a landslide that sent 20 slum shacks and their inhabitants plunging down a hillside.

The bodies of eight persons, including four children, have been recovered. The authorities estimate that 40 to 70 more are missing. The inhabitants of the other 140 crude homes perched above the abyss have been evacuated to safer ground.

The slum, called *Favela of My Loves*, is on an outcropping of rock overlooking the central railway station and the War Ministry in the center of the city. The oldest hillside slum in Rio de Janeiro, it gave its name — *favela* (a kind of wild flower) — to the dozens of similar shantytowns that dot the city.

Jorge dos Santos Generoso, an inhabitant of *Favela of My Loves*, was brushing his teeth when the earth collapsed. "It sounded like a gunshot," he said, "and then everything was falling." He watched the home of his sister and her eight children go over the brink.

A policeman, Mario Martins Taveira, was chatting with a neighbor, known as *dona* Augusta, when her shack fell. Both are presumed dead. The policeman's wife, Ismênia, saw them go over. Friends tried to restrain her but she jumped after her husband.

I envied *dona* Ismênia. My universe, too, was buried in rubble, but I had nowhere to jump.

As a fledgling reporter I had thought that if you get on the right helicopter, on the right luminous morning, fly low over the beaches, the dense neighborhoods, your mouth still tasting coffee and orange marmalade, it's all there, spread out, waiting: The impenetrable exotic paradise. The Brazil of my imagination with its compelling foreignness, and the real Brazil I was discovering for myself with John.

Mike took me to the airport. To my surprise, Walter was waiting for me at the gate. We embraced and kissed one last time. "Don't think badly of us, Kate."

"Oh, my God, Walter, how could I?"

My plane took off into the wind, south by southeast. There it was, out the window a few thousand feet below me, a poet's Rio — a gorgeous, romantic, sexually exhausted, infernal, poetry-loving, frustrating, jealous place. And also, most important to me now, the Rio I had shared with John.

I stretched up out of my seat trying to see the landslide past the wing and glimpsed it just before it disappeared behind us. I could see the coastal mountains — Sugar Loaf, Corcovado with the Christ the Redeemer statue atop, his arms outspread, protecting. Five, six, seven thousand feet. The aircraft banked right, made a broad turn and I caught sight of the open ocean. Then I saw Rio spread before me again, distant, receding. I tried to spot the landslide, but we had already flown too far.

CHAPTER TWENTY

I could light a match to my book
And write another one.
It doesn't matter, it's all the same,
Because I will live to be
One hundred thirty,
The only survivor after World War III.

Every time
I write a poem,
I save a life.

E. Catherine Lawrence
New York
1985

What is passion without trust? It is Brazil, where there are fish that walk, trees that wander, birds that fly backward — and where a man can be pardoned for killing his unfaithful wife. It is unorganized sensitivity. It is sleeping until afternoon without a care. It is transcendent, as if it were love. John's secrets lie buried there.

The day after I got my poetry prize, I slid into the obligatory panic. Where are the poems I'll write tomorrow? I was nostalgic for street riots in Rio and for what came afterward — falling into bed with John, exhausted and exhilarated, making love until daybreak. I longed to be fearless again.

My husband and some friends took me out for a congratulatory dinner. I wasn't in a chatty mood.

"Sorry, darling, I'm bad company tonight. Nothing for you to worry about."

AUTHOR'S NOTE

The year 1968 was a formative time in the lives of many of Brazil's present-day political leaders, including Dilma Rousseff, imprisoned and tortured by the military government and in 2010 elected President of Brazil, the first woman to hold that office.

DISCLAIMER

Many of the political events and personalities recounted in this novel are based on published newspaper reports, although in some cases poetic license has been taken with the names, dates and details. All the main characters and all non-political events are fictional creations. Fictional characters have been put in real offices, such as the executive editor of Macmillan Publishing, Co., Inc. and a number of diplomatic posts. The geography of Rio de Janeiro, including place names, is intended to be accurate.

I took liberties with William L. Shirer's *The Rise and Fall of the Third Reich: A History of Nazi Germany*, inventing an imaginary personage, Friedrich Grabenz, and claiming that he is mentioned in Shirer's book.

ACKNOWLEDGMENTS

No book is born without encouragement, suggestions, editing and rewriting. I wish especially to thank Marcelo Otávio Dantas for his astute advice on this book and his support, Jennifer J. Zeien, who gave magnanimously of her time with insightful recommendations, and Peter Kaufman for editing the final version of the manuscript.

Although I have lived in Rio de Janeiro, heartfelt thanks must go to friends in Brazil who contributed to my understanding of Rio in 1968: Anabela Paiva, Manoel "Kiko" Brito, Tarcisio Zandonade, Renato de Assumpção Faria, Ambassador Marcio de Oliveira Dias and Paulo Moreira Leite.

I also received valuable help from the following friends and I thank them most sincerely: Judy Hallet, Loral Dean, Cecilia Cassidy, Sir Brian Fall and Lady (Delmar) Fall, Béatrice Corrêa do Lago, Laura Brylawski-Miller, George Stone, Giles Roblyer, my sister, Nina Roskin Liebman, and brother-in-law, Theodore Liebman. Their insights and comments on various drafts of this book helped guide me.

Most of all I thank my husband Bernard, who suggested that, in addition to writing poetry, I try fiction. Then he had the formidable patience and intellect to accompany and encourage me every step of the way.

www.ingramcontent.com/pod-product-compliance
Lightning Source LLC
Chambersburg PA
CBHW021957170626
46808CB00001B/186